Paul Thomas was
grew up in New
University of Auc
in journalism and
London, Toulous
several books on sport. *Inside Dope*, his second
novel, was joint winner of the 1996 Ned Kelly Award
for best Australian crime novel. His other novels,
Dirty Laundry and *Guerilla Season*, were also published to widespread critical and commercial success.
All three books have been published internationally.

Also by Paul Thomas

Inside Dope
Dirty Laundry
Guerilla Season

FINAL CUT

PAUL THOMAS

BANTAM BOOKS
SYDNEY • AUCKLAND • TORONTO • NEW YORK • LONDON

Final Cut
A Bantam Book
First published in Australia and New Zealand
in 1999 by Bantam

Copyright © Paul Thomas, 1999

All rights reserved. No part of this publication may be reproduced, stored in a retrieval system, transmitted in any form or by any means, electronic, mechanical, photocopying, recording or otherwise, without the prior permission of the publisher.

National Library of Australia
Cataloguing-in-Publication entry

Thomas, Paul, 1951–.
Final Cut

ISBN 1 8632 5136 7

I. Title

NZ823.2

Bantam books are published by
Transworld Publishers
a division of Random House (Australia) Pty Ltd
20 Alfred Street, Milsons Point, NSW 2061

Random House, New Zealand Limited
18 Poland Road, Glenfield, Auckland 1310

Transworld Publishers (UK) Limited
61-63 Uxbridge Road, Ealing, London W5 5SA

Random House Inc
1540 Broadway, New York, New York 10036

Cover photograph by Louise Lister
Typeset by Midland Typesetters
Printed by Griffin Press

10 9 8 7 6 5 4 3 2 1

To Jeni and to my mother and father.

I'd like to thank Dave Brown, Noel King, and David Matthews for their kind assistance.

I've been bought and sold and
I've been hung upside down
so you can hear me breathing
do you think it's easy?
I've been aching all through summer
I've been aching just to fall
cut me down
cut me down

'Cut Me Down', Lloyd Cole and the Commotions

ONE

My name's James Alabaster. I'm what's known as a white collar criminal.

I used to be a merchant banker. I took home 250K a year plus bonuses. In a good year, that added up to half a mill. I had a three-storey terrace in Paddington, wall-to-wall art deco. I had an investment property and a share portfolio. I had a Saab turbo. I had a twenty-one-year-old blonde secretary who didn't make me use a condom.

Then I got busted for insider trading.

It happened like this. I knew things before the market did. I had a choice: I could do nothing – good boy – or I could use the information to make a shitload of money – bad boy. Gee, that's a tricky one. I wrestled with the dilemma for all of five seconds. This is the real world, right? Everyone's doing it, no-one ever gets caught.

There's a first time for everything. It cost me a year's periodic detention, a few hundred hours of community service and a $75,000 fine. That was just for starters. The merchant bank took away the Saab, the 250K plus bonuses, and the blonde secretary. Then I had to pay my lawyers, the useless fucks. That took care of the Paddington terrace and everything in it.

I did time at the Silverwater Detention Centre, out west. Two and a half days a week, locked up with white trash, black trash, yellow trash, olive trash, punks, losers, misfits, sickos ... I fitted right in.

When I checked out for the last time, this screw said he'd be sorry to see the back of me, it made a pleasant change having a gentleman in Silverwater. As if a fucking screw would recognise a gentleman if he tripped over one.

I asked, 'Can I make a suggestion?'

'Sure.'

'Get rid of the sniffer dogs. They're a waste of time.'

Every time you went in, they put the dogs on you. I pointed out to the screw that I'd sent the mongrels into white powder frenzy half a dozen times. I'd be strip-searched, I'd get the rubber glove up the arse, the works. They never found a fucking thing. There never was a fucking thing.

The screw's explanation went like this: I caught the train to Silverwater at Kings Cross; the Cross was full of junkies; the dogs must've smelt drugs on my clothes. QED.

I said, 'You're missing the point.'

'What is the point?'

'Your wonder dogs went apeshit over me and I wasn't a carrier. Every day, there're guys walking in here loaded like mules – how come the dogs never smell it on them?'

He told me I was talking shit. I told him, wake up, Silverwater was Junk City – whatever your narcotic of choice, someone could supply it.

The screw, who five minutes earlier was going to miss me, said, 'Fuck off, Alabaster.'

While I was waiting for the minibus, another screw came over.

'They bring it in in toiletry containers, don't they?' said Screw Two. 'Toothpaste tubes, cans of shaving cream . . .'

I shrugged. 'Couldn't happen. You can't get it past the dogs.'

He shook his head. 'Those fucking dogs . . . Come on, Alabaster, what do you take us for? Most of these morons, your fellow inmates, couldn't smuggle sand off Bondi Beach.'

'So why don't you stop it?'

He stared at me. 'Tell me something: you've spent a fair bit of time with these blokes – you prefer them in their natural state or out of it?

I didn't have to think about it. 'Out of it. Definitely.'

'Why?'

'Because in their natural state, they're unpleasant going on unbearable. The drugs take that loudmouth, pain-in-the-arse edge off them. All they want to do is sit around all day sucking on a bong.'

He smiled. If I didn't know better, I would've said there was a flicker of pity in his eyes. 'You know, Alabaster, for someone who's meant to be brainy, you're very fucking naive.'

In a funny sort of way, I was almost sorry to finish PD. I read more books that year than in the previous ten. I quit smoking. I had two alcohol-free days a week, like the quacks recommend. I did physical work. I got fit for the first time in my adult life.

It helped that no-one tried to pork me. There were

a lot of jokes about soap soccer in the showers but if they were playing that game, I never got selected.

I got a part-time job in a video rental store, working the seven to midnight shift four times a week. It paid peanuts but then a retarded monkey could've done it. You checked videos out, you checked them back in. You took the money, you gave the customers their change and a smile or a fuck-you look, depending on your mood and their demeanour. You put the tapes away, you put the covers back out on the shelves. When people returned overdue videos, you nailed them. If you let them off, they'd just do it again next time.

The deadshit who worked the day shift had this story about late returns. A well-dressed, middle-aged woman brought in a tape three weeks overdue – a hundred buck charge. She didn't have the money on her and offered him a handjob to let her off. He held out for a blowjob and she did him right there, behind the counter.

The guy was fucked up, even by the standards of hired help in low-rent video libraries, and a chronic liar.

Sometimes customers asked me to recommend a movie. I had four rules. Rule one: the first in a series is always the best. Rule two: if you've never heard of anyone in it, chances are it's crap. Rule three: if it never got theatre release, chances are it's crap. Rule four: no faggot ever felt short-changed by a Barbra Streisand movie.

It was shit work but I needed every cent. I was more or less unemployable. There wasn't a merchant bank in the country which would've hired me to clean the toilets.

At least I had a roof over my head. The only asset of mine the government and the lawyers hadn't got their hands on was that investment property, a one-bedroom shoebox in Macleay Street, Potts Point. It didn't have a view. It didn't get the sun. It had more cockroaches than Tijuana. But it didn't cost me a cent – I'd paid the dump off when I was loaded.

I lived on toast and pasta. I restricted myself to one espresso and two glasses of cheap red a day. I scraped by. It wasn't much of an existence but no-one was offering me a better one.

And the entertainment was free: I watched videos and I watched people.

I'd get to the local cafe early. I'd nab a good table and a copy of the *Herald*. I'd observe the comings and goings from behind my sunglasses. My ears flapped. I sucked information out of the air like an electronic eavesdropping post.

I soon got to know the regulars.

See that bunch of forty-something males over there? They're academics. They teach everything from medieval literature to pop culture. They gather every morning to talk about sport and postmodernism and who's going mad this week.

The pretty boys in the shorts and singlets? Muscle Marys. They talk about work-out routines and waxing their legs and who's dying this week. There go the gangsters with their soft-top BMWs and their mobile phones. There go the model girls with their navel rings and cigarettes. Those two little cuties in black, they're lipstick lesbians. I bet they have fun. There go the middle-aged trendies with their after-thought single child who'd rather be at home having cornflakes, like a normal kid.

And here come the billion-dollar babes.

The brunette used to be Carla Craig, the model. Now she's Carla Sully, Reece Sully's trophy wife. Reece is obscenely rich. He's a corporate raider, a real slash-and-burn merchant. My ex-colleagues thought he was just the big dog's dick. I could say Carla does it for me and leave it there but it goes further than that. A lot further. The fact is, I'm mesmerised by her. I wish I had my old life back, I wish I'd never insider-traded – or more to the point, I wish I hadn't got caught – but not half as much as I wish I had Carla.

I dream about her a lot. The dreams are mind-blowing but waking up's a killer – that kick-in-the-balls moment when it dawns on you that she's not there and she never was.

The blonde's Penny Wheat. She used to be on TV. She married some blueblood. It lasted about a year, then she ripped his lungs out in the divorce settlement. She's always parading her cleavage in the social pages.

And this fucker, I don't know who he is. I call him Engelbert Humperdinck. Carla and Penny always seem pleased to see him – get a load of that ridiculous Frog double-kiss routine. What's he got that I haven't got apart from curly hair, a fake tan and a Rolex?

A life maybe?

The video store, 11.40 on a Friday night. I was checking my watch every five minutes like I had something to look forward to. A guy rushed in to return a tape. It was Engelbert Humperdinck. He slapped the tape down on the counter and pissed off without a word. Fuck you too.

The movie was *To Catch a Thief* – second-rate Hitchcock, a Cary Grant/Grace Kelly caper on the French Riviera. Cary might've been a homo but he wore a tux with conviction. Gracie might've been a nympho but she sure looked good in a red sports car and a Hermès scarf.

I took the tape out of the cover. It didn't have a label – Engelbert Dickbrain had brought back the wrong tape. I stuck it in the VCR to see what it was and got a blast of heavy porn action, a slim blonde slurping cock. I killed it fast when a customer walked in.

When the customer left with his nightly dose of stalk 'n' slash, I checked the computer. The porn fan was Ray Hanna and we were neighbours: Hanna lived in the next building.

I wasn't back in the store till Tuesday night. That didn't suit me at all – I wanted to watch Hanna squirm when he reclaimed his wank flick. I decided to return it in person.

I closed up at midnight and took Hanna's tape home.

I had a glass of wine and recorked the bottle – it had to last three days. I turned on TV and zapped through the channels – universal shit. I cleaned my teeth. As I went to turn out the lights, I saw Hanna's tape on the bench. Might as well have a look, I thought; might help me get to sleep. Or something.

I put the tape in the machine, rewound it all the way and hit play. Talk about cut to the chase. There was no title, no credits, no scene-setting, no dialogue, no background music. One moment the screen was black, next a couple of healthy specimens were going for gold in the missionary position.

She moaned and drummed her heels. He heaved away till the meat musket went off. Cut to more of the same: a different couple going at it like epileptics. This pair hammed it up. The chick looked into the camera and stuck her tongue out. The guy looked over his shoulder and winked. He asked, 'Is she a good root or what?'

The penny dropped. This wasn't product, this was the mother of all home movies. There was no editing to speak of, no camera angles. One set-up per scene, point the camera at the bed and roll it. It had an eighties feel – maybe it was the haircuts.

The cast definitely weren't pros – they were too young, too fresh, way too enthusiastic. The sex wasn't mechanical. These kids weren't gritting their teeth through the same old routine. They weren't bored or even detached. They were into it.

The biggest difference of all? Unlike run-of-the-mill porn, it was a full-blast turn-on. I rodded up, big-time. I felt like I had a gold bar in my jeans.

I hit fast forward and whizzed through some girl-on-top stuff into a masturbation sequence. *Oooh, baby*. I slowed the action down. This girl was a heartbreaker, stone gorgeous. She was blissed out. She was Carla Craig-Sully.

She looked about nineteen or twenty, girl going on woman. The face was a little rounder and the hair was different but it was her all right. It was Carla. No doubt about it.

I sat in the privacy of my apartment watching my dream lover – a woman I studied surreptitiously and with a terrible longing several times a week – wearing nothing but an ankle chain, playing with herself. It was definitely a first for me.

I fast-forwarded. I saw Carla doing lesbianism, body-surfing on the chick who'd poked her tongue out. They weren't taking it too seriously.

I saw Carla getting it fore and aft from a husky tag team. That was serious. That was hard-core.

I came without laying a finger on myself. Which was also a first.

TWO

Sleep came and went like a persistent fly that night. I flopped around the bed, buzzing on Carla going wild.

I got up late and listless. I was going cold on the idea of tweaking Hanna. The fact that the tape was a slice of life as opposed to another unit off the production line changed everything. Then there was Hanna's relationship with Carla. They hung out together. They communicated in murmurs and giggles, the language of intimacy. Maybe it was just me but it wasn't a big stretch to put them between the sheets. Not any more perhaps, but there'd been a time.

The thought of it triggered waves of toxic jealousy.

I decided, fuck it, just get the Hitchcock movie back and be done with it. I threw on some clothes and headed out with the tape. I got as far as the end of the corridor. I couldn't help myself – I had to have one last look. I went back and put the tape on. I jerked off watching Carla give herself an orgasm.

I cleaned up, feeling mildly ashamed. We all beat the meat from time to time but doing it before breakfast isn't too healthy. I had to get rid of that fucking tape.

I tried again. There was foot traffic in and out of Hanna's building. I joined it and slipstreamed in. The apartments were numbered by floors; Hanna's was 51. I took the lift to the fifth floor. Apartment 51 was at the end of the corridor.

The door was ajar.

I knocked. Nothing happened. I nudged the door further open and asked if anyone was home. No-one was admitting to it. I checked out a hallway containing a rug and a flower arrangement on a stand. Potts Point residents like nothing better than poking their noses into other people's apartments and it was a while since I'd had the chance. My eye was a little rusty but the rug looked at least ten grand's worth. Which was more than could be said for me. I saw myself in the oval mirror facing the door. I looked strung-out and shabby, one foot on the down escalator to cask wine oblivion on a park bench.

I called Hanna's name. No reply. It was time to forget the whole thing and go get my caffeine shot but curiosity made me creep across the hall and crane around a doorway.

Hanna was either moving out or he'd forgotten where he'd stashed his drugs. The place wasn't quite a shambles but nothing was where it belonged. Mostly it was on the floor. Maybe there'd been a break-in; if so, the thieves were choosy to a fault.

I picked my way through the mess to the kitchen. Same thing: cupboards and drawers emptied, stuff stacked any old how on the bench, no sign of Hanna.

I kept going. I don't know why. I don't know what I expected to find.

I went down the corridor. The first door opened into a study which had been trashed. Behind the second door was a bedroom. That's where Hanna was and that's where he'd stay till they bagged him and wheeled him out.

He was on the bed, naked. There were a lot of punctures in his chest. There was a lot of blood.

I stood there inhaling death. My engine had seized up. I wanted to scream but couldn't make a sound. I wanted to run but couldn't lift a foot off the floor. It took every ounce of will I possessed to inch backwards out of that bedroom.

The paralysis lifted in the corridor. I strangled a howl and bolted, stampeding through the living room, knocking over piles of books and trampling objets d'art. They must've heard me in the Blue Mountains. I took the stairs – I would've freaked out waiting for the lift. I didn't meet anyone on the stairs or in the foyer. Lucky me. Lucky them.

It wasn't till I was back in Roach Central that I realised I still had the dead man's dirty video.

I got fever shakes. I paced up and down trying to make them go away but it didn't work. I dithered: Should I ring the cops? Did they trace triple-0 calls? Would they believe me?

A siren blared. I went out to the street. A cop car, blue lights flashing, was double-parked outside Hanna's building. An unmarked car pulled up. Two guys in jeans jumped out and charged inside. I went back to my apartment.

I got into bed and pulled the bedclothes over my head. It took ten minutes for the shakes to go away. It took twenty to fall asleep.

I dreamt. I was in Hanna's apartment. I heard sex sounds from the bedroom and went to investigate.

Carla Sully was straddling Hanna's butchered corpse. She was sending him off in style.

Carla stopped humping. Her face darkened. She spat, 'You've seen what you shouldn't've seen.' She unplugged herself, groped under the pillow and came up with a psycho killer's knife. She rushed me, hissing hate.

I woke up sweat-drenched and nauseous. The room spun. I lurched to the bathroom and gushed vomit into the toilet bowl. I fainted. Coming back up was beautiful: I was light-headed; I felt purged. I got the shakes again but that was just puke aftershock. I could handle that.

I stayed in all day. I thought about the dead man and I thought about Carla.

The quote brutal slaying unquote of well-known photographer and film-maker Ray Hanna made the TV news. They ran a sound-bite from a poser in dark glasses who claimed to be stunned, shattered, devastated. A detective with hooded, unshockable eyes said the murder weapon hadn't been recovered.

We got the victim's life and times in a 90-second package. For films read TV ads. They ran a snippet of Hanna's award-winning baked bean commercial, a straight steal of the campfire fart chorus in *Blazing Saddles*. Photography had been his thing lately — apparently he was in big demand as a society photographer.

Watching it, I broke out in a sweat; my armpits foamed. When the doorbell rang, I vibrated with fright. I towelled off before I answered it.

It was the cops, a uniformed constable and a plain-clothes detective, twice-a-week shavers the pair of them. They asked me if I knew a Mr Ray Hanna.

I shook my head, not trusting my voice. They said he lived next door. I tried to look puzzled but eager to help. They said he was murdered last night. I did my best to register shock but my face was out of control. I felt like a contestant in a funny faces competition. If they couldn't tell I was lying, they were in the wrong job.

They asked me if I'd seen/heard anything strange/suspicious. I managed to answer in the negative. They produced a photograph of the deceased. Their body language said they'd given up on me. I told them he looked vaguely familiar, I guessed I'd seen him around. They took down my details. They gave me a number to call if anything occurred to me and went on to the next futile door-knock.

I put the videotape on and fast-forwarded through it, concentrating on faces. Unless he'd had plastic surgery, Hanna wasn't one of the studs. But he had made films. Maybe it was a Ray Hanna production.

Maybe Hanna had bided his time until Carla Craig became Carla Sully, then put the squeeze on her: pay up or Big Reece gets to see his trophy wife whoring in a stag film. She flipped out, punched holes in his chest, then turned his pad upside down looking for the tape.

If it did happen that way, one thing was for sure: right now, Carla would be shitting bricks, wondering when and where the tape was going to turn up.

The more I thought about it, the more far-fetched it seemed. Bad dreams aside, it was hard to imagine Carla hacking pieces out of anyone, whatever the provocation. I couldn't see her going berserk.

I got up at six the next morning and walked up to the video store. I went into the storeroom where we retired slow product when we needed the display space. I put Hanna's tape in a *Showgirls* cover. When it first came out, we'd had twelve copies on display but not even the pervs could be bothered. I got on a stepladder and shoved Hanna's tape and the empty *To Catch a Thief* cover right to the back of the top shelf. On the way home I dropped the *Showgirls* tape in a rubbish bin outside an Indian restaurant.

The Sunday papers went big on Hanna. There was a photo of the cop with the hooded eyes: Dean Donald, a detective-sergeant at Kings Cross. He speculated that Hanna might've tangled with a burglar and described the killer's handiwork as savage. The scribes preferred frenzied.

Donald appealed for assistance. He was sure someone out there possessed information relating directly or indirectly to the crime.

He was dead fucking right.

Two days went by. Carla didn't show at the cafe.

The porno tape ran non-stop in my head. I couldn't blank it out. I gave in. I retrieved it from the storeroom and stayed up till dawn, watching Carla's scenes over and over.

I was in freefall, spiralling into an obsession I couldn't pin a name on. It was too sweet to call lust, too hot to deserve a better label.

There was only one way out. I put in long hours at the cafe. I stretched to two espressos. Late on Friday morning, Carla finally showed up.

She was by herself. She wore tailored black trousers and a white bodyshirt which emphasised her bust and her tan. She sat in the shade and put her sunglasses in her hair.

I deep-breathed. Carla ordered a latte. She picked a glossy magazine from the rack and skimmed it, bored. Her mobile phone rang; she blew the caller off in ten seconds flat.

I watched her like a peeping tom. She didn't look haunted, she didn't look deranged. She looked like a very rich, very beautiful woman with too much time on her hands.

It was now or never. I went over to her. Up close now, close enough to see past the make-up. Carla had no need for tricks of the trade. She was as close to perfect as any human being I'd ever seen.

I'm no stud but I've been around. I'm comfortably into double figures. They were a mixed bunch: romantics who hoped it meant something and realists who knew it didn't; cautious women who eventually concluded that they wouldn't be ashamed to wake up beside me and good-time girls who didn't think that far ahead. There was an American, a southern lady, who took me to bed because I was the only other guest at the dinner party who didn't piss their pants over 'Seinfeld' – it transpired that she didn't particularly care for New York Jews. There was a scriptwriter who aimed to double her tally of lovers every decade to soften the blow of reaching those ominous milestones. There was a Tasmanian woman who said I reminded her of her father. Okay, I made that one up, but you get the idea.

Some were good company but not wildly sexy; a few were both, a few were neither. Some were good-looking, none were ugly. But not one of them was beautiful.

Maybe I've seen too many movies but I've always aspired to a beautiful woman. They're rare but they do exist. And they are different, I firmly believe that. Whenever I saw a beautiful woman, I'd think about the difference. How would it manifest itself? How would it *feel*? I'd think that there was a man – or men – somewhere who knew and I'd shrivel with envy. I'd wonder if my turn would ever come.

When I had money and prospects, I was doggedly hopeful. Now that I had next-to-no money and dire prospects, hope seemed absurd. But I clung to it. The fact was, I'd never met a truly beautiful woman, never got within touching distance of one. Until now.

I said, 'Excuse me, you're Carla Sully aren't you?'

She glanced up, not wildly interested in where this was leading.

I sat down. 'I'm James Alabaster.'

She said, 'It's normal to wait for an invitation.'

The voice thrilled me. I hardly noticed the put-down.

'I need to talk to you . . .'

She raised an eyebrow. 'You need to, do you?'

'It's important . . .'

'I doubt that somehow. Look, I don't wish to be rude but I'm meeting someone . . .'

I got out the sledgehammer. 'Obviously not Ray Hanna – poor old Ray's sipped his last cappuccino.'

She stared. 'What did you say?'

'Hanna was a friend of yours, wasn't he? I've seen you here with him.'

Carla filed me under C for Creep. She got ready to run.

I leaned forward, earnest as could be. 'If you'll just listen to me for a minute, I'm trying to help you.'

'What makes you think I need help?'

'Hanna had a videotape of you and some friends . . . letting your hair down.'

If she wasn't genuinely baffled, she'd missed her calling. 'I've got no idea what you're talking about. What tape?'

'It's a kind of do-it-yourself blue movie. I'd say it's about fifteen years old.'

Carla's eyes got huge. She whispered, 'Oh my God.'

She stared at me for a few seconds then looked away. After a while, she took a packet of Dunhills from her handbag and lit one using a designer version of a Zippo lighter.

She blew smoke, shaking her head. 'That's impossible,' she said. 'It just can't be.' It had the finality of a papal decree.

'Why not?'

She still wasn't looking at me. 'There was only one copy and Adam destroyed it.'

'Who's Adam?'

'He was . . . uh . . . a guy I knew. It was all his idea.'

'Where is he now?'

After a pause: 'He's dead.'

'Well, I don't wish to speak ill of the dead, but if Adam told you he destroyed that tape, he lied.'

Now she looked my way, anger sparking in her eyes. She snapped, 'I was there, I saw him do it. He threw it in the fire.'

I shrugged. 'Maybe he made a switch and burned some other tape – one videotape looks like any other, so how could you be sure it was the right one? Either that or he made a copy.'

I told her how it'd come into my hands. I didn't

tell her that I'd tried to return it. There was a very long silence. I couldn't tell what she was thinking.

It turned out that she was thinking about the next step. 'Assuming you're telling the truth, where's the tape now?'

'In a safe place.'

'What are you going to do with it?'

'That depends.'

'On what?'

'On whether or not you killed Hanna.'

She let go a peal of what used to be called gay laughter. Her violet eyes were as clear as a child's.

'Do I look like a murderer to you, James?'

It was nice to be able to tell the truth for a change.

The fact that I didn't think she looked like a killer seemed to settle her nerves. She changed the subject: could I recommend any good videos? I'm not kidding. One minute it was matters of life and death, the next, what's hot in home entertainment.

I told her my four rules. She thought they made sense. She agreed you had to be gay or at least in the closet to give a shit for La Streisand.

She asked, 'Are you homophobic?'

'What makes you think that?'

'You said faggots. My gay friends don't mind being called queers or poofs but they really hate that word.'

I shrugged. 'I'll bear that in mind next time I'm talking to one.'

'My husband says it all the time and he's definitely homophobic.'

'Does he mind you having gay friends?'

'God, no.' She smiled a private smile. 'He's not silly.'

I wasn't sure what to make of that. I wasn't sure what, if anything, I was meant to make of it. Glancing away, trying to think of something to say to keep the conversation going on that track, I noticed Penny Wheat crawl past in a VW Golf with the roof down. She was looking for a park.

I was disappointed and relieved at the same time. I wasn't ready for the next step; I wasn't prepared for light, loose conversation. I didn't want to tune her out with something leaden like, 'So, Carla, are you doing any modelling these days?'

So I pointed. 'I think your date's arrived.'

Carla glanced over her shoulder and gave Penny a wave. She was frowning when she turned back to me. 'How did you know?'

'It seemed a reasonable assumption – I've seen the two of you here often enough.'

Carla tilted her head, eyes wide. She looked even more adorable. 'Well, aren't you the observant one? You've seen me with Ray, you've seen me with Penny . . . I'm beginning to think you've been spying on me.'

I felt myself go pink. 'No, it's just that I spend a lot of time here – I've got plenty of it.' I wasn't sure if she'd bought it so I threw in some flattery. 'And, let's face it, you and your friend do stand out in a crowd.'

Her eyebrows twitched lazily. Feeble compliments left her cold. 'As long as you're not a stalker. I can really do without a stalker in my life.'

'Do I look like a stalker to you, Carla?'

Her face stayed blank. As far as she was concerned, it was a serious question. 'How would I know? I've never met one. You come across as quite intense . . .'

That was my cue. I stood up. 'I better get moving – my shrink insists on punctuality.'

This time I smiled to let her know it was a joke. She was past caring. She watched Penny crossing the road. Without looking at me, Carla said, 'Goodbye for now. I've got a feeling we haven't seen the last of each other.'

The message was: we have unfinished business. That was fine by me.

I went inside to pay. When I came out, Carla and Penny had their heads together. They raised their eyes in perfect synchrony. Penny was curious, Carla was impassive. She could've been seeing me for the very first time. I walked away knowing that they were talking about me, wondering what she was saying.

That night I took the tape back to the shop. I hid it in the storeroom again, disguised as *Showgirls*. Now that Carla and I were cafe buddies, it didn't seem right to keep watching it.

THREE

That was Friday. On Monday morning I was at the cafe, reading the paper at a pavement table. For once, I didn't see Carla coming. She pulled up a stool and sat down.

'Hi, James.'

'Hi, Carla.'

Her skirt was distractingly short. Her brown legs had a warm, inviting sheen. I ached to touch them.

A waiter arrived. She ordered a latte; I splashed out on another espresso.

She asked, 'How was your weekend?'

The fact was, I'd spent a lot of it thinking about her. Not actually thinking about fucking her, but trying to devise a convincing environment for a fantasy fuck. With fantasy, context is everything. It would've been easy to imagine us in bed but before I could savour her skin, I'd be asking, whose bed? Where's this supposed to be happening?

Think about it. My joint was out of the question: Roach Central would put Carla Sully off faster than bad breath. It would've been frivolous to believe otherwise and frivolity has no place in a fantasy. The more realistic the scenario, the more intense the fantasy – that's how it works. Ditto, her place. Once domestic staff and a husband were factored in, I had to accept that the notion of her taking me home was just as frivolous.

It was a problem. The action couldn't start until I had a narrative and a location. I didn't have friends with stylish or even respectable apartments which were available for assignations. Maybe Carla did. That Penny Wheat looked like a good sport. I could see her coming to the party.

On and on like that – we never even kissed. That was fine. It would all happen in its own sweet time.

I said, 'Bit of a non-event really.'

'Sorry to hear it. Maybe you should get out more.'

'You're probably right.'

She took her sunglasses off and we made eye contact. 'So what'd you do – sit around watching the tape?'

Boxers say it's the ones you don't see coming which do the damage. They know what they're talking about. I went into a verbal clinch. 'Uh, no . . . no, I didn't. I read a book, as a matter of fact, a thing called *The Information*, all 500 pages of it . . .'

'Don't tell me you're bored with it already?'

Careful. 'I wouldn't say that exactly.'

She said, 'What would you say, exactly?' Getting an edge into her voice.

The coffees arrived – saved by the bell. Carla lit a Dunhill, jumpy, and changed tack. 'Well, my weekend wasn't much fun either – I spent most of it worrying about you.'

'You mean . . . ?'

'I don't mean that I was worried on your behalf,' she interrupted. 'I'm the one with the problem, not you. You haven't got a problem, you're part of the problem.'

'How's that?'

'Jesus, put yourself in my shoes. A person I don't know from a bar of soap pops up with something awful out of my past I thought was dead and buried ... how would you feel?'

'I don't know. Vulnerable, I guess.'

'Good guess. That's exactly how I feel – extremely fucking vulnerable.'

I could see where this was heading. She was working up to demanding that I hand over the videotape. I didn't want to do that. That tape was my entrance ticket to Carla's world. The moment I handed it over, I'd be back on the outside, looking in.

'Are you worried that I'm going to cause trouble?'

Carla rolled her eyes. 'What do you think?'

'Why would I want to do that?'

'You tell me. I don't know anything about you so how would I know what you want?'

'I could've given the tape to the cops – that would've really fucked up your weekend.'

'Oh, I get it – you're protecting me.'

I didn't let the sarcasm bug me. 'If you want to put it that way. Look, you don't have to worry about me. I'm not going to give the tape to the cops or anyone else.' She wasn't convinced. I tried again, oozing sincerity. 'Carla, believe me, I'm not going to cause you any trouble. That's the last thing I want to do.'

She didn't overdo it. She didn't break into a melting smile or squeeze my hand. She inspected me gravely for thirty long seconds. Then her expression softened and she said, 'Okay, I believe you.'

It was a long time since I'd experienced such a rush of pure joy. Longer than I cared to remember.

She watched my eyes light up. 'Can I ask you a personal question?'

I was never much of a one for looking on the bright side. After my career crashed and burned, I didn't have much choice: I was sentenced to a lifetime of low expectations. But I was on a high and her request sent me into euphoria overload. I knew what she was going to ask – something along the lines of 'Are you in a relationship right now?' And as we all know, that's code for 'Let's talk about you and me.'

'Go right ahead.'

'Why do you work in a video shop?'

I felt my face sag. 'Well, it's not for the money.'

'I didn't think so.'

'Or the job satisfaction.'

She smiled politely. 'No, I wouldn't've picked that either.'

'Basically, I don't have a lot of choice. I used to work in the corporate sector but that's no longer an option.'

'Why not?'

This was dangerous ground given that I'd just got through doing my Trust me, I'm a man of integrity routine. 'I screwed up.'

'Oh. Sorry I asked.'

'No big deal. Money can't buy happiness, right?'

She laughed. 'Depends where you shop.'

Her mobile phone rang. She answered it and came alive. Whoever it was answered to the name 'darling'. She put on a dumb show to let me know it wouldn't be a brief conversation. It was a dismissal and a pretty offhand one at that.

Burning all the way back to the apartment. Thinking, fucking bitch, one of these days you'll be sorry. Wanting to hurt her back.

Another fucked-up male hating a woman for not falling at his feet.

You might be wondering why is this guy Alabaster so isolated? What about family and friends? Where's the support network? Everybody has somebody, don't they? Even the losers.

It goes like this.

I was born thirty years ago in the town of Cessnock in the Hunter Valley. My father was a coalfield wages clerk. My mother was his wife. Cessnock was somewhere you left behind. My parents never understood that.

I've got a sister, Harriet. She's seven years older than me; it might as well be 107. All she ever wanted to be was a Bride of Christ. The day she turned twenty-one she went into a convent. As far as I know, she's still there.

When I was ten, my parents gave up on their marriage. Dad transferred his affections to alcohol and Mum switched hers to the Country Women's Guild. Harriet's were locked into a long-term contract, so I had to do without.

Dad became the kind of closet drunk who shaved every morning, wore a jacket and tie and did most of his drinking at home. Mum went bananas the way neurotic, ignorant people often do in the bush: the financial system was a Jew/Freemason scam, everyone in Canberra was a commie, the Irish Catholics planned to murder us in our beds if the Abos didn't get us first, the government was putting something in the water to turn us into zombies. Dad was one step ahead of them – he never touched the stuff.

I was friendly with a few kids at school but not too friendly. If you got too friendly, you went to their place to play after school. Some nights you'd stay for dinner and in the holidays you'd sleep over in a pup tent in the backyard. But that hospitality had to be repaid, that was the etiquette. And any kid who spent a night at the Alabasters' would go home with a small-town horror story to tell: Mr Alabaster giggling like a child, Mr Alabaster weeping like a child, Mr Alabaster leaving the table on his hands and knees while Mrs Alabaster barked about kikes and tykes and coons and slant-eyes. And for our pièce de résistance, Mr Alabaster throwing up into the umbrella stand while Harriet damned him with Old Testament hellfire.

I was trying to protect them as well as avoid humiliation. It never occurred to me that the whole town had their number.

I was on my own and I wasn't much good at sport. There was nothing to stop me doing well at school. As soon as I finished high school, I went to Newcastle. I lived in a student hostel and studied accountancy and management. I've been back to Cessnock twice – once to bury my father, the second time to hold a garage sale after the men in white coats took my mother away.

I took it slowly at the hostel. The student life ran on booze and drugs and I'd seen the damage done. I heard that the film society was full of serious-minded girls. I thought they might be easier to talk to. I couldn't do small talk; I hadn't had any practice.

It was one of those French movies in which the characters smoke lots of cigarettes while they talk things to death and the doe-eyed heroine falls hard for Monsieur Wrong. Jane thought it was a work of art and I was happy to agree. Jane was a thirty-four-year-old divorcee who taught English at a local high school. Like me, she was looking for love.

A few weeks later, I moved into her place. Jane wouldn't let me pay rent. She said I could pay her back when I got rich. I promised I would.

Jane showed me that food didn't have to come out of a packet or stay in the oven till it turned to pumice. She showed me that wine didn't have to have bubbles. She did things in bed that school teachers weren't supposed to know about. She made me a worldly young man by Hunter Valley standards.

After I graduated, I got a job with a Sydney investment fund. Every Friday night I caught the train back to Jane. That went on until I joined the merchant bank and became a hot-shot. Hot-shots didn't spend their weekends in Newcastle getting surrogate mother love – it didn't fit the image. Besides, being up there at weekends meant missing out on all kinds of fun, not to mention major networking opportunities.

I told Jane it was the job, I just couldn't get away. When she started making noises about moving down to Sydney to take up a longstanding job offer, we'd reached the end of the line. I had to let her go. I mean, if you showed up at the MD's cocktail party with an old girl from the sticks on your arm, people would start to wonder. In the fast lane, you've got to think about these things.

A few days after the shit hit the fan, Jane left a message on my answering machine. She was sorry to hear about my difficulties but she was sure everything would turn out all right. If I needed someone to talk to or somewhere to get away from it all, I knew where to find her.

I didn't return the call. I had enough problems without feeling ashamed of myself.

My friends and colleagues – most of them fell into both categories – reacted in various ways. Some shunned me from the moment the news broke. I guess the one who dobbed me in was among them. Some stood by me until I was convicted, then spelt out my side of the deal: now I could get the fuck out of their lives and stay there. Some stood by me all the way and would have stuck around if I'd let them. I cut them loose. I appreciated the offer but no matter how hard they tried, things would never be the same again.

I lost interest – in other people, in business, in world affairs, in politics, in sport. Okay, dozing on the couch with cricket on TV was one way to fill in a day but it wasn't like I gave a flying fuck what happened. I certainly didn't want to go to the pub afterwards and analyse it. In fact, I didn't want to talk to anyone about anything. I didn't even want a woman. I couldn't be bothered.

I didn't care about police corruption or paedophile networks. I didn't care about reconciliation or multiculturalism or trailer-park fascism. I didn't care if the bush was burning, if the icecap was melting, if Russia's nuclear reactors were about to blow or if a billion people had AIDS. I didn't give a shit if a meteor hit the Opera House tomorrow.

I was waiting for a sign that any of it mattered a fuck. I was waiting for Carla.

Now you know.

FOUR

There was this Lebanese guy, Eddie, I did time with at Silverwater. He was a real punk – vicious, treacherous, full of shit.

When Eddie wasn't inside, he hung around his uncle's strip club in the Cross, spruiking on the street and doing Christ knows what else. I don't know if he was any good as a pimp but he sure as hell looked the part. He was short and skinny with an evil hook nose and one of those ridiculous westie haircuts – short top and sides and long at the back, greasy black ringlets down to his shoulders.

The punks in Silverwater used to tell each other preposterous sex stories around the clock. It kept them entertained and sustained their conviction that the world is full of wildcat nymphos even if they hadn't actually come across one yet. Eddie pumped out more hot air than any of them. Every couple of weeks, he'd drop in at the video store and blow some over me.

Sometimes his non-stop jabber drove me insane and I'd have to tell him to fuck off. He'd call me a cocksucking anglo loser and kick over a dump-bin display on the way out. Once in a while he'd go quietly, giving me the dead-eye look. Those nights, I looked over my shoulder every step of the way home.

Eddie loved the life. In the Cross, he and his kind were high in the food chain; everyone else was prey. Some of the stuff he came out with, though, you just had to laugh.

Like the Jap tourist with the microscopic dick. The hooker didn't realise he'd cracked a fat; she kept fiddling with him and ended up getting a spunk shampoo. Or the jumbo-hung black American sailor – the girl took one look and demanded danger money. Or the East European wild man who pulled a gun when the hooker tried to put a condom on him. That story went through the Cross like wildfire. The club-owners decided the guy was a point man for the Russian mafia and collectively shat themselves.

That Tuesday night, Eddie had a classic. 'This guy comes into the club, right . . .'

'Un-fucking-believable – a guy comes into a club. Jesus, what next? A guy gets on a bus?'

'Fuck you, cunt. You want to hear this or not?'

'Well, actually, Edward, now that you mention it . . .'

'Just shut up and fucking listen, all right? You'll piss yourself, I guarantee it. This guy, he looks like, I don't know, an accountant or some fucking thing. He's only there because the guys he's with have dragged him along. You know, they're probably in the middle of some business deal and he's scared that if he wimps out, they'll tell him to stick the fucking deal up his fat, fucking arse.'

'That's accountancy for you.'

Eddie gave me a look, not sure if I was having him on. 'Yeah, well, the cunt has three bourbons, right, and he's off his face. Then he spots this chick, Cherie. Now Cherie's okay at a distance – like, if you saw her across the street, you'd think, oh yeah, I'd fuck that – but up close, fucking forget it, man. I mean, she's a fucking junkie, end of story. You should've seen this guy, though ... What do they say when someone reckons a chick's a top sort but the rest of the world thinks she's a fucking sea monster?'

'Beauty's in the eye of the beholder?'

'That's the one. Anyway, this germ couldn't take his fucking eyes off Cherie. Next thing, they're on their way upstairs. Cherie tells him to strip off and get on the bed. He gets his gear off and lies on his side, facing the other way so she can't see his ugly little dick. Cherie strips down to her G-string and cuddles up to him. The cunt just lies there; he doesn't know how it works, so he's waiting for her to do something. But nothing happens. A few minutes go by, nothing fucking happens, Cherie doesn't move a muscle. He says something to her, she doesn't fucking answer. Well, even this loser knows there's more to it than getting a warm arse, so he rolls over to see what's going on. Guess what? Cherie's dead. The fucking bitch is dead as a fucking dodo. Mate, how'd you be? How would you fucking be? Your first time with a hooker and the fucking bitch drops dead on you.'

Eddie howled. He thought it was the funniest story of all time. I half-listened to him rave on – 'Mate, no bullshit, I'm telling you, the fucking bitch croaked on him.' I was wondering when Carla would ask for the tape. I'd just reached the obvious conclusion – the next time we met – when someone walked into the shop.

I thought it'd be one of the Undead. The Undead

were regulars who usually came in between ten and midnight and hired three or four movies at a time. They watched anything and everything. They sat through a truly staggering amount of shit. They were fucking weirdos who avoided sunlight and shunned human contact. I was always pleased to see them. They made me feel like David Niven.

But it wasn't one of the Undead. It was the cop with hooded eyes. He looked Eddie up and down. 'What are you doing here?'

Eddie's eyes skittered to and fro. 'What do you think, man?' he shrugged. 'It's a fucking video shop. I'm checking out the vids.'

The cop said, 'Anything tickle your fancy?'

Eddie pulled a what-the-fuck face. 'Eh?'

'Have you found a video you'd like to hire?'

'Uh, no, I seen most of the good ones ...'

'In that case, get lost.'

Eddie stepped around the cop as if he was a pavement turd. He winked at me and swaggered out of the shop.

The cop came up to the counter. He looked dog-tired and bored shitless. He placed a videotape in front of me and pointed to the sticker with the store's name and address. 'One of yours, I presume.'

I picked it up and checked the title on the spine: *To Catch a Thief*. Oh, shit.

He flashed ID. 'Detective-Sergeant Donald, Kings Cross. I'm investigating the murder of a bloke called Ray Hanna ...'

I said I'd seen something about it on TV.

'That video was in Hanna's apartment. What's strange is we didn't find a cover for it. You don't hire them out without covers, do you?'

'No.'

'What sort of cover would it have?'

'We usually put them in these things.' I showed him one of the standard clear plastic covers. 'But if we've only got the one copy, we leave them in the original covers. This one's got Cary Grant and Grace Kelly in a clinch with a Mediterranean scene in the background . . .'

'Hang on, I better take this down.' He produced a pocket-sized notebook and ballpoint. 'What was that again?'

'It's here if you want to have a look at it.'

'Say again.'

'The cover's here.' I pointed behind me with my thumb. 'In the storeroom.'

'How come?'

'Hanna brought it back.'

Donald put down his pen. He didn't look half asleep any more. 'When?'

'It would've been . . . let's see . . . a week ago last Friday.'

'A week ago last Friday? What time?'

'Pretty late, not long before I knocked off. Say around about half past eleven.'

Donald nodded thoughtfully. 'So far, that makes you the last person to see him alive – apart from the murderer, of course.' His voice rose. 'It didn't occur to you that we'd be interested in any information about the deceased's movements on the night of his death?'

'Well, I'm sorry but it didn't seem that big a deal. I mean, the guy just popped in to return a video. No-one followed him, there wasn't anyone lurking outside with a knife . . .'

'What sort of state was he in?'

I shrugged. 'I couldn't tell. He just dropped off the tape and shot through.'

'What'd he say?'

'Nothing – not a word. Not even hello.'

'You were here by yourself?'

'Yeah.'

'Were there any other customers in the shop?'

'No.'

Donald scribbled in his notebook. Still writing, he asked, 'He obviously didn't bring back an empty cover, so what was in it?'

I was ready for that. 'Some sort of advertising thing, you know, like a demo tape.'

'Where is it?'

'In the storeroom. We . . .'

'Let's see.'

'There's a carton full of odd tapes back there, stuff that people brought in by mistake and never claimed, damaged tapes, crap that no-one ever watched – I just chucked it in there.'

'Could you find it for me?'

'Shit, it'd take me all night. Without a label, you've got no idea what's what.'

Donald sighed. 'Okay. Get me the carton – I'll take them.'

I brought the carton out. There were over fifty tapes in there, all kinds of rubbish including marketing and promotional stuff. I could've told Donald he'd be wasting his time, but I didn't. It was too late to start behaving like a responsible citizen.

'Did you try to get hold of Hanna when you realised he'd brought back the wrong tape?'

'At that hour of night? People usually realise what's happened and come back next day.'

'Okay, let's have your name – I might want to talk to you again.'

I gave it to him.

'James Alabaster – that rings a bell. Now why would that be?'

I owned up to being a convicted criminal. He was probably going to run a check on me anyway.

Donald shook his head. 'No, that's not it. I don't follow the white collar stuff – far as I'm concerned, they're all bloody sharks. That explains what that slimy little Leb was doing here but not why your name rings a bell. I don't think I'm getting it mixed up – it's not exactly a common name, is it?'

There was a glint of amusement in Donald's eyes. It dawned on me that the prick was playing games. He'd known all along.

He snapped his fingers. 'I've got it: I saw your name in a door-knock report. You and Hanna were neighbours, right?'

'Yep.'

'He had a bloody nice view there. How about your place?'

'I'm on the ground floor.'

Donald didn't seem too choked up about that. He put his notebook and ballpoint away and picked up the carton. 'Do you think you could give us a yell next time someone walks out of here never to be seen alive again? Would that be too much to ask?'

'You can count on it.'

He had his hands full with the carton so I held the door open for him. As he went past, I asked, 'So what's the theory: you reckon it was a burglary that got out of hand or is there a psycho loose on the Point?'

Donald stopped and looked at me. 'Most of these things come down to sex or money,' he said. 'This time, my dough's on sex.'

I walked home feeling like the Scarlet Pimpernel. Donald had a way of sneaking up on you, but he'd got no change out of me. I'd kept my cool. I'd fed him a watertight line on the videotape. All he had to show for his night's work was a carton-load of dross. Imagine the poor bastard, parked in front of a TV with his ballpoint and notepad playing spot the clue. Have fun, Sherlock.

But hubris was a hard act to sustain in Roach Central. By the time I'd wiped the bowl clean with yesterday's bread, I was starting to twitch. I'd obstructed a murder investigation. I'd withheld evidence and lied to the police. Christ, what had I let myself in for?

In the morning I rang one of the lawyers who'd worked wonders on my behalf in the insider trading case. I asked him for a crash course in the law relating to obstruction of justice.

'Why do you want to know?'

'A friend of mine might be in a bit of a jam.'

'What is it with friends?' said the lawyer. 'They're always in the shit. Of course, that means I'm now on the clock. If it was for you, I'd do it for free because I figure I punched James Anthony Lewis Alabaster's ticket pretty hard last time around. But if it's for someone else, it's going to cost.'

I told him it wasn't for a friend.

'No shit? What the fuck have you done now, Alabaster?'

'Nothing. That's the whole point – I haven't really

done anything. What I want to know is, where do I stand if I carry on doing nothing?'

I got five solid minutes of legal tongue-flap. I got misprision of felony, I got conspiracy to pervert the course of justice, I got the Lionel Murphy case. To my untrained mind, Lionel Murphy had bugger-all to do with it. He ran me through common law and statutory law. He drew a distinction between non-assistance and active obstruction: 'Take the example of a corporate crime . . .'

'Now you're talking my language.'

'. . . it's one thing to simply not draw the authorities' attention to a relevant document. It's another thing altogether to go out of your way to conceal the existence of that document. You see what I mean?'

I asked, bottom line, how seriously did the cops take it?

'Not particularly' seemed to be the answer. The cops had pretty low expectations of the general public and zero of a suspect's family and friends. At least that was the way it worked with run-of-the-mill criminal activity starring the usual suspects. If it was a high-profile case involving respectable citizens who should know better, they might look at it differently.

'Just as a matter of interest,' I said, 'what's the damage?'

'If it's a common law offence, there's no limit, so theoretically you could get life. In practice, it would depend on the nature of the case but you'd probably be looking at two or three years. From memory, the statutory offence carries a five year max.'

I thanked him for putting my mind at ease.

'Alabaster, let me give you some free advice: you fucked up once, don't do it again. If you have information that's relevant or may be relevant to a criminal investigation, just give it to the police.'

'It's not quite that simple.'

He said, 'I don't think I ever told you this but when we were working on your case, every now and again one of the guys would shake his head and say, "Jesus, that fucking Alabaster, how dumb can you get?" Sometimes they'd even go on to say that anyone that thick deserved to go down. I used to stick up for you. I'd say we could call you a lot of things – naive, greedy, careless, pretty fuzzy in the strategic thinking department – but stupid wasn't one of them. Whatever you were, I'd say, you definitely weren't stupid. But you know what? I think they were right. I think you're seriously fucking dumb.'

'I guess you're right,' I said. 'Why else would I be asking you for legal advice?'

FIVE

I went to the cafe. Carla was there. So was her husband.

I sat down two tables away. Carla didn't acknowledge me. I briefly entertained the possibility that she didn't want to upset Reece. More likely, she simply hadn't noticed me. Either that or she just didn't want to know.

I'd met Reece Sully a couple of times in the old days, not that it would've registered with him. He was a king of the jungle and I was just another scavenger who picked over the carcasses he left in his wake. He was in his mid-forties which made him about a dozen years older than Carla. He was in work mode – dark suit trousers, white shirt, moneyman tie. His jet-black hair was slicked back from a widow's peak Jack Nicholson style and the celebrated glittering black eyes were concealed by dark glasses. The set of his mouth and jaw made you think of snakes – the sort that swallow people whole. He looked the part: Mr Win-at-all-Costs; rapacity in shiny black Prada loafers.

He also looked like he'd bulked up. I didn't remember the swell of pectorals under the white shirt or the telephone pole neck. I wondered if Carla's body beautiful had made him feel inadequate. I wondered if they had his-and-hers personal trainers.

It crossed my mind that Reece could've had a motive for killing Hanna. Hanna might've decided to go direct to the source: instead of blackmailing Carla, put the bite on her husband. Bite a shark, chances are it'll bite back. And the thing about sharks, they don't stop after one bite. That first bite just gets the bloodlust pumping.

A waiter brought out their order and stayed to fawn. They got to talking restaurants. The waiter was twenty seconds into a promo for Sydney's latest hot spot when Reece pulled the plug: he'd eaten there and wouldn't feed that shit to his dog, not that he actually had a dog because his wife wasn't a dog person.

Business as usual for big, bad Reece. Take no prisoners.

The waiter slunk back inside. If Reece did have a dog, and if he'd taken to it with a studded belt, the body language would've been much the same. Carla chided him in a low voice. I couldn't hear whether it was for being mean to a nice young homosexual whose only crime was being too eager to please, or for airing their domestic disagreements. Reece didn't bother to defend himself. He just sat there with a shit-eating grin.

He finished his coffee and stood up, dropping a ten dollar note on the table. He bent down to kiss Carla. It wasn't the lingering farewell of a couple who counted the seconds they were apart. Then again, she didn't turn her face away.

He sauntered over to a Maserati. According to the Reece Sully mythology, he had a different car for each day of the week. Carla waved and he took off, scattering pigeons. She put her nose in a newspaper. A few minutes went by. I stewed on my dismissal from her presence last time and the bad thoughts bubbled up again.

Eventually she looked around. 'James, I didn't see you there. Why didn't you say hello?'

'I didn't want to disturb you.'

'I was only reading the paper.'

I took my coffee over to her table and sat down.

She held her smile for longer than I had any right to expect. 'James, when was the last time you got out of Potts Point?'

That was a good question. 'I can't remember, to be honest. At least a month . . .'

She got her things together and stood up. 'Come on, we're going for a drive.'

Carla's ride was a dark-green Audi. A nice set of wheels but I'd expected something more exotic and said so. Cars weren't such a big thing for her, she said. She wasn't going to drive a bomb but as long as it started when it was supposed to and the seat belt didn't crush her boobs, she didn't really care what it was. Besides, she could always take her pick from Reece's fleet. That month it consisted of a Rolls for taking his mother out for dinner, a Ferrari for showing off, a Range Rover for adventures in the wild like visiting their vineyard in the Hunter Valley, some kind of high-tech Jap speed machine which he'd gone off already and an old Jag and an old Merc for tooling around the eastern suburbs at weekends. Plus, of course, the Maserati for sitting in CBD gridlock bawling obscenities.

We went down through Elizabeth Bay and headed

east on New South Head Road. Carla seemed relaxed and it rubbed off on me. I did some mental arithmetic. 'So he really does have a different car for each day of the week?'

'Oh yes.'

'You must have plenty of room at your place?'

'As a general rule, if you can afford to run seven cars, space isn't going to be a problem. It's kind of vulgar though, don't you think?'

I shrugged. 'It's his money, he can spend it how he likes.'

'That's not the issue. The issue is how he exercises that choice.'

We were passing through Double Bay. I said, 'I thought a certain amount of vulgarity went with the territory.'

Carla laughed. 'That may be so but a different car for every day of the week? That's vulgar, even by Double Bay standards.'

'Have you told him that?'

'Of course I have. He doesn't take any notice. Reece doesn't give a damn what anyone thinks of him. He works on the assumption that, whether they admit it or not, the whole world would like to be in his shoes.'

'He might be right.'

I felt Carla glance at me. I wanted to meet her eye but my nerve failed. I didn't want to push my luck: I wasn't sure she'd welcome a follow-up meaningful look, especially if it turned lecherous. Carla's skirt had been short to start with and now it had ridden right up her casually parted legs. If my gaze had strayed down there, it mightn't have come back up.

We went out through Vaucluse to Watsons Bay.

Carla turned off Old South Head Road and followed Military Road down through Dover Heights into Bondi. When we hit the strip, she pulled into a parking place overlooking the beach.

'Let's go for a walk,' she said.

It was midday. Heat poured out of a deep blue sky. By the time we reached the sand, there was a film of sweat on my face. Carla got ahead of me when I stopped to take off my shoes. I took my time, watching her fabulous behind churn brazenly beneath the clinging skirt.

The sun worshippers were out in force. Some of them were young, female and topless. She said, 'Titty City. You don't see that in Potts Point.'

'You've seen two, you've seen 'em all.'

'Well, that's a minority view. You're not a boob man, then?'

'I've got nothing against them but they're only one element in the mix. I'm more interested in the total package.'

'I'd keep my voice down if I were you. They don't go for that sort of talk around here.'

'And how about you – what do you admire in a man?'

'That he doesn't snore and that he's capable of tenderness.'

I wasn't sure if she was being serious. 'It just goes to show,' I said. 'Appearances can be deceptive.'

'Who are you referring to?'

'Your husband: going by his public image, you wouldn't think he had a tender bone in his body.'

'With Reece, what you see is what you get. And what's more, he snores like a pig. It's what they call a marriage made in heaven.'

Her tone was still light. The fact that the man she'd married struck out on both counts was presumably just another of life's little ironies.

'Getting back to tits,' she said with a fake guileless smile, 'can I take it that your girlfriend isn't over-endowed?'

'I haven't got a girlfriend.'

'Why not?'

I shrugged. 'I went through this phase – I just couldn't be bothered.'

'Are you over it now?'

I nodded. 'Yeah. I'm slowly rejoining the human race.'

'So how did you cope?' She was grinning now, getting a kick out of teasing me. 'I mean, you're a normal guy, right, with normal appetites?'

'There's a couple of ways. There's cold showers and there's the one I used.'

'James, you're beginning to sound like a bit of a wanker.'

I wondered if she'd forgotten what was on the tape. I was tempted to remind her, to point out that I'd seen her arch her back as she made herself come. But then she soothed me. She toned the grin down and added, 'That makes two of us.'

We walked on. Suddenly she laughed out loud, shaking her head. 'This is so weird, isn't it?'

'What is?'

'You and me walking on the beach, chatting away like this. You've got to admit – under the circumstances that we met, it's pretty weird.' Before I could think of a reply, she stepped in front of me. 'I've got a confession to make: I found out what happened to you. I mentioned you to a woman I know who's a finance journalist. She knew all about it.'

I said, 'I guess it was a big talking point around the market for a while there – my fifteen minutes of infamy.'

'Linda said you were unlucky. She reckoned the authorities needed a scalp to justify their existence and because they couldn't nail any of the big boys who were doing far worse things, they picked on you. She was tactful enough not to mention any names – I don't think Linda approves of Reece.'

As long as she was going to take that attitude, I was happy to play the stoic. 'I happened to be talking to one of my lawyers this morning. He didn't think luck had anything to do with it. According to him, it boiled down to the fact that I was quote fucking dumb unquote.'

'Your lawyer said that? What a turd.'

'Don't get me started.'

'Listen, if this is a sensitive subject for you . . .'

'Shit, I'm well past that stage.'

'You're sure?'

'Positive.'

'So what was jail like? As bad as you'd imagine?'

'I did periodic detention, two days a week. There's a hell of a big difference between that and a stretch on Cadbury Row.'

'What's Cadbury Row?'

'Cadbury Row is what the guys at Silverwater called full-on prison, somewhere like Long Bay. Cadbury makes chocolate, chocolate's brown – you get the picture?' She didn't. 'The implication being that your high-security, seven-days-a-week prisons are hotbeds of homosexuality, not necessarily of the consensual variety.'

Carla raised her eyebrows. 'Oh. So the place you were in wasn't that bad?'

'Much as I'd like your heart to bleed for me, no, it wasn't that bad.'

'Even so, it must've been pretty traumatic going from being rich to not being rich almost overnight?'

'I was never rich, not by ...'

'Reece's standards?'

'No, definitely not by Reece's standards.'

'Well-off then. By most people's standards, you were pretty well-off ...'

'And now I work in a video store. It was hard at first but you get used to it. At the end of the day, you don't have much choice – you either adjust or you jump off a tall building. So you adjust.'

'I don't know. I don't think I could.'

We walked on. She wanted to know why I'd talked to my lawyer. I told her about my tete-a-tete with the cop, Donald. She asked if I was really worried about it.

'There's something I didn't tell you: I was at the scene of the crime. I went to Hanna's place that Saturday morning to return the tape – this was before the cops got there. I saw the body.'

'Jesus.'

'Yeah, it wasn't pretty.' Call me Mr Nonchalant. 'I don't think I've got anything much to worry about, but still, it's not a situation you'd choose to be in.'

'That bloody tape ...'

'Don't worry about the tape. The cop wanted to know what was in the cover Hanna brought back but I had an answer worked out.'

I ran her through what I'd told Donald. She seemed impressed.

'So what's happening? Have they got any leads?'

'He said these cases were usually about sex or money and this time he was picking sex.'

That didn't get a big reaction. 'All that proves is that he's talked to a few people who knew Ray,' she said. 'Not only was Ray a serious party boy, he was a little ... off-centre. I remember someone – I forget who it was – saying sex would be his downfall one day. I doubt getting murdered was what they had in mind.' She stopped and threw out an arm. 'See that white building, the one with the roof garden?' She was pointing at a medium-rise apartment building a block back from Campbell Parade. It was as undistinguished as most of man-made Bondi. 'That's where it happened.'

'The stuff on the tape?'

'No need to be coy, James. That's where the orgy took place.'

'Who was behind the camera?'

'Who do you think?

'Hanna?'

She nodded. 'He liked to watch. Among other things.'

Carla had a lunch date. She didn't say who with. She dropped me at Bondi Junction and I got a train to the Cross. Back home, I relived our little jaunt to the seaside, weighing the significance of every word, every gesture, every look.

She wasn't starry-eyed over Reece, that was for sure. Mingled undercurrents of contempt and reluctant admiration ran through everything she said about him.

It was like a mother discussing her adorable but

vacuous teenage daughter. 'Dear Katy, she's absolutely hopeless – I really don't know what we're going to do with her.' Then she remembers the boys, the constant stream of tongue-tied boys with puppy dog eyes. And she says, 'Well, I suppose if you can't be bright, you might as well be a man-magnet.'

At this point the proud father, who probably has to pound his dick with a cold spoon whenever he sees Katy sun-bathing in her string bikini, chips in with, 'Just as well she didn't take after her old man, eh?' Ho-ho.

And mother smiles and thinks of the Swedish tennis pro at that Hawaiian hotel. Oh my, the things he did for her return of serve while hubby was at his sales conference, catching a chill from the air-conditioning.

What did you expect? Goodwill to all men, women and children and their little fluffy dogs? I'm a casualty, remember.

So much for Reece. What did Carla think of me? She'd asked her friend the finance journalist about me – that had to mean something, didn't it? Why bother if you don't give a shit? She wasn't put off by my shady past. I guess that should've been the least of my worries. You don't play house with Reece Sully if you're squeamish about what it takes to stay ahead of the field in the money race. The only rule is there are no rules. For every winner, there's got to be a loser. If you're not inside, you're outside. That's the way it is downtown, baby. You don't like it, get back to the suburbs.

In fact, she sympathised: I was a scapegoat who'd paid for the sins of others with almost everything I had. But she didn't pity me, that was the important thing. Sympathy was okay, sympathy I could live with. But there was no percentage in pity. Pity is for the children and for the terminal, the mangled, the irretrievably lost, the totally fucked. Women like Carla don't contemplate sleeping with men who fit those descriptions under any circumstances.

Which of course was what all that analysis, that painstaking reconstruction, was leading up to. Did Carla find me attractive? Had the concept of *us* crossed her mind? Did she lie awake in a vast bed in a vast bedroom in a vast house, with Reece beside her blasting nose-noise at the ceiling, and think of me? Did she wonder how much I wanted her and imagine that pent-up desire exploding? Did she visualise us coming together, panting and trembling, with a moist smack of humid flesh?

Well, it beat the shit out of counting sheep.

I used to work with this guy who had a reputation as a ladykiller. I never saw him in action but the guys who hung out with him afterhours reckoned his hit rate was phenomenal. We got teamed on a project, putting in brutal hours. Over a midnight beer and pizza, I asked him what his secret was. There was no secret: all things being equal, the best-looking guys got the most fucks. If there was some kind of celebrity in the room, forget it, try somewhere else. Beyond that, nothing had changed – you had to get over the fear of rejection, you had to be persistent, you had to be able to talk about whatever they wanted to talk about, you had to speculate to accumulate.

He said a common mistake was not letting the woman know she turned you on in case she took offence. If it was done the right way, why the fuck should she be offended? The thing was, once a woman knew you were attracted to her, she became more aware of you, she couldn't help it. At the back of her mind she's thinking, I could have this guy, it'd be so easy – all I'd have to do is go with it. It was like at high school. If a girl told you that her friend liked you, you started taking more notice of the friend. Before that, she mightn't have done a thing for you; after that, you started to entertain the possibility.

That didn't apply to Carla, though. She would've got used to seeing desire in men's eyes years ago. She'd take it for granted. So you dream about me, do you? Join the club.

But things were different between us now, she'd said as much herself. We'd got away from the cafe and beyond the videotape. We could go for walks on the beach and chat about all sorts of stuff. Like the place of tits in the grand scheme of things. Like jerking off.

We were on the fast track to intimacy.

There's one problem with this sort of obsessive analysis. Sooner or later you come to something which doesn't necessarily lend itself to favourable interpretation; at that point, your beautiful scenario turns to shit. Was it just a coincidence that we'd ended up opposite the building where the orgy was staged or had Carla planned it that way?

Hanna had the tape. Hanna liked to watch. Someone tried to cut Hanna's heart out.

Now I had the tape. The first time we'd met, Carla told me, 'I'm beginning to think you've been spying on me.'

Maybe I'd got it around the wrong way and she

didn't take me to Bondi for some sea air and flirtation. Maybe she was giving me a warning: You're playing a dangerous game, little man. Look what happened to Ray ...

SIX

A few days went by; no Carla sightings. Probably just as well seeing I was having trouble working out whether she wanted to fuck me or kill me. By the time she showed up at the cafe again, I was leaning towards other possibilities, somewhere in between.

She was with Reece. She fluttered fingers at me, briefly and, I suppose you'd have to say, surreptitiously. Reece was otherwise occupied hounding a waitress, I think for not saving him a chocolate croissant. Whatever it was, it was enough to make him cancel breakfast. He huffed off. As soon as he was out of sight, Carla came over.

They'd been down to Melbourne. They went every year for the tennis. I'd watched the finals on TV and we post-mortemed like a couple of sun-dried has-beens in the courtside studio. She mentioned – again, the faint twang of contempt – that Reece had prowled the practice courts smacking his lips over the 52nd-ranked woman in the world, a pouty little baseliner out of Vilnius, Lithuania, via Florida – pure jailbait. I didn't say so but it sounded like male menopause kicking in.

Carla went quiet. She made a production of

spooning out the dregs of her latte. I assumed that concluded our round-up of the Australian Open. Eventually she said, 'I ran into Pete Grayson in Melbourne.'

I thought, it's a small world.

'Do you know him?'

I didn't. She explained that he was the son of Brian Grayson who'd made a bundle in real estate and whom I also didn't know. I was beginning to wonder what the point was when she got to it: 'Pete's on the tape.'

I couldn't see a cue there either. She said, 'There are three guys, right? He's one of them.'

I gave a meaningless nod. What was I meant to say? So which hole did Pete plug?

'Pete was saying that Shelley Lendich, who's also on the tape, died a couple of weeks ago.'

'Which one was she?'

'The blonde who couldn't get enough.'

'What'd she die of?'

'A drug overdose.'

'Did that come as a shock?'

'I'm always shocked when someone my age dies. Aren't you?'

'That depends. If she was a junkie I might be upset, but I wouldn't be shocked.'

Carla shrugged. 'I can remember her taking heroin once. Apart from that, she used to do pretty much the same amount of drugs as everyone else. I suppose that, given what I've heard about her since then, it's not that much of a shock, but I didn't really think about that. The first thing that went through my head was that there were six of us, plus Ray makes seven. Now there's only four.'

'Oh, yeah, Adam. What happened to him?'

'He jumped off a high-rise balcony a couple of years ago. So of seven people, aged between say nineteen and twenty-five, who hung out together in 1983, three aren't around any more. What do you think the odds on that would be? One in a thousand? One in ten thousand?'

'Well, you know, shit happens.'

'That's it? That's all you've got to say?'

'What do you want me to say – that it's too much of a coincidence? Is that what you think?'

'It did cross my mind.'

We stared at each other for a while. We could've stared at each other all morning as far as I was concerned but I had the feeling Carla was expecting a little more from me. I said, 'You want to tell me what happened back then?'

It was late summer. Two couples – Adam and Carla and Pete and Shelley – were flatmates in the Bondi apartment. It was a slightly eccentric set-up. Six months earlier, Pete and Carla had been an item – they had the apartment to themselves then – while Adam and Shelley had been in one of those 'Drop by if you're in the neighbourhood and feel like a fuck' type relationships.

One hot Sunday, Pete bumped into his old schoolmate on the beach. Adam was between addresses so Pete invited him to move into the spare bedroom. Big mistake.

Carla had never come across anything quite like Adam. There was the soft voice and the slow, dazzling grin. There was the long blond hair and the lithe swimmer's body. And those eyes! Like cat's eyes, green and glowing. And not just a pretty face: au contraire, he was *sooo* cool. When he wasn't surfing, he was playing guitar in a rock 'n' roll band. Or painting or writing poetry or earning some change as an artist's model, striking a Greek statue pose while a bunch of baby-boomers with Georgia O'Keefe fantasies counted the veins on his dick.

The first time Pete left Adam and Carla together for any length of time, they wound up in bed. They were still there when Pete came home six hours later. That night Carla moved her stuff down the hall.

No-one could stay pissed off at Adam for long, not even if he'd helped himself to your girlfriend. He softened the blow by setting Pete up with Shelley. When she moved in, things started to get a little blurred. Pete wasn't really over Carla and Shelley found it difficult to keep her hands off Adam. Adam didn't go out of his way to discourage her or any other girl with the same problem. He had a good line in Dada agitprop which reclassified many forms of questionable if not downright shitty behaviour as a refusal to conform to bourgeois morality. Self-serving bullshit, but plenty of people seemed to buy it.

They were doing a lot of drugs – Adam had the connections, Pete had the cash. Carla was spooked when she came home early to find Adam and Shelley shooting up. Just experimenting, they said. She made Adam promise not to do it again.

Carla was a sound sleeper but we all have the occasional nightmare. One night, she rolled over to cling to Adam but Adam wasn't there. She found him in the living room, sprawled in an armchair with his head thrown back. Shelley was on her knees, her head nodding over his crotch. Carla was outraged.

Adam told her it didn't mean a thing: they'd both got up to get a glass of water and one thing just led to another.

Pete came out to see what all the noise was about and for a while it looked like turning ugly. Pete was easygoing to a fault but it's hard to refrain from killing someone who's made it his mission in life to fuck your girlfriends. But Adam could play Pete like his Fender Stratocaster, maybe better. He always knew which string to pluck. If Pete and Carla ever wanted to get it on for old times' sake, it'd be cool with him. That chilled Pete out but re-ignited Carla. She moved out, but went back the first time Adam asked her to. She was addicted.

Another couple were admitted to the magic circle. Gareth and Alex lived on the ground floor. Gareth was Welsh; he'd come to Australia to follow a rugby tour and stayed on. He was pretty mainstream until Adam started messing with his head. Once Gareth discovered his creative side, there was no stopping him. Depending on which way the wind blew, he was going to be the next Dylan Thomas, the next Augustus John, the next Richard Burton.

Alex was a local girl, a law student. She found it all a bit overwhelming but did her best to keep up. It couldn't have been easy. Adam liked to mock her diligence and, as in most things, the others followed his lead.

The apartment was still ankle-deep in New Year's Eve party debris when Pete came home with a videotape. It featured a guy Pete knew and his ex-girlfriend exploring the fifty-seven ways to please your lover. It was a DIY job, intended for their eyes only, but she'd dumped him and now he was getting even by putting it out on general release. Carla found it embarrassing, Pete sniggered, Adam watched it intently without saying a word and Shelley got wet. As soon as it was over, she whisked Pete off to bed. When Adam suggested they could do their own version, Carla told him, no fucking way.

So Adam went to work. Carla was familiar with the technique: plant the idea then make it a running joke so that it kept coming up in conversation. At first, it was just something that was fun to talk about, their very own blue movie, any mention of it guaranteed to get a laugh. The next stage was What if . . . ? Still not treating it as a serious proposition but getting into this kind of thing: Okay, hypothetical situation – say we did decide to do it, how'd we go about it? Then came the hard, ideological sell. It would be liberating. It would be subversive. It would be a happening. Shit, man, it wouldn't be pornography, it'd be performance art.

Shelley didn't need convincing. She was on heat most of the time anyway and probably saw it as a way of getting around the embargo on Adam. Pete started out lukewarm but was soon running hot. For him, too, it represented a chance to turn back the clock. Adam could get Gareth to agree to anything if he packaged it in enough avant-garde guff. The problem there was Alex.

After a few weeks of this, Carla realised it was a matter of when, not if. If she said count me out, Adam would simply recruit someone else and go ahead without her.

They were having breakfast on the Parade, the six of them. Adam announced that he'd sourced a video camera so it was time to make a decision: were they going to do it, yes or no? Shelley and Pete said they were up for it. Gareth looked at Alex, putting her on the spot. The look said, if it was up to me ... Shelley told her, Come on Alex, it'll be a blast. Carla felt sorry for Alex. It wasn't her scene but she was going to cave in. She didn't want to be a drag. Alex said I suppose so and everyone looked at Carla.

Carla had known it would come to this. She'd worked out how she was going to play it. She looked straight at Adam, shrugged as if it was no big deal, and said Yeah, why not? It was almost worth it just to see the expression on his face.

The big day arrived. So did Ray Hanna with his video camera. Ray suggested that, seeing he'd shot some pretty way-out stuff in his time, maybe Adam should concentrate on his performance and leave the camerawork to him. The implication was, if I have to go, the camera goes with me. Adam thought Ray had a point. The others – Alex apart – had got used to the idea of having an audience. Besides, they just wanted to get started. They were fizzing.

Adam had in mind a free-for-all but Alex finally put her foot down. She was going to do it once, with Gareth, and that would be that. Shelley was coked to the eyeballs. She was ready for anything. Carla had primed herself with a jug of margaritas. Normally, she watched what she drank because booze loosened her up in a way drugs never did. There'd been times when she'd had a few too many and done things she'd regretted in the morning. But this wasn't normal. The best way – in fact, the only way – to handle this scene was to get right off her face.

Alex and Gareth did their brisk thing then left. Gareth went reluctantly, so it was no surprise when he sneaked back an hour later. By then, things were pretty much out of control.

The next night, I got the tape out of the storeroom and took it home. Now I had the God's-eye view. I looked down on the sinners seeing beyond their skin, knowing their characters and motivations, their pasts and futures. In a couple of cases, their fates.

It started with Gareth and Alex. Gareth was built like a rugby player. His shoulder muscles bunched and flattened as he lunged at Alex. The relationship didn't last. Alex didn't mind eccentricity but she drew the line at weirdness, especially when the weirdness took on a dark, unnerving edge. After they split up, Gareth got religion, reinventing himself yet again. He joined a born-again Christian performing group which roamed the state bewildering country folk. Then one day he strapped on his backpack and walked into the sunset.

Alex looked like the girl next door. At first, she wore an expression of pained concentration like someone undergoing dentistry, knowing it was going to hurt but determined to be brave. Her eyes stayed shut but gradually her bland features relaxed. By the end it was working for her, in spite of herself.

Alex had come a long way from that Bondi bedroom with the print of Magritte's 'The Lovers' on the wall and the Chinese-lantern-style light fitting. She became a corporate lawyer. The nineties were a good time to be a woman in Corporationland. You didn't have to be Rupert Murdoch in drag. They just wanted your photograph in the annual report to get the sisterhood off their backs. No glass ceilings around here, no ma'am. She'd even starred in one of those spurious magazine articles: 'Mahogany Row Here We Come: The women changing the face of Australia's boardrooms.'

Next up were Shelley and Pete. They were much more at home. Shelley was pale, trim, almost boyish, with Slavic cheekbones. And she burned. She plunged into the debauchery with the zeal of a true believer. Before the curtain came down, she'd go one-on-one with Carla, Gareth and Adam, one-on-two with Gareth and Pete and stow a cucumber where the sun didn't shine. Shelley would take the other fork in the road. She opted out. There were steady drugs; there were pilgrimages to India; there were stints in a Melbourne urban commune and Byron Bay. And there were men, lots of them, and everyone a fuck-up.

Pete was big and blond and flying high. In those days, Carla would've picked him as the one who'd flame out. But he lucked onto the rich kid's two-step survival and personal growth plan. Step One: Stay alive to spend the fortune that Daddy amassed in a lifetime of toil and/or chicanery. Step Two: Anchor yourself in the everyday world – get married, have kids, buy such a fucking expensive house you have to have a mortgage.

Adam was a natural, I had to admit. He had the equipment – heart-throb profile, sinewy physique, a pretty solid hunk of pipe. He had the technique and he had the stamina. He sure as hell didn't look like a potential jumper. The world wasn't a cruel place then. So what happened?

Nothing happened, that was the problem. None of his creative endeavours brought overnight success and he didn't have the temperament for the long, lonely haul. Meanwhile, Carla was starting to make it as a model. She had to work hard; she had to be disciplined. Adam's refusal to play by the rules which once seemed cool now seemed feckless. His disdain for materialism and the straight life now seemed like a licence to bludge with her as the first port of call. She moved out. They still saw each other but the gap got wider each time.

Eventually, she called it quits. Whenever she came across him, he was the same old Adam – still charming, still self-consciously bohemian, still going nowhere. He seemed stuck in a time warp, clinging to memories of Bondi and that golden summer when the sky was the limit and he walked among them like a young god.

It ended eleven floors below a friend's balcony, in a concertina of burst skin, splintered bone and pulped flesh.

I zoomed through Carla's scenes on fast-forward. By now I knew every flex and shudder by heart. There was nothing more I could learn from them. As we parted, she'd told me that she hadn't been that abandoned before or since. She wanted me to know that.

SEVEN

It was thunderstorm season. That night we had a biggie. At its peak, it sounded like Armageddon had broken out in the penthouse. It must've been a bad night for the little old ladies cowering in their widows' flats and the deadbeats grappling with their demons in hostel dormitories and piss-soaked boarding houses.

In the morning the streets were carpeted with litter blown down from the Cross like a shower of propaganda leaflets. Junk food rules. The future belongs to McDonald's. Resistance is futile.

The storm whirled out to sea but the rain stayed the night. It fell steadily, rhythmically, as if it was pacing itself. I listened to the rain and thought about tomorrow. Tomorrow I was going to test Carla's proposition that the secret seven's fatality rate was unusually high. Suspiciously high. I was going to look into the deaths of Shelley Lendich and Adam Lomas. For the time being, I was prepared to leave Ray Hanna to the police.

You're going to do what? Well, we'll all sleep a little easier knowing Alabaster's on the case.

Sure, it was laughable. What can I say except, whatever it takes.

The next morning I rang the Glebe Coroner's Court. I asked the woman who took my call if they had an information officer. She chuckled, grimly.

I said, 'I assume that's a no.'

'You assume correctly.'

'Perhaps you might be able to help me.'

'You never know your luck.'

'Does the general public have access to coroners' reports?'

'No.'

Take your time, think about it. 'Under no circumstances?'

'Correct. Next of kin, accredited researchers, insurance companies – that's it.'

'But coroners' findings get written up in the papers, don't they?'

'Of course. Inquests are open to the public.'

'I don't suppose you supply details of a deceased's next of kin?'

'Certainly not.'

I thanked her and hung up. You can't take any shit from these people.

The day before, still distracted by the memories she'd stirred up, Carla had given me her mobile phone number. She'd said I better have it, just in case. Just in case what wasn't spelt out but I didn't get the impression she wanted me cooing in her ear seventeen times a day.

I rang the number.

She answered, 'This is Carla.'

'And this is James.'

'James?' Sounding as if she was having trouble placing me.

'Remember me? We spent a couple of hours yesterday discussing sex, drugs and untimely death.'

'Oh, that James. What can I do for you?'

How about that? From playful to businesslike in ten words or less. 'I'm glad you asked. I need your help.'

'To do what?'

I'd rehearsed this line. 'To find out whether shit just happened or someone gave it a push.'

'I assume you're talking about Adam and Shelley?'

'Yep.'

'How are you going to do that?'

'You mean we – how are we going to do that.'

'Actually, I've got quite a lot on today . . .' Her voice faltered evasively. Perhaps the storm had blown away yesterday's anxieties.

'Who's Adam's next of kin?'

'His mother. Why?'

'Do you know her?'

'Sure, we got on fine.'

'Do you know how to get in touch with her?'

'Well, it'd be a stab in the dark but I'd probably look in the phone book under I. Lomas, Edgecliff Road, Edgecliff.'

'It's not much to go on, but let's give it a try.'

'Give what a try?'

I said, 'The coroner's report on Adam's death would explain why he came to the conclusion that it was suicide. The general public doesn't have access to that report but his mother, as next of kin, should have a copy.'

'And when she asks, as she's bound to, why the sudden, belated interest, what am I meant to say?'

'You'll think of something.'

'Come on, it's a serious question. I doubt I've seen the woman more than once this decade and that was at the funeral.'

'Carla, you know her, I don't. You'll figure out the best way to handle it.'

'That's easy for you to say.'

I pretended that she was trying my patience. 'Well, if you don't feel you can do it, we've either got to think of another way to get hold of the report or just forget the whole thing.'

A stony silence followed. I was afraid that I'd overplayed my hand and she'd go for the second option, but she hesitated on the brink. 'I'll think about it, okay? I just don't want to upset her. I'm sure it's the last thing she wants to talk about.'

'There's something else . . .'

'I thought this was a joint venture – what's your contribution?'

'You make two phone calls, I'll do the rest. That's fair, isn't it?'

'What's the other thing?'

'Your friend the finance journalist: where does she work?'

'At the *Herald*.'

'Can you ask her to ask the police reporter if he or she'd be prepared to make a couple of calls about Shelley?'

'I'll have to think of a reason for that as well.'

'Just say Shelley was a friend of yours from way back and you'd like to know exactly what happened. What's wrong with that?'

'I don't think she'd believe me.'

'You mean she wouldn't believe that any friend of yours could die that way?'

'Well, there's that. She'd probably also wonder why I'd go about it in such a roundabout way when Reece could do it much more directly.'

'That's a point.'

'Oh, what the hell. She's a finance journalist, she must be used to being lied to. You better give me your phone number. I mightn't be at the cafe for a while.'

'Why not?'

'Reece threw a tantrum yesterday because they didn't have what he wanted; now he's boycotting the place. He does that sort of thing from time to time.'

'How long do the boycotts last?'

'As long as it takes him to find fault with the new place or get sick of driving out to Bondi. In other words, a few days.'

I relaxed. 'Bondi, eh? Well, after you've had breakfast, you could go for a walk on the beach, point out the sights.'

There was another silence, then a slow, almost reluctant chuckle. 'Eat shit, James.'

How much shit could one man eat?

Carla rang back an hour later. Tony Stark, the *Herald*'s police reporter, was expecting a call from me. She was still thinking about Mrs I. Lomas of Edgecliff Road, Edgecliff.

I rang Stark. I asked him if, without going to too much trouble, he could get the cops' off-the-record assessment of Shelley's death: was it a straightforward drug overdose or not that clear-cut? He told me I needn't worry about him going to too much trouble.

Stark didn't muck around. Ten minutes later he was telling me that it was a routine OD, according to a detective who'd worked on the case. The deceased and her partner were known drug-users; there was nothing to suggest anyone else had been present at the time; there were no suspicious circumstances. Case closed. Just another statistic for the War on Drugs brigade and the decriminalisers to throw at each other.

'Her boyfriend claimed they weren't on smack,' said Stark. 'But as the cop said, "How do you tell when a junkie's lying? His lips move."'

'The boyfriend reckons she never used the stuff?'

'Not quite. He says she wasn't a regular heroin user. Of course, there's a school of thought that casual users are more likely to overdose than addicts – lower tolerance, less experience calculating the dosage.'

'Where was he at the time?'

'Otherwise engaged. Forget about him – he had a rock-solid alibi. Let me ask you a question: what makes you think she got a hot-shot?'

'A what?'

'You obviously think someone gave her a killer dose?'

'No, I just wanted to know if it was cut and dried.'

Stark said, 'For what it's worth, I've heard more than one cop say that if you want to take someone out, a hot-shot's the way to go. That probably tells you how much of a shit they give about ODs. Dead druggies are very low priority – the way a cop looks at it, anyone who's on the needle's just killing themselves in slow motion. Shit, take this case – they're a fucking sight more interested in the stolen goods than the overdose.'

'Which stolen goods?'

'They found a shitload of stuff in Lendich's flat.

Her boyfriend's up on a bunch of B and E charges.'

'Is he inside?'

'No, he got bail – on compassionate grounds. We wouldn't want a white man hanging himself in a jail cell, would we now?'

'No, that wouldn't do at all. Where do I find this guy?'

Shelley's boyfriend, the last in a long and undistinguished line, was called Shane Salter. Stark gave me his address. And he reminded me what the detective had said about junkies and their attitude to the truth.

Weeds were taking over the paved front yard of the Surry Hills terrace, the scene of the final spasm of Shelley Lendich's jitterbug life. Soon the junk – the wheelbarrow without a wheel and the rusting paint cans, the grease-caked chip pan and the plastic toilet seat – would be hidden from view, awaiting discovery by yuppie renovators in the next inner-city property boom. The stucco facade was crumbling and black polythene covered for a missing windowpane. Long-dead flowers shrivelled in a hanging basket by the door. Two kinds of people lived in places like this – those who simply didn't give a fuck and those who were heading down the lost highway towards the last exit to nowhere.

I had to knock long and hard to get a response. The door was opened by a visitor from the twilight zone wearing only torn black jeans if you didn't count the tattoos and the nipple rings. He looked about as bad as a human being with a heartbeat could look, tall and POW-thin with blood-filled eyes burning low in the bony ravages of his face.

He said, 'Yeah?' There was no truculence in his tone and certainly no hope.

'Shane Salter?'

He sighed and looked over my shoulder. 'Shane's not here, mate. He's gone.'

'Gone where?'

'Don't know. Left town, I think.'

'Is that right? Don't you have to report to a police station every day when you're on bail?'

The man I was pretty sure was Shane Salter took his time over that one. 'Yeah, well, if he's around, I ain't seen him.'

I took a folded piece of newspaper from my hip pocket and handed it to him. It was an account of my day in court under the headline 'Merchant banker convicted of insider trading', with accompanying photo. I was expressionless to the point of utter blankness. I'd spent hours practising that look.

Salter stared at the cutting as if he'd never quite got the hang of reading. He had the slowest blink I'd ever seen.

'That's me, okay?' I said. 'Obviously I'm not a cop; I've got nothing to do with the cops. I just want to talk to you for a few minutes. I'm here on behalf of someone who knew Shelley years ago. This person wants to know what happened. She doesn't think Shelley would do something like that.'

He handed the cutting back without giving any sign that he understood it or, if he did, that my chequered past made an ounce of difference to him. He said, 'What's it to her?'

'I think she just feels she owes it to Shelley – for old times' sake.'

'Why don't you go to the cops? They'll tell you what happened.'

'They'll tell me their version. I thought you might have another version.'

Salter sighed again, shaking his head. He was disoriented, groping his way like a blind man in a strange house. He said, 'Suit yourself', and went inside. I took that as an invitation and followed.

He took the first left off the hallway into a grimy front room. There was a threadbare sofa parked a metre and a half from a TV set with a rabbit ears aerial. There was a tape deck and speakers on the floor with a stack of tapes. There was a faded poster of Dubrovnik on the wall. And that was about it except for the five bottles of Appleton Estate Jamaica rum on the mantelpiece above the bricked-up fireplace. Four of them were empty.

Salter saw me looking at the bottles. He said, 'Yeah, I drunk some piss lately.'

He ground his knuckles in his eyesockets as if sight had become a source of torment. 'Shel going like that ... it really knocked me around, you know, it fucking killed me, man. Then getting done by the cops ...' His legs seemed to retract like a telescope and suddenly he was slumped on the sofa. His chin was on his chest but I didn't need to see his face to know that tears were just seconds away. 'Everything's fucked, man.' The voice wobbled. 'So fucked.' Then he put his head in his hands and let himself go.

I thought about getting him a drink but decided against it. It didn't look as if the booze was helping much. I waited. I remembered the fatalism of an ex-friend's wife whenever her little boy embarked on one of his fierce and, to a childless outsider, disturbing crying jags. 'Kids cry,' she'd say. 'And then they stop. You can't hurry it.'

After a while Salter stopped. He wiped his eyes with the heel of his hand, mumbling an apology. I told him he had nothing to apologise for, but he kept saying sorry. Eventually I realised that he wasn't talking to me.

When he looked at me again, I said, 'Did you ever think there was a possibility that it might happen?'

'No, mate, never ... not to Shel.'

'But she did use heroin now and again, didn't she?'

Salter finally took an interest. 'We had two rules with smack, Shel and me. Always get it from someone you know so you're sure of what you're getting and never shoot up alone in case something goes wrong. Mate, I've asked every fucker we ever got stuff from – Shel hadn't scored from any of them lately.'

He started rambling then. I tried to ask questions but he just talked over me. Shelley's family came from Croatia and for years she'd had her heart set on going there. Here he ducked out of the room and came back with a 1988 Fodor's guide to Yugoslavia, held together with sellotape, which she used to study for hours on end. The pilgrimage was put on hold when things fell apart over there but just lately they'd started making plans again. They'd been working, him doing odd jobs, her waitressing, trying to save.

But it was slow going. They weren't cut out for the workforce and no matter how hard they tried, their consumption ate up their income. Then he met a guy who had this neat little scam, breaking into beach houses up and down the coast. He was creaming it but he needed a hand. Salter signed on. Once a week, usually a Tuesday or Wednesday night, they'd take a van up or down the coast to places like Pearl Beach and Palm Beach and Kiama and Batemans Bay. Jesus, some of the joints were fucking mansions and crammed full of all sorts of gear – state-of-the-art appliances, jet skis, windsurfers, rubber dinghies with outboard motors, mountain bikes, you name it. And lots and lots of booze – some places even had full-on wine cellars. They'd load up the van and come home.

About there he ran out of steam. I said, 'That's what you were doing the night it happened?'

'Yeah, it was our first run for a while. We got fuck-all – still too many bastards on holiday.'

'You were gone most of the night?'

He nodded, looking at the floor.

'And Shelley was dead when you got back?'

Another slow, sorrowful nod.

'Does the name Ray Hanna mean anything to you?'

'No.'

'Did Shelley have a videotape of her and some people she knew years ago, you know, fooling around?'

It was clear from his expression that there was some part of the question he didn't understand. Leaving nothing to chance, I added, 'They videoed each other fucking.'

He shook his head, frowning.

'Did she ever mention it?'

'I don't know what the fuck you're talking about.'

'Forget it,' I said. 'Okay, what about this as a possibility: Shelley's here by herself. Someone she knows drops by with some heroin. They take it but something goes wrong and Shelley starts to look pretty sick. The friend panics and takes off. Now the friend's keeping quiet because they're scared of getting themselves in the shit. Could it've happened that way?'

Salter took an age to answer. He sat there hugging himself with his stick-insect arms, eyes screwed shut. Maybe he was remembering Shelley or maybe he was reflecting on the choices they'd made.

He said, 'Shit, who knows? Could've, I suppose. You know what some people are like.'

Don't tell me, I got the message. I know what happens when a junkie's lips move.

EIGHT

I don't often sleep through the night.

In the good old days, that was because of the booze – most nights I'd hit the bed face-first, tanked to the eyeballs. In the good old days, I started work at seven-thirty and finished at eight, maybe nine. That was an average day. When something big was going down, as we used to say, it was hardly worth going home. Working those sort of hours, you don't feel like tidying your desk and heading straight home to the empty apartment or the wife and kids. You feel like unwinding. You feel like going out with the team to sink a few and pump up each other's egos. Wimps went to bed at a sensible hour. Guys like us, we worked hard and we played hard. You were one or the other.

There's this idea that alcohol's a knockout drop – take ten units of Tanqueray with ice and tonic and forget about breakfast. It might work like that for some people, not me. I'd flake out for a few hours and then it would start: the brain-rattling shockwaves from the back of the cranium, the static crackle of torched neurons, the gravel-road mouth, the beachball bladder. If you can sleep through that, you're drinking way too much.

Nowadays, three glasses of cheap red is as close as I come to getting loaded. I still wake up, though. I don't know why but I just can't seem to sleep through. And when I wake up, my mind starts ticking.

At first, things just pop into my head, random, out of context stuff, like sound-bites from a weirder-than-usual dream. Alone in the night's eternal, curving act. Excuse me? Alone in the . . . Where the fuck did that come from? It takes a while but eventually it comes to you: Jane's Dylan Thomas record. Jane the high school teacher from Newcastle, Jane who loved me, had this record of Dylan Thomas reciting some of his poetry. Here's some more: Teach me the love that is evergreen after the fall leaved grave.

One of Jane's favourite lines, as I recall.

The trouble is, the mental effort required to track that fragment of memory back to the source gets your mind racing. It's like cranking the oven up to 220 degrees to soften a tablespoon of butter. Half an hour after you turned it off, the oven's still cooking. You've solved your little brain-tickler, now you just want to get back to sleep. Try telling your brain that. It's humming now, chewing over the day's leftovers. And once it gets its teeth into them, you never know where you'll end up.

Well, that's not quite true. I always knew where I'd end up.

That night I found myself thinking about a coroner's report and the fifteen bucks I'd spent cabbing it to and from Surry Hills to shoot the breeze with Shane Salter.

Fifteen bucks, Jesus. Why did I do that? Because I

cared about Adam and Shelley? Give me a break. How could I? I never knew them. To me they were just images on an old videotape, a couple of spaced-out kids having dirty sex. And from what I'd heard about them, I didn't miss much. She was a slutty little wacko in freefall. He was a preening hustler who peaked way, *way* too early.

RIP and all that but I never knew them. And the fact is, we don't feel a thing when strangers die. We pretend we do but we don't. It's different with celebrities. Millions weep for Princess Diana because they got it into their heads that they knew her. They didn't know her at all. They just looked at the photos in crap magazines and believed in fairytales. Only the near and dear weep after road accidents and drownings. Only the near and dear weep for the disappeared ones who go into hospital and never come out. All those routine exits, those one paragraph death notices, they're just numbers. Just background noise.

And if people dying mundanely in their ones and twos across town, in the bush, out of state, are just background noise, where does that leave the multiple check-outs in faraway places? The earthquakes, the floods, the epidemics, the overladen ferries and the forty-year-old unlovingly maintained aeroplanes. Christ, in Bangladesh it's just one damn thing after another. There's always something sweeping them away in their hundreds. Those folks know only too well what an act of God can do to a neighbourhood.

Maybe I could interest you in an unnatural disaster, say a massacre in Algeria? They're running at one a week right now, straight out of the Dark Ages: impaled babies, ten-year-olds raped and beheaded, foetuses ripped from mothers-to-be. How much compassion do you have? How much cruelty can you stand before you turn your face away? Before you change channels?

We might like to kid ourselves but the truth is we're a hard-hearted species. We have to be. There's so much death out there.

So no, it wasn't because I cared about those flickering phantoms. And I certainly didn't spend fifteen bucks on taxis because I wanted to see justice done. No-one believes in justice any more, do they? Maybe I'm a little biased here. I got taken to the cleaners, I got fucked over by experts, because I bought some shares for $1.70 in the morning and sold them for four bucks in the afternoon. The law says I ripped off the people who sold me those shares because I had inside knowledge that they were about to go gangbusters. If I hadn't bought their shares, so this argument goes, they could've sold them for $2.30 more a few hours later. But if I hadn't bought them, somebody else probably would've. Those people were sellers at $1.70. Their shares were on the market. I couldn't have got my hands on the fucking things otherwise.

After I was charged, I returned the profits I'd made on the transaction to the people who'd sold me the shares. The 'victims' actually made on the deal – $2.30 a share over and above whatever profit they'd made when they quit the stock. In effect, they got the benefit of my inside knowledge.

I'm not saying I did nothing wrong. I knew it was against the law but I went ahead and did it anyway, so I had to take the consequences. What I am saying is that the system is too detached, too arbitrary, too clumsy to deliver justice. Even if it was run by idealists. Which it isn't, not by a long stretch.

I committed what could well have been a victimless crime. It certainly ended up that way. On a one-to-ten measure of antisocial criminality, it was down there in the very low single figures, along with serial parking offences and housewife shoplifting. And look what the system did to me. I lost the lot. I can't practise my trade. I'm forced to lead a basically shitty life. If I'd smashed someone's head in or gouged them with a broken bottle leaving them disfigured and traumatised and jumping at shadows for the rest of their days, I would've got off easier.

It doesn't make sense. In the unlikely event that I'm ever in a position to inside-trade again, I won't do it. I've learned my lesson. A process of careful empirical analysis led me to conclude that it wasn't worth it. But how many slaps on the wrist does it take to persuade the headkickers of the error of their ways? In my experience of them, they don't reason, they react to certain stimuli. They do what they do because they are what they are. All that's stopping them from shattering some other poor bastard's skull is their conscience. That, I think you'd have to admit, is a good one.

Justice? I don't think so.

So I wasn't driven by a sense of loss and I wasn't on a crusade. But you already knew that. You knew from the word go that I was only doing it to get next to Carla. Ice Station Carla. Where I always ended up at four in the morning.

And where the outlook, however promising it was to start with, always turned bleak. I was temperamentally incapable of lying there thinking rosy or merely salacious thoughts, imagining it all coming true, until I drifted back to sleep. Sooner or later, I'd throw the switch to pessimism. I'd start to think, what if Carla had a hand in Ray Hanna's murder? What if I didn't mean a thing to her?

If I didn't mean a thing to her, why had she let things get this far? What was in it for her? There was no obvious answer to that. But there was a less-than-obvious answer.

Say, for the sake of argument, that Carla killed Hanna. Now it was a matter of getting away with it. And the surest way to get away with it was to pin it on someone else. In other words, find a fallguy.

Maybe that was why she'd let things get this far – she was setting me up. Shit, I'd even told her I was in Hanna's apartment that morning. I'd practically fucking volunteered.

If you thought sleep would be out of the question after that, you're wrong. That scenario didn't change a thing. I wasn't going to walk away. I was going to carry on doing whatever it took to make the connection.

Eyes wide open.

I was killing time at the cafe, putting off the return to Roach Central. I read the business section for the first time in months. It felt like English as a second language. I even read the personal finance supplement: Your essential sharemarket survival guide. Cashed-up and conservative – an investment strategy. How to save on school fees.

Yeah, you've got to watch out for those school fees. They can come at you out of nowhere.

A waitress came over to tell me I was wanted on

the phone. You-know-who, she said. Maybe mine wasn't the only imagination in which Carla and I were lovers.

I said hello. Carla said, 'Isn't it about time you got yourself a mobile?'

'I'd never be off the phone.'

'Of course, all your admirers. Are you free this afternoon?'

Well, let's see ... 'Yep.'

'We've got an appointment with Irene – Adam's mother.' She told me when and where.

I said, 'You don't have to be there – the deal was, you set it up and I do the rest.'

'Oh yes I do – Irene insisted on it.'

I was half an hour late. There was no way Carla would be bang on time and if strange men made Irene Lomas nervous – and under the circumstances, who could blame her? – then getting there first would've been counterproductive.

She lived on the fifth floor of a sixties orange-brick apartment block, a minor-league eyesore. I pressed the intercom, identified myself, and got buzzed in.

Carla opened the door. She had her hair up and was wearing a classic white linen Chanel suit. The society beauty look was a new one on me and seemed to tone down her vibrant sexuality. Not that the effect was noticeably different. As always, I felt as if a voracious parasite was feeding on my heart.

She didn't smile or say hello. She didn't say a word. She just glanced at her watch – one I hadn't seen before; it managed to look tasteful yet colossally expensive – and raised an eyebrow.

I said, 'There's an explanation.'

She said, 'James, never apologise, never explain.'

She spun on her heel like an ice-skater and led me down the hall into a large living room. A ceiling fan rotated laboriously. Sliding glass doors opened onto a balcony where a platoon of pot-plants wilted in the afternoon sun.

Irene Lomas was poised over a low table, pouring tea. You could see where Adam got his looks from. She was a strikingly well-preserved fifty-five or so and I suspected her appearance owed nothing to cosmetic surgery. It might've been the surplus skin around the throat or the lack of jut beneath the white silk blouse. Or maybe she just didn't look the type.

Carla introduced us. I apologised for being late. Irene said my timing was perfect, it'd given her and Carla a chance to catch up. I was invited to take a seat. The sofa was oriental, in keeping with the theme of the room. There was a black lacquer sideboard, a silk screen, a jade Buddha, a herd of ivory elephants, a wall-mounted folding fan and a couple of those kiddy paintings featuring a moon, a river, a hillside and a dwelling. All up, it looked like a week's worth of promiscuous shopping somewhere on Asia's beaten track.

Naturally I led off with, 'Have you spent some time in Asia?'

Irene seemed momentarily flummoxed by my powers of observation. Eventually she said, 'We were in Hong Kong for ten years. We came back so Adam could go to college here. Unfortunately, my ex-husband never really settled down – he skipped back to Hong Kong when Adam was fifteen. He's got a lot to answer for, that man.' She brightened up. 'I hear he lost his shirt when the market there crashed recently. I think I'm entitled to a little schadenfreude, don't you?'

I said, 'Absolutely. As much as you can handle.' I glanced at Carla. She didn't have a clue what we were talking about. 'Wouldn't you agree, Carla?'

She was smart enough to play dumb. 'It's a perfume, right? Dior, I think . . . or is it Boucheron?' Then she poked her tongue out at me.

Irene looked puzzled. She had every right to be – it was a strange situation. I wondered what she made of it all. She offered me tea or something stronger. I declined both, signalling that I was ready when she was. She fortified herself with a gulp of tea and got to it.

She wasn't going to show us the coroner's report because it covered some private family matters. But she'd re-read it after Carla's call and was prepared to answer questions. Within reason.

I asked why the coroner concluded that Adam had committed suicide.

Irene took her time. She seemed quite composed. 'He'd been down in the dumps, although exactly how far was a matter of opinion. Some of his friends just thought he'd lost a bit of spark – hadn't been himself lately, that sort of thing. Others described it as depression. The problem was that he wasn't going anywhere. One after another, his various endeavours petered out. The response to his novel seemed to bring things to a head. He was convinced it would take the world by storm but he couldn't get it published. One rejection letter described it as unpublishable, which seemed rather harsh when you consider some of the stuff around. Adam had always taken it for granted that he was special, you see, but after that I think doubt really set in. He was drinking and drugging heavily and did so the night it happened, which raised the possibility that it was simply a stupid accident – he might've gone out onto the balcony pie-eyed and somehow managed to fall off. The coroner pointed out that that was easier said than done given the balcony's design. The fact that he was alone at the time and petrified of heights ruled out some sort of stunt or horseplay which went horribly wrong.'

Carla said, 'That's what I couldn't get over. I've never known anyone as scared of heights as Adam. You know that movie *Blade Runner*?' I nodded. 'That was his all-time favourite – he had it on video. He used to watch it all the time but he just could not sit through the ending – you know, when Harrison Ford's scrambling around on the roof. If other people wanted to watch it, he'd have to leave the room.'

I asked Irene, 'Were there any witnesses?'

'No. It happened about 1.45 in the morning. His flatmate worked in a nightclub and didn't get home till five.'

'Did he leave a note?'

'No. There was some debate about that at the inquest. One expert said it was quite unusual, another said it wasn't unusual at all, there weren't notes in over half the cases he'd studied.'

'Had there been any previous attempts?'

'No.'

'Did he ever talk about it?'

'Certainly not to me and there's no mention of it in the report.'

'The family stuff – I know you don't want to discuss it, but can you tell us if it ... strengthened the case for suicide?'

Irene plucked at her throat. 'I suppose it did.' Her words hung in the air. I waited for her to elaborate. After an awkward fifteen seconds, she gave in. 'There was the situation with his father, obviously' – she paused – 'and the fact that one of his ... relatives had committed suicide.'

'When was this?'

'Two or three years earlier.'

'By what means?'

'She didn't throw herself off a balcony, if that's what you're getting at.'

I nodded. 'How old was she?'

Irene frowned, letting me know I was pushing my luck. 'She was about the age at which life is supposed to begin.'

'Were she and Adam close?'

'They were family.' Her clipped delivery indicated that the subject was closed.

'What do you think, Mrs Lomas? Do you think your son killed himself?'

She got up to pour herself another cup of tea. She went over to the sliding doors and stood with her back to us. 'It's a hard thing for a parent to come to terms with. Terribly hard. I never saw Adam in that light but then what parent would? The older he got, the less I felt I knew what was going on inside – we didn't communicate all that well. Of course, the drugs didn't help.'

'What effect did they have?'

'As I said, Adam always had big plans. He was surrounded – or surrounded himself – with people who were forever telling him how talented he was. Unfortunately, he wasn't very disciplined by nature and the drugs just made it worse. I think it boiled down to him despairing that he'd ever fulfil his potential.'

I left it there. That was as far as she was going to go.

On the way down, Carla asked me what I thought. I said I thought Irene had constructed an explanation which enabled her to make some sort of sense of it. It tripped off her tongue with the smooth gloss of hindsight.

I asked her how she'd broached the subject.

'I told her the truth.'

'The whole truth and nothing but?'

'I might've left out the cucumber. No, I just said there seemed to be a jinx on our little group and it made me nervous. She didn't press the point; she was a lot less uptight about it than I thought she'd be.'

'How did you explain me?'

'I said I'd roped you in because my ex-boyfriends were one of Reece's least favourite subjects, especially if they were better looking than him.'

'How many of them were?'

'All of them.' By now we were outside the building. I hoped Irene couldn't hear us laughing. She might've got the wrong idea.

Carla was stunned to learn that I'd walked to Edgecliff. I didn't point out that the previous day's foray to Surry Hills had blown a hole in my discretionary spending budget. I just accepted the offer of a lift.

On the way to Potts Point, I ran her through my session with Shane Salter. Her view was that we hadn't come across a hint of anything sinister. I didn't quite see it that way. If Adam had left a note, if he hadn't been terrified of heights, if Shelley had just scored from one of her usual sources, I would've gone along with her. As things stood, though, there was an element of doubt in both cases.

Carla didn't ask where I wanted to be dropped off. She just pulled up outside the cafe. Maybe she thought I lived there.

She said, 'We haven't got very far, have we?'

'I wouldn't say that.'

We made eye contact. I was unprepared for the intensity of her gaze. I felt exposed to the core, as if she could see into the secret place where my obsession raged against its confinement.

Amusement or maybe satisfaction tugged at the corner of her succulent mouth. She turned away and put the car into gear. As she checked the wing-mirror she said, 'Ciao, James.'

I got out of the car and looked in the window. Carla sat there for a few seconds, letting me worship her goddess profile. Then she drove away without a backward glance.

NINE

It was a slow night at the video store. I was in conference with the Prof, one of my regulars. The Prof was a nine-stone weakling with a triple-A brain and tufts of coarse black hair growing out of his ears. It was hard not to stare, but he didn't notice. In fact, he was oblivious to the whole situation. That's what I chose to believe anyway. The alternative was that he cultivated the ear fuzz, he considered it *becoming*. He was one sick fuck, the Prof, but not that sick.

Notwithstanding his otherworldly IQ and his chair in philosophy, the Prof was a huge fan of Hollywood action extravaganzas. The more bloated the production, the more cataclysmic the mayhem, the more inane the premise, the better he liked it. He liked the way the hero's buddy, usually a straight-arrow family man, invariably bought the farm. He liked the way the bad guys just could not put a bullet in the hero, even when their lives depended on it. He liked the way in hand-to-hand combat the hero could sustain enough physical punishment to destroy a tank and still come out on top. He liked everything about them. I already knew this but I would've heard it all over again if Detective-Sergeant Donald hadn't backed his way into the shop.

He was carrying a carton which he dropped on the counter with a brittle clatter, saying, 'I'm returning your videos.'

'Oh, right,' I said. 'I'd forgotten about them. Any joy?'

'A complete and utter fucking waste of time.' Donald enunciated as if he was addressing an Eskimo. 'But thanks for asking.'

The Prof couldn't handle real-life confrontations. He skedaddled into the night.

Donald leaned on the counter. He'd undone the top button on his white shirt and pulled down his tie to expose a grime-caked collar. When he shifted position I got a clout of gamy body odour. He smelt and looked as if he'd had a screaming bitch of a day. There were blue-black rings under the hooded eyes and deep seams in his face. He wasn't a pretty sight and he wasn't in a hurry.

I put the carton on the floor behind the counter. Donald watched me the way a drunk watches a barman. I asked, 'So how's the investigation going?'

'Slowly. Mr Alabaster, are you a hundred per cent certain you put the tape Hanna brought back into that carton?'

'Yeah, absolutely positive.'

'You said it had advertising-type stuff on it?'

'That's right.'

'I made a list of all the companies and commercial projects which appear on those sort of tapes and showed it to Hanna's accountant. Not a single name rang a bell and he's been Hanna's accountant for ten years.'

I shrugged. It seemed the only appropriate response.

Donald mimicked the shrug. 'What's that meant to mean?'

'It means Hanna made TV ads for a living, so there could be all sorts of reasons why he'd have copies of stuff he didn't do himself.'

'Such as?'

'He might've wanted to see what his competitors were up to. He might've wanted to check out a certain cinematographer's work. Ditto an actor, ditto an editor, ditto, Jesus, I don't know, some postproduction outfit . . .'

'What's that?'

'Beats me, but film people are always talking about postproduction. I hear them at the cafe.'

Donald pulled a packet of Winfields out of his breast pocket. He slotted a cigarette in his mouth and offered me one.

'No thanks. I gave up.'

'Bully for you.'

'When I was at Silverwater, as a matter of fact.'

Donald dropped the hardbitten cop act. Maybe he found it hard work. 'That's the spirit, son – turn a negative into a positive.' He lit the cigarette with a throwaway lighter. 'What else did you do in there?'

'Read. Slept. Lost weight.'

Donald looked down at the tube of fat which ran around his waist like a moneybelt. 'Welcome to the country club, eh?'

'Yeah, five-star all the way. And you get to meet such a nice class of person.'

'I'll bet. That little Lebanese mongrel, for instance.'

I hadn't seen Eddie since the last time Donald had dropped in. That didn't surprise me. I'd attracted heat; I had bad karma and that could be contagious.

I said, 'Eddie's not that bad . . .'

'Piss off,' said Donald mildly. 'He's a complete shitbag.'

'That's what I was going to say – he's not that bad, for a complete shitbag.'

Smoke streamed from Donald's nostrils. Even before he'd finished exhaling, he was into his next drag. 'Interesting case this,' he said conversationally. 'We got Hanna's cleaning woman in to tell us what was missing. All that's gone are his videos.'

Donald prompted me with his eyebrows. I obliged. 'What videos?'

'Don't know, that's the point. That's why I had to wade through that crap you gave me. Hanna had a couple of dozen videotapes. They were there when the cleaning woman did the joint on Thursday, they weren't there when we arrived on Saturday – except for your one, Grace Kelly and whatsisname. Nothing else was taken. What does that tell you?'

'That he was murdered for his collection of Disney videos?'

Donald's worn face crinkled into a slightly menacing smile. 'That's one possibility.' He hunched closer. It was the body language of a gossip, however unlikely that seemed. 'I've got a pretty good idea what's on those tapes. See, Hanna was also a photographer. He specialised in portraits – kids, families, graduation – and what's known as glamour photography. You know what that is?'

'It speaks for itself, doesn't it?'

'Ah, but this isn't for magazines. This is vanity

stuff, women who want a photo of themselves looking like a movie star – or whose husbands or boyfriends do. They go along to a studio, get their hair and make-up done, get dressed up to the nines and the photographer does the rest.' He paused to let me know we were getting down to the nitty-gritty. 'We found some negatives in Hanna's office. Some of those sessions got pretty steamy.'

Donald paused again. I tried to look suitably expectant.

'Let me put it this way,' he said. 'They're not the sort of photos any self-respecting woman would show her parents. Shit, some of them no self-respecting woman would show her gynaecologist.'

'I think I get the picture.'

'I've talked to most of the clients. Apparently he used to get some white wine and maybe some weed into them, just to get them relaxed, then lay on the bullshit with a trowel. These aren't nineteen-year-old trainee hairdressers with tattoos on their bums, they're eastern suburbs types – mostly married and pretty well-off. The reactions vary: some were mortified, some couldn't give a shit, a few went to pieces. I suppose if I was a QC's wife and snaps of me looking like the guest of honour at a gang-bang were doing the rounds, I might drop my bundle too.'

I couldn't be bothered playing dumb any longer. 'Was Hanna backmailing them?'

He nodded approvingly. 'A couple owned up to it, but I'm bloody sure they're not the only ones. Hanna lived well and usually paid cash. Looking at the books, it's a bit hard to see where all the money came from.'

'Well, at least you can't complain about a lack of suspects.'

Donald was smiling again. 'Oh, we're narrowing the field down, don't you worry.'

I walked home at midnight thinking about what Donald had told me. And why he'd told me. He didn't strike me as a blabbermouth, someone who got off on spilling juicy inside dope to civilians. That wasn't his style. He struck me as a smart operator; there'd be a reason for everything he did. So what was the reason for that little exercise? Was he letting me know that he hadn't been fooled, that he knew bloody well I'd held out on him? That didn't explain why I'd got the lowdown on Hanna's candid camera racket – unless he thought I knew something about that as well.

These were disquieting thoughts to be taking home to bed. Or so it seemed at the time. In fact, the night was just getting started and so were the disquieting thoughts.

I walked into the flat and kicked over a pile of books which hadn't been on the floor when I left. I'd had a break-in. The bathroom window didn't have a lock or bars and the intruder had just levered it open and slithered in. I'd never worried much about security. When I was the landlord, I didn't give a shit. If the tenants didn't want midnight prowlers and strung-out dope fiends invading their personal space, they were perfectly welcome to turn the place into Fort Knox – at their own expense. Now I relied on the professionalism of the criminal fraternity. It was fairly obvious that Roach Central was the pokiest, seediest apartment in the whole building, so why would they bother?

Everything I'd ever owned that was worth stealing

was long gone. The custom-designed cluster oak veneer table, the turn-of-the-century Austrian Secessionist dining chairs, the Biedermeier sofas, the dinner and cutlery sets from Tiffany in New York, the Tibetan rugs. All sold off to pay for my lawyers' skiing holidays in Colorado or Tuscan food and wine tours. Speaking of wine, I'd assembled a 500-bottle cellar for the long term. After my first interrogation by the nerdy little zealots from the Australian Securities Commission, I resolved to swill the lot before anyone else got their hands on it. It took eleven months and probably kept me sane.

What was left was the personal stuff, the stuff that wasn't worth selling and hardly worth stealing. An unremarkable and heavily dated CD collection. Does anyone listen to 'Born in the USA' these days? Does anyone admit to owning it? The books. Burglars aren't bookworms and vice versa. People who like to read like to buy books – that's half the fun. Think of all those unread masterpieces occupying space on your shelves.

And the clothes. I have a confession to make here: I just couldn't bring myself to sell my corporate-wear. It wasn't that I expected to get any use out of it or even that it would've fetched a fraction of what it cost. It served a purpose. Every time I opened the wardrobe, I saw a wall of pin-stripe and plaid, a who's who of men's fashion in cellophane wrap. There it was, right there – the story of my life: The Rise and Fall of James Alabaster.

So what was worth stealing – fifteen suits, a TV, a VCR and a CD player – hadn't been stolen. Several things occurred to me as I was putting things back where they belonged. They all scared the shit out of me.

It wasn't a burglary. The intruder was looking for something. It had to be the tape.

The intruder hadn't torn the place apart. The search had been methodical, almost considerate, not unlike the scene in Hanna's apartment.

Whoever had been in Hanna's place had been here. They knew I had the tape. They knew where I lived.

I thought about getting out of there, spending the night somewhere else in case the intruder came back. Yeah, like where? No-one in this town wanted me on their doorstep at one in the morning. I could've gone to a hotel but what about the next night? And the night after that?

I had some bad times during the insider trading case. Not so much the trial – by then I knew the score. I knew the worst-case scenario and the best-case scenario and my Einstein lawyers were predicting the judge would come down in the middle, which he duly did. No, the worst moments were early on. When I found out they were on to me; when I realised they were going to get me; when I saw my future.

Those were bad moments, let me tell you. I churned with panic brought on by the recognition that it wasn't business as usual, it wasn't something that could be sorted out or glossed over or finessed. It was for real and it was unstoppable. I was tied to the tracks and they couldn't halt the train, even if they wanted to. There was no escape. I was fucked.

You don't want to know how bad that feels.

But I'm here to tell you there's an even worse feeling: the feeling you get when you think a killer's got your number. A killer was out there, that was a fact. Someone had been in my flat looking for the tape. The logical conclusion was that the killer had been there and he – or she, or they – would be back.

I thought I knew what fear was. I didn't know the half of it.

Imagine your entire body feeling like part of your face does after a dentist's local anaesthetic. You're numb all over. Your flesh no longer feels like living tissue. It's as if all those cells and nerves and corpuscles have just downed tools and walked off the job.

I sat there until it started to get light. I don't remember much of what I thought about but it was mostly to do with death and dying.

I do remember trying to imagine what it would be like to be on Death Row when the last legal manoeuvre has failed and the last loophole has been plugged. The governor's consulted his opinion pollsters and decided you're not worth saving. Your last meal's sitting there, untouched. The priest's been and gone. That wasn't a total success – if there's a heaven, then it stands to reason there's got to be a hell, right? This thing's been hanging over you forever but you never believed it would come to this. There'd always be another legal avenue to explore, another roll of the dice, another delay. But this is it. This is the end of the line. Next time you hear the key in the lock ...

I can also remember thinking that I didn't want to die by the knife.

I went to bed at dawn. It wasn't the greatest sleep I'd ever had but for a few hours I was able to block out the fear and the morbid images clogging up my head.

I woke up just after nine. There'd be no-one at the video store until ten. I got dressed and walked up there, wired on paranoia. I looked over my shoulder; I peered into passing cars; I stared right into the faces of everyone I met. I made a few people nervous but they'd get over it. No-one followed me as far as I could tell but that was no great distance. If they were good at it, I wouldn't have been any the wiser.

I got the tape out of its hiding place in the storeroom and took it to the Macleay Street post office. I hired a post office box and locked the tape in it. It cost me 80-odd bucks but my financial situation was the least of my worries now.

TEN

I walked up to Kings Cross. I wanted people around me, even the sort you find there.

Some hookers were having smoko outside Hungry Jack's. They were the pits, thirty-buck street-meat. Something terrible had happened to these women. With their dumb animal expressions and skin like wet tissue paper, they looked like the product of tainted genes.

How low can you go? Not much lower than these zombies selling their putrefying bodies on the street in broad daylight. Not much lower than the men who use them.

Twenty metres further along the strip two young men lay on the footpath. They were dusty and half naked, defaced by sprawling, childish tattoos. Their eyes were watery slits in pink, booze-boiled faces and the gastric stench of vomit clung to them like a losing streak. A shopkeeper looked in vain for beat cops while pedestrians made faces and changed course.

Street life. Don't you dig it? In some parts of the world, the state has a way of dealing with these rag-tag elements, a little unofficial social engineering in the form of a bullet in the back of the head and a shallow grave in a rubbish dump on the edge of town. We leave ours to decay in public while we hurry past, holding our noses.

Someone came up behind me and thumped me on the arm. I spun around and found myself staring into the shining, villainous face of Eddie Sarkis.

I made a spur-of-the-moment decision. 'Just the man I was looking for.'

'Oh yeah?' He said it with a sneer, but I didn't take it personally. Eddie would've sneered at a kitten.

'Yeah, I want your advice.'

'You want my advice, do you? What do you think I am – your fucking father?'

'You're many things to me, Edward, but a father figure isn't one of them . . .'

'You're full of shit.'

'No, I'm serious. Come on, I'll buy you a coffee.'

We set off for the Fountain Cafe on a collision course with one of the whores I'd seen earlier.

Eddie elbowed me. 'It's your lucky day – get in there.'

'I'd rather go blind.'

'You will, mate. You fucking well will.'

We crossed the road. The whore waved and called out, 'Hey, Eddie. How's it going, darl?'

I said, 'Sorry, I didn't realise she was a close personal friend of yours.'

Eddie ignored us both.

The moment we sat down, he went to work on his mobile phone. 'Al, it's Eddie. You know that filthy old slag, Denise? . . . Yeah, that's her. I was walking down the street with this dude just now' – Eddie winked at me; his eyes glittered with malice – 'and the fucking bitch yelled at me as if I was her fucking best friend ... Right, as if ... Yeah, fucking great for the image. Do us a favour, would you? Give her a fucking good smack next time you see her, make sure she gets the message ... Good on you, mate.'

He ended the call. He was showing his teeth now. I suppose you'd call it a grin. 'She's no fucking friend of mine, pal.'

It was all for my benefit. He was letting me know that Denise would have me to thank for the pummelling she was about to receive.

Point made, he asked how come a brainbox like me needed advice from a dumb prick like him. I told him I'd had a break-in.

'Shit, is that right? What'd the cunts take?'

'Nothing.'

'So what's your fucking problem?'

'Remember a couple of weeks ago a guy called Ray Hanna was murdered just down the road? Right next door to me, in fact.'

'Yeah, maybe. What about it?'

I told him about Hanna dropping off the wrong videotape the night he was killed and what I'd seen in his apartment the next morning. I told him that Donald seemed to think Hanna's missing tapes had something to do with it. I didn't tell him about Carla or the contents of my post office box.

Eddie's confusion was comical. 'I don't fucking get it,' he spluttered. 'What the fuck are you trying to tell me here?'

'I'm trying to tell you that I'm in the shit. I think the killer's after me now.'

Eddie let fly with his shit-himself laugh. It jangled the nerves like a jackhammer outside your window. After ten seconds of it, you were looking around for a weapon. 'Mate,' he brayed, 'here's my advice: go home, have a cold shower, take a couple of Disprin and go to bed. And for Christ sake, leave your slug alone – all that jerking off's making you paranoid ...'

There was a lot more in that vein. When he'd had his fun, I said, 'This is how I see it. Whoever put the knife into Hanna was looking for something; whoever broke into my place was also looking for something. Donald thinks I know more about the tapes than I've let on – maybe he's not the only one.'

Eddie sniffed and sat up straight to show he was taking it seriously. 'Listen, man, if you really believe that, don't fuck around – just get yourself a gun.'

'A gun?'

'That's right, dickhead, a gun. Some cunt messes with you, you stick it in his face and listen to him crap his pants. I can get you a good deal.'

'A couple of minor points.'

'Yeah, what?'

'In the first place, I've never handled a gun, let alone fired one.'

'You point the fucker and pull the trigger – how fucking hard is that?'

'As a matter of interest, do you carry a gun?'

'Depends what's going on, doesn't it?' Even without the studied nonchalance, I would've assumed he was lying. Eddie had that effect on people.

'Okay, what if he doesn't crap his pants?'

'You blow his motherfucking head off, what do you think?'

'I'm not sure I'm ready for that.'

Eddie heaved a sigh. You try to help someone ...
'Well then, get a knife.'

I shook my head. The thought of shoving a knife into someone was almost as sickening as the thought of someone shoving a knife into me.

'Fuck, what's the problem now?'

The explanation earned me another spray. I was talking shit: deep down, we were all wild animals – back us into a tight enough corner and we'd do anything, bite a guy's nuts off if we had to.

When I pointed out that the combination of knives and that sort of mad-dog behaviour got people killed over a spilt beer, Eddie ran out of patience. 'You really give me the shits sometimes, you know that? You don't want a gun, you don't want a knife, you can't afford protection . . . So what the fuck are you going to do?'

'I don't know. Maybe I'll just lie low for a while.'

'Well, fuck me, why didn't I think of that?' Eddie stood up. 'I'm out of here, I got better things to do.' He walked away, abandoning me to my fate. When he did a U-turn, I assumed he'd come up with a particularly tasty sign-off which he couldn't bear to waste. But he'd moved on. 'Hey, what about that fucking weasel, Donald?'

'What about him?'

'You reckon he's bent?'

'Donald? What gives you that idea?'

Eddie shrugged. 'You hear things.'

I was saying I thought it was pretty unlikely when Eddie put his hands flat on the table and poked his evil hook nose into my face. 'How many times did I tell you when we were in that shit-hole: everyone's got their angle. You hear me? Fucking everyone.'

It was true that I'd never handled a gun but I'm not averse to them in principle. Knives, yes, but not guns.

Unless I was extremely hungry and all the shops were shut, I don't think I could shoot an animal but, given an incentive – life or death, for instance – I could see myself shooting a human being. It's easy. As Eddie said, you point it and pull the trigger, how hard is that? And you can keep your distance – that's the part I like.

I'm a fan of gun movies. Of course, Clint Eastwood is Hollywood's top gun. No-one looks more relaxed with a gun in his hand; no-one kills with the same cool authority.

Take the bank robbery scene in *Dirty Harry*: He's in a diner when all hell breaks loose. He says, 'Aw, shit', through a mouthful of hot dog. He strolls, loose-limbed and unhurried, out to the street and goes to work. When the smoke clears, he's got a flesh wound and a few more notches on his .44 Magnum. And he's still chewing on that mouthful of hot dog.

Guns even things up. Anyone can be dangerous with a gun in their hand – in the wild west, they called them 'equalisers'. In *The Wild Bunch*, perhaps the greatest gun movie of them all, the legendary outlaw and killer Pike Bishop is shot dead by a boy soldier using a rifle he can barely lift.

I liked the idea of having a gun; I liked the idea of being cool and deadly even more. But if someone was shooting at me, I wouldn't keep chewing rhythmically on a mouthful of hot dog. Even if I was armed with the most powerful handgun in the world.

I was thankful for a rare busy night at the video store. At midnight I made a dash for home, scuttling from streetlight to streetlight like a cockroach trying to dodge the obliterating stamp.

I'd ordered a grille for the bathroom window but that would take a week. Until then I had to make do with a chair jammed against the bathroom door and a broom handle under the bed. I lay awake running heart-in-the-mouth ID checks on the noises of the night. Every indeterminate creak, every convulsion of the plumbing, foreshadowed the stealthy turn of the doorknob. It was going to be a long week.

I drifted in and out of sleep, more out than in. I tried to make up lost ground by dozing in. That's never a good idea. I rolled out of bed at ten, fogged-up and frazzled. I stood under the shower like a statue in the rain, waiting for my head to clear. It didn't.

That only left coffee.

At the cafe I thumped down a double espresso and soaked up the sports pages. I had a second and head-line-hopped through the other stuff, the sideshows.

There were rumblings of another war in the Middle East, another laser-guided turkey-shoot, another bloody nose for the Butcher of Baghdad. Apparently he was hiding a bio-arsenal capable of depopulating the planet in an afternoon. That had a familiar ring.

We grew up in the shadow of The Bomb. We didn't put too much faith in life's promises. We understood that the whole deal could go up in a mushroom cloud at any moment. We knew that somewhere there was a warhead with our name on it. Ours and 250,000 others. This one's for you, James Alabaster. You and all the other imperialist jackals in the Hunter Valley.

Sure, Saddam Hussein didn't seem a suitable person to possess the power of life and death over the human race. But who was? Certainly not those dumpy proles in the Kremlin whose fingers caressed the Doomsday button for forty years. Those old Reds didn't quail at the thought of mass extermination, no way. They were quite comfortable with it. They'd spent the best years of their lives drawing up death lists, organising midnight swoops, making the cattle trains to Siberia run on time.

And the boys in DC also knew a thing or two about megadeath. Dresden, Hiroshima, Nagasaki, Hanoi ... Bombing other folks back to the Stone Age was their *thing*.

I heard the click of high heels and glanced up like a Pavlov dog. The high heels belonged to Penny Wheat.

She walked right up to me. 'We haven't met but you're James, aren't you? I'm Penny Wheat.'

She offered a brown hand. I handled it with care. She had long, slender fingers and a smooth touch.

She pulled out a stool. 'May I?'

'Of course.'

She sat down, crossing her legs. They were long and slender too. Her low-cut top showed off the familiar scoop of cleavage. In my furtive youth I often read about 'proud' breasts. Penny's breasts were proud, all right. Those babies were as proud as Punch. They were hefty, protuberant, *Californian*. You wouldn't bet against her in a wet T-shirt contest. I suspected a cosmetic surgeon deserved some of the credit. Penny did look the type.

She was the sort of woman who caused road accidents – *Jesus fuck, get a load of that*! The warrior-queen blonde mane, the centrefold chest, the catwalk sashay, the whole vamped-up, voluptuous package screamed, *Look at me!* Don't worry about that pram, forget the geek on the bike, just look at me.

Compared to Carla, though, she was a blunt instrument – good-looking but in a slightly coarse way. Prominent features crowded her face like bulky furniture in a small room and, beneath the make-up, faint acne scars roughened her cheeks.

She said, 'I don't mean to pry ...' and laughed disarmingly. 'Actually that's a lie, that's exactly what I intend to do. About Carla, of course. I hear you two have been seeing quite a bit of one another.'

'Where'd you hear that?'

'Oh, you know, girl-talk.'

I smiled politely. 'In that case, you know all there is to know – which isn't a lot.'

'Oh no, I'm pretty much in the dark. You see, Carla didn't go into detail. And I didn't ask.'

'That doesn't sound like girl-talk. I thought you told each other everything.'

'You've got a lot to learn about girl-talk, James. It's all about getting approval: if we don't think our little secret will meet with approval, we don't share it.'

'Well, let me put your mind at rest: there's nothing to disapprove of.'

'Damn, I hate anticlimaxes. So what do you two actually do?'

'Have coffee, chat about this and that, the usual stuff.'

'That's it?'

'That's it.'

'And that's okay with you?'

'What sort of a question is that?'

Penny shrugged. 'Well, I know one thing: if I was a man and Carla Sully crossed my path, I wouldn't settle for coffee and a chat. I'd be setting my sights a little higher.'

'You're forgetting something.'

'What's that?'

'Carla's a married woman.'

She regarded me with heavy-lidded cynicism. 'So she is. Whatever was I thinking of? I'm still curious, though: Carla doesn't exactly make a habit of this sort of thing.'

'What sort of thing?'

Penny dropped her chin onto the heel of her hand and gave me a let's-quit-messing-around look. 'Hanging out with men who don't seem to have a job to go to.'

'Well, that's where you've got it all wrong. I work nights.'

'Do you now? And what do you do at nights?'

'I'm in the entertainment industry.'

'That could mean all sorts of things.'

I tried to look enigmatic, leaving her to figure out if I tore tickets in half or ran Twentieth Century Fox.

She said, 'Actually, I'm relieved to hear it's all perfectly innocent. It just wouldn't be fair if Carla was having more fun than me – I'm the single one, after all.'

Because I couldn't think of any other way to change the subject, I said, 'Sorry about your friend, Ray Hanna.'

'Wasn't that awful? I feel ill just thinking about it. Did you know him?'

'No. I just used to see him here, with you and Carla.'

'Poor Ray. We really miss him.'

Yeah? Carla didn't give the impression that something precious had gone out of her life, but I guess we all have our own way of grieving.

Penny stood up, shouldering her handbag. 'Well, I'd better be running along.'

'Aren't you going to have a coffee?'

Her wide mouth curved into a flirtatious smile. 'Oh, I only come here for the company.'

ELEVEN

When the phone rang at the video store, nine times out of ten it was a customer checking the availability of a new release or trying to track down some flick that time forgot.

Ring, ring. 'Potts Point Video, can I help you?'

'Well, I certainly hope so, squire.' Male, middle-aged and, like a lot of people in this neck of the woods at that hour of night, half cut. 'I'm trying to get hold of this movie I saw, shit, it'd be at least twenty years ago now. Haven't got a clue what it's called but it's set in Venice and it's got that bloke from *M*A*S*H* and I think Julie Christie in it. Whoever it is, they have a pretty raunchy sack scene – got me fizzing, I can tell you. More to the point, it got the bird I was with fizzing too. Oh yeah, and the killer turns out to be a dwarf, would you believe? Any of that ring a bell?'

Even down a telephone line, you can sense the desperation behind the bulldozing heartiness. A lonely forty-five-year-old sitting in his crummy apartment, remembering his first date with the one it might've worked with if he'd just tried harder, if he'd just put himself in her shoes occasionally. You don't want to watch *Don't Look Now*, friend. It'll only make it worse.

If it wasn't a customer inquiry, it was either a wrong number or a 'how fucking long does it take to choose a video' hurry-up for someone who'd been dispatched with a fairly tight set of guidelines half an hour earlier.

One night I got a call from this chick Megan who came in from time to time. She asked if I'd mind telling her boyfriend to get his arse back to the flat, like now. There was no-one in the store. I asked her what he looked like: medium height, well built, wearing a black leather coat – as opposed to a jacket – and a totally cool hat. I hadn't clapped eyes on anyone fitting that description all night.

Megan took the news badly. She'd spent two fucking hours cooking a meal for that arsehole so what'd he do? Went out on the piss with his mates, that's what. She had an idea: rather than let dinner go to waste, why didn't I come over? I said thanks but no thanks, I couldn't leave the shop. She pointed out that it was ten o'clock on a Wednesday night and not a customer in sight. Who the hell was going to know or care if I closed up early?

I was tempted, because Megan gave the impression she'd be serious fun when the lights went down. But it was a set-up. She just wanted the boyfriend to find her nuzzled up to some other guy when he got home. But what if he came home smashed and looking for trouble? What if he brought home a bunch of mates in the same state? Being the instrument of Megan's revenge looked like a high-risk gig and I wasn't that eager for a home-cooked meal.

Megan showed up the next night, wanting to

know why I'd knocked her back. I explained that I didn't want to get caught in the crossfire when the boyfriend got home.

She said, 'What boyfriend?'

'What?'

'Read my lips. I haven't had a boyfriend for over a month.'

Talk about short-term memory loss. 'You rang here with a message for him, remember? Dinner's on the table.'

'There wasn't a dinner either.' Megan was in her Friday night kit, which verged on overkill. She put her hands on her hips. 'I mean, for Christ's sake, do I look like I'd spend two hours slaving over a hot stove? I'm a five-minute cook. I do toast and cup-a-soup and real basic pasta, that's it.'

I'd clearly fucked up but I wasn't sure how or why. I said, 'I'm sorry, I'm missing something here.'

She looked pleased with herself. 'You certainly missed something last night.'

I felt like the straight man in an under-rehearsed double act. 'Let me get this quite clear: there was no boyfriend and no dinner – you just wanted me to come round?'

'That's about it.'

'Why the fuck didn't you say so?'

'Well, it's like this: a guy's got to be pretty special before I come right out with it. Don't take it to heart but you don't quite make the grade. I set you a little initiative test, to see how keen you were, and you failed it.'

'Do I get a second chance?'

I got a blast of scorn. 'Get real. You know what they say: no guts, no glory.'

Just to rub it in, the next time the bitch came in, she was coiled around this black dude who looked like Mike Tyson's evil twin. He didn't take his hand off her butt the whole time, not even when he paid.

So I had low expectations when the phone rang just after eleven. But this was my lucky night.

'I'm in the bath,' said Carla. 'If we get cut off, it means I've dropped the phone. It's a very big bath and I've overdone the bubbles so the salvage operation could take a while.' *Jesus Christ*. 'I've got this theory that you're either a bath person or a shower person. Which are you, James?'

'I'm a shower person. I've got no choice – my place doesn't stretch to a bath.'

'You poor thing. I can't imagine life without a bath. A long, hot bath with all the works, a glass of champagne, a few glossy magazines, the phone of course – that's pretty much my idea of luxury.'

'It sounds very inviting.'

'It's meant to.'

'Well, one of these days . . .'

'One of these days, what?'

'One of these days I'll have to get myself a place with a bath.'

'I'm not sure I can wait for that.'

Before I could think of a reply, she changed tack – abruptly. She had a habit of doing that, but I still hadn't got used to it.

'Irene Lomas rang,' she said. 'She wants to talk to us again.'

'What about?'

'She didn't say but it's obviously about Adam. What do you think?'

'We might as well. She must think it's important.'

'That's what I thought. Does eleven in the morning suit you?'

'Yep.'

'Do you want me to pick you up?'

'If it's not too much trouble.'

'For you, James? Ten to at the cafe, okay? I've got to go – my rubber duck's getting jealous.'

Irene Lomas was still growing old gracefully in her east-meets-west apartment but the atmosphere had turned sombre. Last time, she'd been determinedly brisk and composed. Now the brave face wouldn't stay put and melancholy clung to her like cigarette smoke to a party dress.

She poured tea for Carla and half-heartedly tried to interest me in various beverages. I declined on the grounds that I'd just had two strong coffees.

She visibly steeled herself before addressing Carla. 'My dear, in all honesty, I still haven't quite grasped why you're going through this exercise but you obviously have your reasons and I'm sure they're valid. I've given it a lot of thought since you were here the other day and I've decided to tell you the whole story. Hopefully, it'll put to rest whatever it is that's bothering you.' Her eyes moved, drawing me into a triangle of confidence. 'Does the name Lesley Croft mean anything to you?'

It did. There was a time when Lesley Croft was one of the most talked-about people in Sydney. Or at least in that part of Sydney where what's on TV doesn't set the conversational agenda. Lesley and her husband Will Hunt had ranked high on Sydney's alternative A-list. The establishment A-list reflects power, wealth, influence, mainstream fame – the conventional measures of success. Success in those terms isn't enough to get you on the alternative A-list. It doesn't disqualify you, it just isn't enough.

The alternative A-list is more about how you make it rather than how much you make. It's okay being loaded as long as you've made your pile doing something creative. The alternative A-list is about style, about cool, about looking good, about individuality and, paradoxically, about fashion. Heart and mind also come into it: you have to be a beautiful person inside as well as out. You can be the niftiest interior designer in town but if your attitudes are shabby or stick-in-the-mud, if you aren't on the side of the angels, forget it.

Lesley Croft was a publisher who'd made her name championing gay and feminist writing. Will Hunt was a doctor. He came from a long line of eminent surgeons but had forgone a lucrative medical career to crusade for Aboriginal health. Will and Lesley cared. Whenever people took to the streets in a righteous cause, they'd be up there at the head of the march. The ALP made no bones about it: Lesley and Will only had to say the word and they'd be on the political fast track. Neither of them ruled out an eventual move into politics.

They also liked a good time. The media were plugged right into that hip Sydney scene so, for a couple whose minds were on higher things, Lesley and Will got a lot of ink in the social pages.

For a healthy fee which they donated to the Women's Refuge, they allowed '60 Minutes' to do a week in their lives. It was a politically correct fairytale. Lesley in designer specs, a heady mix of brains and sex appeal, talking cover design with the author of *Murder at the Mardi Gras*. Will in the outback, a sweat-stained bandanna around his head, ducking kamikaze blowflies and cradling an Aboriginal child with eternity in her eyes. Will and Lesley marching for an independent East Timor. Will and Lesley grunged-down at a cut-and-thrust dinner party in their funky Newtown terrace. Will and Lesley in perfect harmony with their cute, perky kids. Will and Lesley hand-in-hand on a beach at sunset, reassuring the nation in voice-over that, yes folks, there is such a thing as wedded bliss.

I've always thought that it's tempting fate to go public with that higher love stuff – 'Lesley's not just my wife and lover, she's my best friend, my inspiration.' Take Hollywood. Whenever some movie star starts gushing on the talk-show circuit that she's finally found her soul-mate, you know it's just a matter of time before her lawyer's telling the court that Mr Soul-mate's a twisted swine who liked to tie his client down and piss on her. Call it Roseanne's Law.

That '60 Minutes' story seemed to kick-start the rumour machine. At first, it was low-impact stuff on the theme that things weren't quite as peachy as they'd have us believe. No kidding? Then the poison darts started flying. Not for the first or last time – and what does this tell us about ourselves? – the tittle-tattle cast the female as a sexual predator and the male as a closet queen. So we heard that Lesley had blown a pretty-boy soap actor in the back of a cab, that Will had blown a slab-chested model in a restaurant toilet, that Lesley was screwing a Very Important Person in Canberra, that Will had been seen in an Oxford Street S and M club on all fours, being led around on a leash.

There's no smoke without fire, the gossips reassure

each other as they shred another reputation. Their vindication came with a terse trial separation announcement coupled with an appeal for space and privacy while Lesley and Will tried to work through their difficulties. Then suddenly it was over. There was talk that some hair-raising filth would emerge from the custody battle, but they drew back from the brink. Lesley ceded custody. That, it was assumed, was the price she had to pay to avoid humiliation.

A few months later, Lesley Croft got in a hot bath and opened her veins.

Irene said, 'Lesley Croft was my sister. Will came home early from a trip to Alice Springs and found her in bed with their nephew. My son. Will's a saint, but even he couldn't forgive that, not after Lesley admitted that it'd been going on for three years.' Irene squeezed back tears. When she spoke again, her voice was thick with pain and perhaps anger. 'I've never had the slightest doubt that Adam killed himself. If there can ever be such a thing as a good reason to commit suicide, he had it.'

When the lift doors closed, Carla said, 'Jesus.'

I could only agree. 'Yeah.'

'Why do you think she told us?'

'You heard what she said. Maybe it bothered her that she'd given us a version she didn't believe herself. Call it good, old-fashioned honesty.'

Carla said, 'No wonder it's going out of fashion.' We reached the ground. 'I'm trying to remember, when did all that happen?'

'The rumours started midway through ninety-two. I know that because I was working on a deal for this client who had all the scuttlebutt.'

'And they'd been at it for three years.'

I had a pretty good idea what was on Carla's mind. As we exited the building, she said, 'Adam and I broke up for good at the end of eighty-nine. I wonder if Lesley and I overlapped.'

We walked to her car in silence. Carla leaned against it and stared up at Irene's apartment building. 'I was twenty-five in eighty-nine. How old would she have been?'

She was trying to sound vaguely curious, as if she was asking whatever happened to whatsisname. She didn't quite carry it off.

'From what Irene said the other day, Lesley must've been around forty when she died. That'd make her mid-thirties.'

'The older woman syndrome, eh? Guess I shouldn't knock it.' She pushed off the car and focused her sunglasses on me. 'So: are you convinced now?'

I nodded slowly. 'I was a bit dubious about the tortured genius scenario, but you can't quibble with that.'

'That means I can relax a little, doesn't it?'

The coroner had got it right: Adam committed suicide. That made it two out of seven which, statistically, was a lot less implausible. And if the cops were right about Shelley's overdose, that made it one out of seven. One murder could be isolated and rationalised. After a while, it could be shrugged off.

Most murders are the result of either a sudden escalation in domestic skirmishing or rotten luck – that lethal quinella of being in the wrong place at the wrong time. Hanna was probably just plain unlucky, firstly that the psycho or the burglar or the whacked-out junkie chose his place and, secondly, that he happened to be there at the time. Shit happens and there's always some poor bastard in the vicinity. And if it didn't happen that way, then maybe the blackmail racket blew up in his face. Or he put his clammy hands on the wrong woman. Or he drew the short straw at a satanic rite. All those scenarios were more likely than that he was hacked to bits because of his link to a fifteen-year-old dirty video.

I wished I could've spun it out for a little longer but Carla could see for herself that we were out of the grey, into the black and white. There wasn't much point in pretending otherwise.

I nodded. 'I'd say so.'

'Well shit, James, this calls for a celebration.'

TWELVE

I was wishfully thinking of a lost afternoon, a slow, wine-tinted dissolve to intimacy. Knees grazing under the table and cleansing vodka and tonics at five o'clock and ... well, who knows? Afternoons like that can take on a life of their own. Carla had something else in mind. Her idea of a celebration was a quick lunch: one course, one glass of wine, one coffee. She was pushed for time, she said. She had a lot on and too much of anything in the middle of the day slowed her down.

I hadn't been to the Bayswater Brasserie for a couple of years. Nothing much had changed. It was still full of people with expense accounts – PR people, advertising people, publishing people, fashion people, film people, even a few people who'd strayed in from the real world. All discussing projects over swordfish and chardonnay. All doing lunch.

Most of them wouldn't achieve anything that they couldn't have achieved in a ten-minute phone conversation, but that wasn't the point. The point was that over lunch they could develop relationships. They could drink too much, talk about themselves, shamelessly overstate their place in the scheme of things, toss around a few ideas they'd had in the taxi on the way over, make a few promises they'd forget in the taxi on the way back ... Before they knew it, they'd have a relationship. It's that easy. And relationships are important. Never underestimate the value of relationships. Ignorance breeds distrust; acquaintance enhances understanding and communication. If everyone had a corporate credit card, the world would be a better, safer place.

Carla surprised me by opting for the non-smoking section. I estimated she had a ten-a-day habit which probably blew out to twenty and counting when she partied. She explained that she was an active smoker, not a passive smoker.

We were led to a table next to a group of eight young women. It was someone's birthday. They were still on their first courses and already sounding like a riot in the typing pool. In half an hour they'd be telling first-fuck stories and screeching like pterodactyls. In an hour we'd be bleeding from the ears.

Carla took one look and told the waiter, 'On second thoughts ...'

She asked the waiter to hang around while we looked at the menus. The clock was ticking all right. When we'd ordered, I told her about the time I was in a restaurant in North Sydney with a bunch of guys from work, sat next to another all-female birthday group. After dessert, the birthday girl got her presents, which included a pair of naughty knickers. She went to the ladies to try them on. When she got back, the others wanted to see how they looked on her. Birthday girl ordered the other diners not to look, hoisted her skirt and did a slow circuit of the table.

'You looked,' said Carla.

'I felt it would've been rude not to. She can't have been all that offended, because she came over and introduced herself.'

'I suppose you're going to tell me she ended up marrying someone at your table?'

'Not quite. One of my colleagues did fuck her in the back seat of his car – I think he also felt it would've been rude not to. When they came back into the restaurant, we all sang Happy Birthday.'

Carla shrugged. 'These things can happen on a girls' night out.'

'Were yours like that?'

'What makes you think they still aren't?' Giving me the slow raise of the eyebrows.

'Well, now that you mention it, I imagine your pal Penny's hell on wheels when she gets going. She and I had a little chat at the cafe the other day.'

'I don't remember introducing you.'

'You didn't. She introduced herself.'

'And?'

'We had a brief chat.'

'What about?'

'Have a guess.'

The food arrived. Carla's was a dainty piece of fish, mine a Bible-sized hunk of sirloin which ran red when I cut into it.

'Let me think,' she said. 'Penny's favourite topic of conversation is her sex life, past, present and future. Her second favourite topic of conversation is other people's sex lives. Am I getting warm?'

I was. 'Yes and no. She was intrigued that you were spending a fair bit of time with someone who, as she put it, didn't seem to have a job to go to. She said you didn't make a habit of it.'

Her eyes narrowed cagily. 'What did you say?'

'I told her I worked nights. I also told her there was nothing going on that she could disapprove of.'

'That doesn't rule out much – when Penny disapproves, you know you've really gone too far.'

'Well, it seemed to satisfy her. She was pleased to know that you, being a married woman, weren't having more fun than she was.'

'That's our girl. So what did you make of her?'

'She seemed like a nice person.'

'Really?'

'She's not my type.'

Carla snapped her fingers. 'That's right, I forgot – you're a total package man. Penny must've wondered what was going on. She's used to getting a reaction.'

'I imagine so.'

'She's not the blonde bimbo people take her for, though. She's quite tough – and resourceful. You know what she did when her ex-husband kicked her out? Hired a private detective to dig up some dirt on him to strengthen her negotiating position. It worked, too.'

'Why did he kick her out?'

'You need to ask?'

Not really. After we'd paid some attention to the food, Carla surprised me by asking, 'What would you do if you found out your wife was having an affair?'

'Jesus, I don't know – that's a bit hypothetical for me.' I was glad she'd raised the subject, though; I'd been wondering how she felt about adultery. 'You're the married one – what would you do?'

I half-expected her to avoid the question, but she didn't. Before they were married, she and Reece had sorted out the ground-rules, just like the textbooks say you should. Reece's basic attitude was that if he'd wanted to keep playing the field, he wouldn't have got married. He fully intended to be a one-woman man, but there was always the Elle Macpherson scenario.

That went like this: Mr X, a happily-married Australian, is in, say, New York on business. It's late and he's watching TV in his lonely hotel room. There's a knock on the door. It's [insert the name of your supermodel or film star of choice] and guess what? She's kinda lonely too.

I said, 'I hear it happens all the time.'

Carla smiled. 'Well, they do say it's lonely at the top.'

Reece's argument was that promises were only good for foreseeable circumstances. But what if, out of the blue, one of the most desirable women in the world knocked on your hotel room door? What were you going to do – shut the door in her face? Like fuck. You'd pounce on her like a speed-crazed lab rat and any man who said otherwise was either a liar or a fag. In that situation, promises and good intentions weren't worth a tin of shit.

He argued that there was no point in them making hope-to-die promises they mightn't be able to keep. What really mattered was that they didn't go looking for it. If the Elle Macpherson thing happened, it happened and it wouldn't be worth splitting up over. But if they went looking for it whenever the other's back was turned, then the marriage was shot. There wouldn't be much love left and even less respect.

It seemed like one big grey area to me, but maybe that was the idea. I asked, 'Does it work?'

She opened her mouth to reply, then closed it as if she was having second thoughts. Eventually she said, 'Well, we're still together. It's probably harder for Reece – the fact that he is who he is can be an attraction in itself, but most guys are going to think twice before they go sniffing around Reece Sully's wife. Mind you, there's the odd one who doesn't give a toss.' Was it my imagination or was there a note of approval in her voice? 'Like this guy who works for Reece – he tried it on at the company Christmas party, would you believe?'

'What happened?'

She shrugged. 'I told him to go home, take a couple of aspirin and play with himself.'

'Someone gave me similar advice just the other day.' Carla looked interested, but I didn't want to change the subject or spoil her mood by bringing up the break-in. 'A long story which I won't bore you with. Actually, what I meant was, what happened when Reece found out?'

The waiter was hovering. Carla indicated she was finished and he swooped to clear the plates away. We ordered coffee and she lit a cigarette. 'I didn't tell him,' she said. 'It was kind of a complicated situation . . .'

'What's so complicated about hitting on the boss's wife?'

'In the first place, we were doing coke at the time and Reece is a little old-fashioned when it comes to drugs. Secondly, I was looking for an alternative supplier and this guy was perfect. As was the timing seeing that, three weeks later, Ray Hanna went out of business.'

'Hanna was a coke dealer?'

'Why do you think I put up with him?'

I was glad we'd cleared that up. While we were on the subject, I passed on the news about Hanna's glamour photography racket.

It didn't surprise her. Nothing would where Hanna was concerned. 'He was such a sleaze. How about this? He once tried to get me to do a glamour shot for an ad he was putting in the *Wentworth Courier*. As if I wanted to appear half-naked in that bloody thing. When I refused, he threatened to tell Reece that I was buying coke.'

'What did you do?'

'Threatened him with instant social death. He almost wet his pants.' She put on a wheedling voice. '"Only joking, darling, you know I'd never do any such thing." I wouldn't wish what happened to him on anyone but there weren't too many tears shed for Ray Hanna, let me tell you.'

'How much coke do you get through, if you don't mind me asking?'

'Not much – a few hundred dollars worth a month, I suppose. In Reece's terms, that's a couple of bottles of wine.'

'Peanuts.'

'You have a problem with that?'

'Shit, no. If it turns you on and you can afford it, go for it. I mean, if you can't handle it, you should stay away from it, but that goes for a lot of things.'

'Can you handle it, James?'

It was a loaded question, but I played it straight. 'Coke? Sure. In fact, I could never quite see what the fuss was about.'

'Remind me never to waste any on you.'

If we got to that, it'd be the last thing I'd do. Carla

paid the bill with a gold Amex card and I walked her to her car. As we turned into Ward Avenue, she said reflectively, 'So after all that, it really was just a coincidence.'

'Looks like it. If we hadn't gone to the trouble, though, we'd still be wondering.'

'I know.' She gave my arm a lingering squeeze. 'Thanks, James. I wouldn't have known where to start.'

As we reached the entrance to the carpark, she said casually, 'I must get that tape off you.' I must've looked startled because she quickly tacked on, 'You've still got it, haven't you?'

I nodded like a woodpecker. I could feel the post office box key taped to my right instep with a band-aid.

She said, 'Okay, see you.' I got the regulation cheek-to-cheek and she disappeared into the parking building. I hadn't even thanked her for lunch.

I'd started running again. It'd be stretching things to say it made me feel good about myself, but it did represent progress. Seeing my natural inclination was to sit on my arse and do nothing, each run was a small triumph of the will.

I usually ran at dusk, when it had cooled down a bit. Up Macleay Street towards the Cross, past the Asian tourists filing in and out of the hotels and duty-free shops. Past locals flocking back into the most densely populated square mile in Australia to squat like battery hens in their little boxes. Turn left at Greenknowe Avenue and freewheel down the hill into Rushcutters Bay Park.

Past the floodlit tennis courts. Check out those

slo-mo serves and spastic backhands. Past the Reg Bartley Oval and the dim shapes of footy players at pre-season training. Listen to them pant; listen to them moan. Whoops, someone just called the coach a cunt and it's not even autumn.

Past the hand-in-hand strollers and the tree-huggers. Past folks walking the dog. The dog–master nexus has many manifestations these days, including young women in sports bras and bicycle shorts power-walking with their rottweilers. Those chicks don't mind the park at night. Why should they? Mess with them and Brutus will have your windpipe for supper. Chicks with nice little dogs, dogs which take the man's best friend role seriously, walk them before breakfast or hurry home after work.

Past faddists windmilling at their personal trainers' punching pads. Past the ethnics cooling down after their pick-up soccer games. Past other joggers. Fellow plodders nod or blip their eyebrows. The serious distance guys, gaunt creatures who prance like show jumpers, stare straight ahead as if in a trance.

Past the marina, shifting and creaking like a forest. Past the Moreton Bay figs, hearing the bats shriek as they glide overhead like black kites. Past the yacht club, dodging yachties back from a twilight sail. Past clandestine lovers tangled up in parked cars, rehearsing the lies they'll tell when they get home. Past Yaranabee Park with its view of the city shimmering like an electric Legoland.

Hit the dead end, admire the Harbour Bridge, turn around and head home. If I was feeling really good I'd tackle the hill up to Darling Point, past Tom and Nicole's place. But it was a pretty steep hill and I didn't feel that good that often.

I'd also started lifting weights again. When I got back from the run, I spent half an hour with my second-hand dumb-bells. Exercise is like banging your head against the wall: it feels good when you stop. And there's nothing like going through a little pain in the cause of self-improvement to make a person feel, well, virtuous. It's all relative, of course. Most of the Muscle Marys at the cafe had better bodies than I'd ever have and I was no paragon of virtue, even in this depraved time and place.

I went into the bathroom, stripped off and examined myself in the full-length mirror on the back of the door. Working out makes you do that sort of thing.

The hair was more or less okay – still dark and still there, although the hairline had begun its long retreat. It wasn't as manageable as in the days of the monthly fifty buck cut from a hair consultant. I missed the tarty trainee who used to shampoo me. I missed the soft nudge of her thigh. I never worked out if it was for her benefit or mine.

You've got a lot of forehead there, pal. My mother believed that a high forehead was a sign of intelligence but then she would've said that. It came from her side of the family. Jane thought my hazel eyes were soulful, but then she would've said that. She loved me.

The nose was good. The nose I liked. Not too big, not too small, not too thin, not too pointed and very straight. Geometrically straight. The mouth was small without being prissy and the jawline was clean without being heroic.

If that all sounds pretty satisfactory, there was a

downside. It has to be said that the overall picture wasn't as impressive as the sum of its parts. There was something lacking, something, I'm afraid to say, known as character. If you believe that faces reflect personality – and let's be honest, who doesn't? – then you wouldn't look at me and think, There's a guy who'd never let you down. Or, There's a guy I wouldn't mind on my side when the going gets tough. On the other hand, you wouldn't find anything particularly disturbing about this face. It wouldn't give you the creeps. You wouldn't think, Jesus, imagine how that guy gets his kicks. Or, Jesus, I wouldn't like to meet him down a dark alley.

I guess we're talking bland here but ... but if you were a woman who wasn't looking for a hero, you might give me a second glance. We're certainly not talking handsome but then handsome, like beautiful, is rarer than the media would have us believe. And if it's handsome and hetero you're after, pack some sandwiches, honey – it could take you a while.

I stand 182 centimetres tall, exactly six feet in the old measurement. My mother claimed that Our Lord was exactly six feet tall. Don't ask where she got that from – she just knew, okay? During my going out, getting drunk and not doing much exercise phase – which lasted almost four years – I blew out to 85 kg. Now I was down to 77, slightly below my post-prison norm. Since I'd met Carla, I just hadn't had much of an appetite. I was in reasonable shape: square shoulders, flat stomach, some upper-body definition, some bicep bulge. The legs were to scale and the equipment was standard issue. Whether it was in full working order was another matter.

Summing up, then: although of limited appeal to the high-income, status-conscious consumer, this product should find a niche in the market given an appropriate targeting strategy.

THIRTEEN

Saturday morning at the cafe. I got there late after another drawn-out, jittery night. All the tables, inside and out, were taken. So were all the newspapers, so was the shade. I sat and sweated on a plastic milk-crate. They'd forecast 33 degrees and they were probably going to be right.

At least I was dressed for it in a T-shirt, shorts and thongs. The pair next to me were in shirts and ties and shoes that needed socks. Real estate agents. No-one else dressed that way on a Saturday morning.

They were soon talking shop. One of them just couldn't believe that queen knocking back a million. A million was way above the market. The other couldn't believe the way people were prepared to pay a premium just because a property had appeared in a home beautiful magazine. He thought everyone knew that if you hired a good photographer and a few nice pieces, you could make any dump look okay.

I was wondering how long I could take the heat and the rising camp when one said, 'By the way, do you know Peter Grayson?'

'I know who he is. Why?'

'You mean was – he's dead.'

Jesus fucking what?

'The plague?'

'Oh, God no, he wasn't a candidate. He had a wife and kiddies.'

'So do some of our best friends.' Titter, titter.

'Actually, he was run over.'

'Ugh. When did that happen?'

'Yesterday. There's something about it in the paper.'

The woman sitting opposite me in the shade was studying the movie listings, so I borrowed her news section. The story was low down on a local news page under a two-deck headline: Hit and run kills real estate man.

According to the *Herald*'s story, Peter Grayson, only son of late real estate bigshot Brian, was thought to have left his Vaucluse mansion for his regular early morning run at around 6 a.m. He usually showered and dressed downstairs to avoid waking the family and went straight to work, so the alarm wasn't raised until 9.30 when his wife got back from taking the kids to school. She could think of various mundane reasons for her husband's car still being in the garage, but none for his work clothes still hanging in the downstairs bathroom.

Grayson was already in the morgue when his wife rang the police. Three hours earlier, a paperboy had reported a body on a street corner five minutes jog from the Grayson residence. A police spokesman said they were still awaiting the full pathologist's report but the deceased's injuries were consistent with having been struck by a vehicle. They were treating it as a hit and run.

Grayson had been dead for almost thirty hours. Carla must know by now. Why hadn't she been in touch?

I'd thought Irene Lomas had laid Adam to rest: with the benefit of hindsight, it was understandable, almost predictable, that Adam would kill himself. But hindsight can distinguish a pattern in random events and life isn't a straightforward process of cause and effect.

Would you call this a pattern? Neither Adam nor Pete nor Shelley Lendich lived alone, but they all died alone.

Adam was home alone in the wee small hours because his flatmate worked in a nightclub till dawn. Shelley's boyfriend left her at home when he went out stealing once a week, on a Tuesday or Wednesday night. Pete got mown down on his regular early-morning run.

Someone who knew the flatmate's hours could've dropped by after midnight. Adam would've been out of his skull by then, easier to lure onto the balcony and send on a space-walk.

Someone who knew about Shane Salter's scam could've watched him drive away then dropped in on Shelley with some lethal junk.

Someone who knew Pete was an early-morning jogger could've parked with the motor running near a corner where he crossed the road and knocked him over like a tenpin.

The killer could've watched them, learned their routines, worked out the how, when and where. The killer could've had a head-start from knowing them from way back.

Ray Hanna lived alone, so timing wasn't as critical. And if the killer knew that Hanna was playing dangerous games, there wouldn't have been the same need to make it look like something other than murder. There'd be no shortage of suspects.

Four down. Three to go. Where the hell was Carla?

The call came early on Monday morning. There was no hello, how are you, did you miss me like I missed you? Just, 'James, it's Carla. You know about Pete Grayson?'

I said yes. She asked if I was going to the cafe. I said yes again. She said she'd try to be there by ten and rang off.

I got there on the dot. Carla was waiting for me. She was dressed down – white jeans, black T-shirt, flat shoes, no make-up – with a mood to match: subdued and slightly anxious, as if her hair stylist had just died or moved to the Blue Mountains.

'Hello, Carla.'

'Hello, James. How was your weekend?'

'Better than yours, I suspect.'

'Oh, mine was fine until yesterday afternoon. We went up to the beach. It was brilliant: perfect weather, hardly any kids – what more could you want? When it's like that, I turn off the mobile and don't look at a newspaper. Yesterday we had some friends for lunch. The first thing they said was, Have you heard about Pete Grayson? You know how it is – you try not to let these things put you off your sushi, but . . .'

Her voice trailed off. She lit a cigarette. It wasn't the usual unhurried routine culminating in a lazy tilt of the head to direct a vapour trail into someone else's air space. She practically swallowed the cigarette and exhaled in short bursts, as if she was sending a smoke signal.

She said, 'Okay, so what are the odds on four out of seven being a coincidence?'

'Pretty long.'

'Does that mean you've changed your mind?'

I said carefully, 'It means that I think the balance of probability no longer favours a coincidence.'

Carla snorted and took another fierce drag. 'Christ, you sound like a fucking lawyer.'

Thinking about it afterwards, I wondered if it was meant as the usual knockabout but her downbeat mood caused her to get the tone all wrong. At the time, though, I took it at face value and it stung me.

I didn't stop to think, I just stung back. 'Fuck you.'

She sucked in her cheeks and her violet eyes flared. 'What did you say?'

I suppose it wasn't such a daft question. She was putting the onus on me to decide how far it went. I could repeat myself and declare war or I could back down.

Or I could bounce it back to her. 'Hey, you asked me a question, I answered it. If you don't like my answers, maybe you should ask someone else.'

She stood up abruptly, tossing cigarettes and lighter into her handbag. She said, with icy sincerity, 'What a fucking good idea', and walked away with a long, implacable stride.

I watched her leave. I hadn't realised how tight those white jeans were. Suddenly I felt nauseous. I flushed and my heartbeat shot towards the red zone. I asked myself, 'Why the fuck did you do that?'

After a while, I gave up waiting for a reply.

I should've seen it coming. We were both on edge: Carla was shook up over Pete Grayson and I was feeling like the hired help. She'd summoned me as if she thought she only had to click her fingers and I'd come running. I wonder what gave her that idea.

But it happened so fucking fast. Out of nowhere, like one of those late afternoon summer storms. You notice a few smudgy clouds out west and make a mental note to take an umbrella tonight, just in case. Half an hour later, thunderheads the size of Mount Everest are colliding 50 metres above the TV aerials and your garden gnome's going down for the third time.

Things had been going so well, too. The flirting was getting more pointed and the conversation kept coming back to sex. For a while there, in my private moments, I'd made much of her admission that she masturbated. I extrapolated bullishly from that throwaway remark until I realised I was romanticising again. The only way a married man could get my attention on the subject of masturbation would be by claiming he never spilt a drop.

And, intoxicated as I was, I was aware of her probes and gambits, aware of being assessed, weighed up. She'd implied that she still kicked up her heels from time to time – Did her wedding ring spend those nights in her handbag? I wondered – and let it drop that she made a habit of doing things behind her husband's back. She'd hinted that she admired men who didn't care that she was Reece Sully's wife. She'd asked me, can you handle it? All the time watching me react, wanting to know what I was made of.

I stewed on it for twenty-four hours. That's too long to stew anything. The reality, as the boys at the bank used to say, was that it was up to me. Carla wasn't going to make the first move. Even if she was having second thoughts about the lawyer jibe, that was a long way from concluding that maybe she'd asked for it. That, in turn, was a long way from picking up the phone and conceding that it takes two to tangle. I couldn't see her covering that amount of territory, not in this life. So there it was: unless I went cap in hand, I'd be back on the outside looking in, snatching glimpses of Carla's world through a hole in the fence.

Of course, if Carla wasn't the forgiving kind, I was already banished. But I had to know one way or the other. I had to kick this feverish speculation, one minute convinced she'd never want to see me again, the next wondering if her heart went pitter-patter each time her phone rang. I just didn't want to grovel. I was prepared to repent but I really didn't want to grovel. If it came to that ... Jesus, who was I trying to kid?

I tried ringing her on Tuesday morning but her mobile was switched off. Bad sign. I tried every half-hour for six hours – same thing. She was shutting me out. She was severing the connection.

Each time I got the recorded message, I sank a little further. I didn't want to go to work. I thought about calling in sick, buying a bottle of vodka and getting trashed. It wasn't the fact that I didn't get sick pay which stopped me. I just couldn't afford to let go, not even for one night. Curling up in Roach

Central with a bottle could've been the beginning of the end.

I didn't dart home from the video store in a funk that night. I really didn't give a fuck.

FOURTEEN

I tried Carla again the next morning. She was still off the air, making sure I got the message.

I went to the cafe. When I went inside to pay, the owner was in a talkative mood. When I finally got out of there, Carla was sitting down at the table I'd vacated.

She crossed her legs in a flurry of suntan and inched her hem southwards. That still left a lot of tantalising flesh exposed. Her eyes, though, were blanked out by impenetrable sunglasses, like movie stars sealed off from their fans behind the smoked-glass windows of their limousines. She ducked her head to light a cigarette. I just stood there; I didn't know what to do. Her demeanour wasn't encouraging but if she didn't want to see me, all she had to do was pick another cafe. There were plenty to choose from.

I could *hear* my pulse. I went over to her. She didn't look up.

'Hello, Carla.'

She turned her head to exhale and squeezed a throwaway hello through ventriloquist's lips.

I placed a tentative hand on the spare stool. 'May I?'

She shrugged, aiming her sunglasses at my right

armpit. I sat down. I gave her half a minute or so to enter into the spirit of conciliation. She passed up the opportunity, so I took the plunge. 'I'm sorry for what I said. I was out of line.'

The sunglasses swivelled. She took a long drag on the cigarette, averting her face just enough to avoid blowing smoke in mine.

I played my only card. 'Okay, you're pissed off, I can understand that. And if you've made up your mind to stay pissed off, there's not much I can do about it. But we need to talk.'

'What is there to talk about?'

It was a rhetorical question, but I didn't let that stop me. 'At the risk of sounding like a lawyer, the law of averages suggests there's something strange or worse than strange going on. You need to make a few decisions.'

'Such as?'

'Well, for a start, have you told Reece?'

'Oh, now he's a comedian.'

I nodded slowly. 'If you're not prepared to tell Reece, you're obviously not prepared to go to the police.'

'You catch on quick.'

'Even though you might be in danger?'

That met with another sulky shrug. I felt like a parent trying to negotiate a Saturday night curfew with a sixteen-year-old.

'What's the security like at your place?'

'State-of-the-art, of course.'

'Does that include guards?'

'We've got people on call twenty-four hours a day – buzz them and they're there in five minutes. Happy now?'

'If I was you, I'd have a couple of big security guys on site. Tell Reece you've seen a suspicious-looking character hanging around, or something. You need visible protection and you need to start taking precautions.'

No reaction. I stood up. If she'd given me a hint of encouragement, I would've hung in there; I might've even grovelled. But she hadn't given me a thing and I had just enough pride left to walk away. 'Well, it's up to you now. See you.'

Carla said, 'What's the rush?'

I stared, incapable of playing it cool.

'Have another coffee.' She was still expressionless but the dismissive chill had left her voice. That was good enough for me. I sat right back down. We looked at each other for a while. I was beginning to wonder what came next when she said, 'I'm sorry too, James. It was a bitchy thing to say.'

It was okay. It was going to be all right. I was going to be all right. 'Well, maybe, but I still went over the top . . .'

'Hey, you've already apologised; you don't have to do it again.'

'I wasn't sure it'd been accepted.'

She treated me to a smile straight out of a toothpaste ad. It warmed me all over. 'I came, didn't I?' she said. 'I couldn't make all the running.'

'Is that why your phone was switched off yesterday?'

'So you did try to call me. I wondered about that.'

'I assumed you'd take it for granted.'

She nodded. 'That was the problem, wasn't it? You felt taken for granted.'

I didn't say anything. I didn't have to.

'I don't take you for granted, James, but if you got that impression, I'm sorry.'

'Carla, you've apologised once; you don't have to do it again.'

'That was for something else.'

'Well, we must've covered everything now.'

She said solemnly, 'Our first tiff.' Then the straight face collapsed and she was laughing, a low, bubbling laugh. I joined in. I could hear the creak of relief in my laughter.

Suddenly Penny Wheat was standing there. 'Well, well – the sights you see when you get up early.'

I said, 'This is early?'

Penny said, 'Depends what time you went to bed.'

Carla looked her over. 'Just off to the supermarket, are we?'

Penny was wearing a black sheath dress and dominatrix stilettos. The dress was split to the thigh and as tight as a tourniquet. 'Something like that,' she said, her smile giving nothing away. 'But don't let me interrupt – I just popped in for a takeaway.'

She went inside. Carla raised her eyebrows. 'Where were we?'

'Making up.'

'Before that.' It took her a moment. 'That's right, you were saying I should get security guards. Were you serious?'

'Sure, even if it's just for a couple of weeks while we try to find out what's going on.'

Penny came out of the cafe carrying a sealed styrofoam cup. She asked Carla, 'What's on your agenda today, darling?'

'Nothing special.'

'Well, I'm sure James will keep you entertained.'

I said, 'It's a tough job but someone's got to do it.'

Penny told Carla she'd call her later. We watched her sway to her car. I said, 'The supermarket, you reckon?'

'You can never tell with Penny – she'd get glammed up to go out for a carton of milk. She's got an image to live up to. I suppose we're all playing roles to some extent, but Penny . . .' Carla shook her head slowly '. . . she plays hers to the hilt.'

'What's your role?'

'Surely you've worked that out?' I shook my head. 'Cool, collected Carla, the woman who has it all. Or, as Penny sometimes calls me, Australia's Jackie O.'

'That's a role?'

'Come on, James, you should know that by now.' The way she said it made me wish she'd take her sunglasses off.

I said, 'Do you think I play a role?'

'You know you do.'

'What is it?'

She took a few seconds to sort out the words. 'You pretend to be the detached, cynical guy who's kind of pulled back from everything and just sits on the sidelines watching everything turn to shit.'

'That's no role, that's the real me.'

'No, it's not. I can understand why you put it on, but it's not the real you.'

'What is?'

'You're not as detached as you make out. You wouldn't have done what you've done for me if you didn't give a shit.'

'I give a shit about you.' I could hear my pulse again. 'That's not quite the same thing.'

'It is to me.' Carla leaned across and placed her palm gently on my cheek. 'That's why I'm here.' She removed her hand and sat up straight. 'So what do we do now?'

'What've you got in mind?'

She tilted her head and gave me a look: try to keep up. 'You mentioned trying to find out what's going on.'

So I did. 'I think we should talk to Alex – apart from anything else, she ought to be aware of the situation. And she might know what happened to Gareth.'

'Then there were three.' Carla rubbed her bare forearms as if there was a sudden chill in the air. 'Isn't that a cheery thought?'

'Okay, the odds have moved, but it's still possible that there's only been one murder,' I said. 'There are four deaths which fall into four different categories: Adam's, which was probably suicide . . .'

'Only probably?'

I shrugged. 'All bets are off now.'

Carla was looking gloomier by the second. 'You were saying?'

'There's Grayson's, which was a hit-and-run but not necessarily deliberate; Shelley's, which is a toss-up; and Hanna's, which isn't. Even then, it doesn't automatically follow that Hanna's murder had anything to do with the tape: this guy wasn't just an arsehole, he was an arsehole who dealt coke.'

'I can't keep up with you – you change your tune with the wind.'

'I know. It's that sort of situation – nothing's definite so everything's open to interpretation. It's like the bottle, half-full or half-empty, depending on your point of view. You can look at those four deaths one way and it's mundane, nothing to get worked up about. Look at them another way and what you see is very, very scary.'

'But the law of averages favours scary, doesn't it?'

'Okay, so let's assume they were all murdered because of the tape. Now you've got to ask yourself, who would do that and why?'

She took it head-on. 'You'd start with the three who are left . . .'

I nodded. 'Well, we know it's not you.' Carla watched me through her dark glasses; I hoped the thought which I tried to keep quarantined at the very back of my mind wasn't showing on my face. 'We don't know if Gareth's still in Australia or, for that matter, if he's still alive. That leaves Alex: I can see that the tape could spell trouble for her but whether she'd commit serial murder over it is another matter . . .'

'You can forget about Alex,' said Carla, shaking her head, 'until you've exhausted all other possibilities.'

'Including you?' I said it with a smile.

'Including me.' Managing to raise a smile of her own.

'Well, anyway,' I said, 'let's see what she's got to say for herself. Then after the three of you, there's potentially a cast of thousands. If you think about it, between them Adam and Hanna had that tape for fifteen years. It's pretty hard to believe they kept it to themselves.'

Carla bowed her head and began massaging her temples. In a low voice, she said, 'You're right, that is hard to believe. But why would seeing the tape make someone want to kill the people on it?'

'I guess that'd depend on the person concerned and the circumstances. For example, what would Reece do if someone played him the tape and threatened to put a copy in every letterbox in the eastern suburbs unless he paid up, big-time?'

She took her sunglasses off. There were no illusions in her violet eyes. 'He'd probably dump me,' she said calmly. 'Then it wouldn't be his problem any more.'

FIFTEEN

Alex Towle kept us waiting all day. It was half past six and I was on my way out the door when Carla rang. Alex had finally returned her call. She wanted to put us off for a few days, she was up to her eyeballs. When Carla told her it really couldn't wait that long, Alex said it'd have to be tonight.

I rang the video store to tell Max, the freak who worked the afternoon shift, that I'd be late. I throttled his bleating by reminding him that I often came in early just so he could get to an AA meeting.

Carla picked me up from the cafe just before seven. We zipped down through Woolloomooloo and up the expressway to Macquarie Street, past a slow-moving column of worker ants filing out to the suburbs. She had a parking spot under Chifley Tower, where Reece holed up between raids like a corporate Geronimo. We walked down Hunter Street and crossed George Street to that other tower of power, Grosvenor Place.

Carla had rung ahead. A young woman with a ponytail and retro glasses was waiting for us on the other side of the glass doors. The doors slid open and we went in. In a finishing school drawl, ponytail said, 'Hello, I'm Lucy, Alex's PA.'

Lucy led us to the lift and we rocketed up forty floors. The decor up there hollered top-dog law firm: smoked glass and marble, dark wood and leather, carpet that sucked at your shoes. And when you needed a break from the small print and serpentine language, you could soothe your soul with the million-dollar art collection and views the rest of us only get from the window seat of a Boeing.

Alex was obviously keeping her partners happy. They'd given her a corner office with a view from Hunters Hill to the Heads. These were dizzy heights. Once you'd clawed your way up there and breathed the sweet, rarefied air, the prospect of an abrupt and undignified return to street level wouldn't bear thinking about. Some people might do just about anything to avoid that hard landing.

The bookshelf behind her desk was loaded with files, boxy legal volumes and texts on conflict resolution and business ethics. But anyone who stereotyped Alex as a one-dimensional litigation-head hadn't noticed works by such big brains of our time as Naomi Wolf and Robert Hughes or the biographies of Madonna and Princess Diana.

The de rigueur Aboriginal art hung on the wall along with several framed degrees and diplomas, a framed cover of a business magazine featuring guess who and a photo of guess who with Hillary Clinton. On her desk was a silver-framed studio shot of Alex and a beefy specimen in a sweethearts pose. Maybe the girl had a thing for rugby players.

Alex didn't look all that different from across the room. I hadn't picked it up from the videotape but now it was apparent that she had a few years on Carla. Her appearance hinted at a split personality or perhaps the image-makers were unable to resolve their creative differences. The navy-blue pinstripe suit went one way; the white shirt unbuttoned to reveal a triangle of weathered chest went the other. The man's-size sports watch clashed with the pearl earrings while the long, blonde hair, which she tossed and teased constantly, and barmaid-bright lipstick seemed like leftovers from a discarded persona.

She and Carla played long time no see, you haven't changed a bit. Carla observed that Alex had done really well. Alex didn't deny it but complained about her hours and the imbalance between work and life outside work. Did Carla still do any modelling? Carla didn't, she was a lady of leisure. Alex would've loved to just please herself, do nothing if she felt like it. Instead, she was programmed from dawn till dusk, scrambling from one end-of-the-world situation to the next. If Carla realised she was being condescended to, she didn't show it. Maybe Alex was thinking that the wheel had come full circle and now it was Carla's turn to suffer by comparison.

Carla introduced me. Alex thought she'd heard the name somewhere.

I said, 'That's James Alabaster, insider trader.'

Alex's gaze bounced around the room. I wasn't sure if she was avoiding my eye or doing a stocktake in case I pocketed something. Carla chipped in with a character reference, telling Alex that I'd been a big help.

Alex said, 'Why don't you sit down and tell me about it?'

As she went behind her desk, Carla said quietly, 'You might want to close the door.'

Alex did so. She was still frowning when she sat down. Carla and I perched on high-backed chairs as Alex appraised us across the desk, like a marriage guidance counsellor trying to decide if we were worth the effort. She said crisply, 'Okay, I'm all ears. What is it that simply couldn't wait?'

Carla said, 'Something we both thought we'd heard the last of – our naughty video.'

Alex's face flashed red like a traffic light. Carla felt obliged to beef up the character reference. 'James knows about it; I can vouch for his discretion.'

And she thought I sounded like a lawyer.

Alex decided she'd deal with me later. She zeroed in on Carla, her voice taking on a hard, haranguing edge. 'Carla, you promised me that tape had been destroyed. Remember, I raised it with you and we agreed it wasn't a good idea to have it floating around? When I rang you a few days later, you assured me . . .'

'I thought it had been destroyed, Alex. I told Adam he had to get rid of it and he threw a tape in the fire. But unless there was more than one copy, it wasn't the tape. That turned up a few weeks ago.'

'Where is it now?'

'In a safe place.'

'Don't give me that crap, I want to know where the fucking thing is. Do you realise the damage . . . ?'

'Alex, I don't need a lecture about how much harm that tape could do. We've both got a lot to lose, let's just leave it at that.' Carla's composure was impressive; you would've thought she was the high-flying professional. 'It's safe, take my word for it. Right now, we've got bigger things to worry about.'

'Like what?'

'The last person to have the tape was Ray Hanna – remember him?'

'He was murdered.'

'That's right. And I presume you know about Pete Grayson?'

Alex nodded uncertainly.

'What you probably don't know is that Shelley Lendich also died not that long ago – of a drug overdose.'

'Shelley?' It took Alex a few moments to place her co-star. 'You mean that Shelley?'

'Yes, that Shelley. And of course Adam's no longer with us. Do you see a pattern here?'

Alex seemed lost. She sat there wide-eyed and open-mouthed, like a child watching magic tricks.

Carla nodded at me to take up the story. I said, 'Four of the seven people involved in the tape are dead, three of them in just over a month. We know what happened to Hanna; we don't know for sure what happened to the others. What we could have here is a series of suspicious deaths with the videotape as the common denominator. If that's the case, you and Carla may be in danger.'

Alex's complexion faded to white. Glowing earlobes were all that remained of her epic blush. 'What about the police? What are they doing?'

Carla said, 'The police don't know about the tape and I'd prefer to keep it that way, at least for the time being. God knows what they'd do with it once they got their hands on it – we'd have absolutely no control.'

'But if he's right, if someone's going around killing . . .'

I said, 'It's a possibility, that's all we're saying. It may just be a bizarre coincidence. But even if we did go to the cops, we'd have a hard time getting them to take it seriously. As far as they're concerned, there's nothing untoward about what happened to Adam and Shelley and we've got no hard evidence to convince them to have another look.'

Alex pressed her hands to her face. Her eyes darted back and forth between me and Carla, as if she was watching tennis. So far, she'd given a fairly convincing portrayal of someone hit by a bombshell.

'Anyway, now you know,' I said. 'You mightn't thank us for it but at least you can take precautions. What about Gareth? Any idea where he got to?'

'Gareth?' Alex wasn't functioning too well. This wasn't like playing conference-call poker with someone else's money.

'Your boyfriend at the time. He's the only one unaccounted for.'

Her head wobbled. 'I haven't seen Gareth for, Jesus, I don't know, ten years.'

'Do you ever hear from him?'

'I used to – quite regularly, in fact. He sent me postcards from all over the place.'

I asked, 'When was the last one?'

Alex kneaded her forehead as if she had mental cramp. 'Three or four years ago, I suppose. He'd met a New Zealand woman on his travels and they'd gone back there to live on a commune run by some kind of quasi-religious group. One of their rules was that you had to cut all ties with the outside world for a certain length of time, I can't remember how long. Anyway, I haven't heard from him since.'

Carla said, 'That's a lot of information for one postcard. All I ever get is the weather and the exchange rate.'

'That one was a letter, come to think of it. Gareth signing off, I guess.'

I said, 'Have you still got it?'

'I might have. Why?'

'We should try to get in touch with him. He's in the same boat.'

'I could have a look,' said Alex airily. She was recovering her balance and getting back in character. 'But don't you think you might be getting a bit carried away? You must admit, it's pretty far-fetched.'

I said, 'I'll tell you what I told Carla: the law of averages suggests there's something strange or worse than strange going on.'

Carla said, 'We did some research on Adam and Shelley.'

'And?'

I said, 'Adam still looks like a suicide. Shelley, you'd have to say, is wide open. Personally, I think there's reasonable doubt that it really was an accidental overdose.'

'Do you have any expertise in that field?'

'No, but I was curious, which is more than the cops were.'

Alex looked dubious. She obviously rated expertise well ahead of curiosity. 'If you don't mind my asking,' she said, 'how did you get involved in this?'

The question was really directed at Carla, so I left it to her. 'Ray gave James the tape by mistake. When he was murdered, James got in touch with me.'

'So you two already knew each other?'

I said, 'No, we didn't. Carla was the only person on the tape I recognised.'

Alex looked away. She had no more questions.

'Did you ever hear anything more about the tape,' I asked, 'or the ... events that gave rise to it?'

'No, absolutely nothing. Apart from those conversations with Carla, I never discussed it with anyone. When she told me it'd been destroyed, I assumed that was the end of the matter. I never gave it another thought.'

I found that hard to believe. 'So the subject never came up when you were talking to any of the others?'

'No. Look, everyone knew how I felt about it.' She was getting worked up again. 'I didn't want to do it, did I, Carla?' Carla shook her head. 'Nor did you. We were against it from the word go.' Alex's face had taken on a purple tinge; her complexion was as changeable as a chameleon's. 'If there's one thing I'll regret to my dying day it's that I ever let those pricks bully me into it.'

I asked Alex if she'd kept in touch with any of those pricks. She said the term only applied to Adam and Shelley and, to a lesser extent, Peter, not that she wished to speak ill of the dead. To answer the question, apart from Gareth's postcards, few of which she'd bothered replying to because he was constantly on the move, she hadn't maintained contact with any of them, pricks or otherwise.

In the lift, I asked Carla what she thought of Alex's performance.

'You saw what happened – she freaked out. I told you, you can forget about her.'

'Yeah, she was convincing, I'll give you that. But say she has got something to do with it: she would've figured out why we were coming to see her, wouldn't she? She would've had her response worked out. And most lawyers are pretty good actors – they have to be to hide the fact that, half the time, they're making it up as they go. I'm speaking from bitter experience here.'

'You know what else you're doing? You're clutching at straws.'

'What else is there?'

The lift touched down. I asked, 'How old is she?'

'Four years older than me. Why?'

'Just wondered. She's starting to look her age.'

We walked out of the air-conditioning into the still, cosy night, heading south along George Street. Carla said, 'It'll be interesting to compare us in ten years time – if we're still here, that is. Most people would have their money on Alex having a rosier future.'

'Why's that?'

'Oh, I'm sure a lot of people think that, in ten years time, Reece will've traded me in for a younger model and I'll be one of those ladies who lunch with their overdone tans and their little dogs and their drinking problems.'

I shook my head. 'I can't see it.'

'Why not?'

'You don't like dogs.'

Carla laughed. 'Fuck off. I can see it sometimes – Reece trading me in, not the other stuff.'

'You don't really believe that.'

'Why not? It happens all the time, so why should I assume it couldn't possibly happen to me? I can tell you one thing, though: if it did, I sure as hell wouldn't become another tragic eastern suburbs divorcee. I'd take my share of the loot and go and live on a beach somewhere. Find a nice young man to look after me.'

We turned a corner and started the climb up to Chifley Square. We passed a pub. People had spilled out of the bar onto the footpath. I registered brown forearms and midriffs, hair gel and toenail polish, body odour and perfume, European beer and American cigarettes. Déjà vu – I'd done time in that scene.

Carla stopped. 'Shall we have a drink?'

Like a fuckwit, I looked at my watch. Carla saw me. 'You're not working tonight, are you?'

'Yeah, but it's pretty loose ...' It was almost eight o'clock. I'd told Max I'd be there by quarter to at the latest. Well, fuck him.

'What time do you start?'

'Oh, any time from seven ...'

'You should've said so.' She checked her watch. 'Shit, it's nearly eight o'clock. Come on, I'll drop you there.'

'Carla, seriously, it's no big deal – I warned them I'd be late. We've got time for a drink.'

Carla shook her head and broke into a power-walk. 'Doesn't matter. I should get home anyway.'

I caught up with her, silently cursing my crassness. She misinterpreted my expression. 'How do you stand working there – or have I already asked you that?'

'We covered it. Nothing's changed.'

'You've got to get out of that place, James, it's just not a good look.' She put her hand on my arm. 'Sorry, that's a silly thing to say. What I meant was, there must be lots of other things you could do.'

'It's not that easy.'

She hesitated, then said carefully, 'I could ask around. I don't mean Reece, people I know.'

'Thanks for the offer but I wouldn't want to put

you in an embarrassing position. You saw how Alex reacted.'

'Well, yeah, but you kind of shoved it under her nose.'

'They're going to find out sooner or later.'

She shrugged. 'Anyway, the offer's there.'

'Listen, I really appreciate it, but let's just get this thing out of the way first.'

She agreed but offhandedly. When she hardly said a word on the way back to Potts Point, I began to rue my diffidence. Under the circumstances, I would've settled for another feathery touch of her cheek as we parted. But she leaned over and pressed her lips to my neck. She brushed them lightly to and fro, working her way over the jawline onto my cheek.

I could hardly believe it. For a few seconds, I just sat there letting her nuzzle me, like a jaded roué waiting for the rhino horn to kick in. Half in a daze, I turned my face to hers. She looked up at me, her eyes smoky, her mouth slightly open, waiting for mine.

We kissed, jaws working. A bone – I'm not sure whose – clicked and our lips squirmed and stretched as we slurped greedily at each other. Her mouth was hot, moist, luxuriously soft. I could taste her through the lipstick. The taste was sharp and clean yet heady, like water from a mountain stream laced with the purest vodka.

When her tongue slithered into my mouth, I reached for her breasts. She pulled away. Her chest rose and fell and she was breathing hard through her nose. Her eyes flamed then dwindled, like matches struck in the dark. 'Not now, James,' she whispered. 'Not like this.'

I stared at her, more exhilarated by her advance than deflated by her retreat. She leaned across me and opened the car door on my side. Her expression was calm now, almost serene.

'Call me,' she said. 'I'll be switched on.'

I floated into the video store. Max glared at me, his facial muscles wriggling like maggots. 'About fucking time,' he whined.

Detective-Sergeant Donald stepped out from behind a wall of video covers. He said, 'I'll second that.'

SIXTEEN

Donald was in better shape than last time. Maybe he'd caught up on his sleep. Max was even more spazzed-out than usual. Maybe it was full moon. They stood there waiting for me to say something – apologise perhaps, or go jabbering off on one of those 'You're not going to believe this' narratives. I looked at my watch and did a double-take. 'Shit, is that the time?'

Max cuffed himself on the side of the head. He had quite a repertoire of tics, twitches and convulsive gestures, but that was a new one on me. 'You're a bullshit artist, that's what you are,' he foamed. 'Where the fuck have you been, eh?'

'Don't take this the wrong way, Max, but that's none of your fucking business.'

Max turned his back on me and began muttering to himself. Donald had watched this battle of wits from a few feet away, hands in his pockets, rocking on the balls of his feet. Now he came over and leaned on the counter, next to me, and said, 'I get that all the time – "it's none of your fucking business". Not a hell of a smart thing to say to a cop, really. We decide what's our business and what's not – and let me tell you, there's bugger-all that's not. It becomes a sort of challenge. You think, righto mate, I'm going to get that information if I have to beat it out of you.'

I went behind the counter. Getting that close to Max was a health hazard, but having Donald in my personal space made me uncomfortable. Body odour-wise, it was line-ball. I said, 'Listen, don't get out the testicle clamps on my account. If you really need to know about my private life, I'll tell you. It won't take long.'

For a moment, I thought Donald was going to take me up on it. Instead, he came out with, 'You know, I'm surprised you didn't tell your mate here about Hanna coming in that night. People who've had a brush with crime – especially murder – usually can't wait to tell every man and his dog about it.'

There was an easy answer to that and Max supplied it. 'Doesn't surprise me, one little bit – he never tells me anything. Might as well talk to myself.'

'You do talk to yourself,' I said. 'All the time. I don't like to butt in.'

Donald's face contracted with irritation. He squinted at Max. 'You still here? I thought you were in a lather to be somewhere else.'

Max started to give Donald a filthy look but thought better of it. He redirected it at me and slouched into the night like a mongrel on the scavenge, his exit line lost in the oily growl of a kick-started motorbike.

Donald said, 'Christ, where'd they find him?'

'I don't know and I don't want to know. So what brings you here this time?'

'Still looking for those tapes. I had a little brainwave this afternoon: where would be the best place to hide a bunch of videotapes?'

Too late, Sherlock. That pony's long gone. 'In a video library?'

He made a pistol sign with his thumb and forefinger.

There were well over a thousand labelled tapes stacked on the shelves behind me. I hooked a thumb at them. 'Help yourself.'

'Oh, your mate and I had a bit of a hunt before. We went through all the old tapes out the back and a few off the shelves. I suppose the problem with hiding them in among the current stock is that someone might hire them?'

I nodded. 'Putting them in covers would be a better bet.' I pointed at the rows of empty videotape covers on display. 'Look at them all – half of them wouldn't be picked up from one month to the next. Anyone could walk in here, pretend to be having a browse and quietly slip a tape into a cover. You'd just have to remember which one.'

'Yeah, I thought of that. I checked them.'

'You mean you checked every single cover?'

'I didn't open them, I just shook them to see if they had a tape inside.'

'And?'

Donald gave me a long, unfriendly stare. I was starting to fidget when I remembered what Carla had told me about Hanna. 'Have you considered the possibility that it was a drug thing?'

'What the fuck are you talking about?'

'I heard Hanna was a cocaine dealer.' Donald's eyelids rose fractionally. 'Drug-dealing does have the reputation of being a high-risk profession.'

'Who told you that?'

'I forget who it was. As you can imagine, Hanna's

been a hot topic of conversation around the Point lately.'

'What exactly did they say about him?'

'Just that if you were in the market for coke, Hanna was your man.'

I thought Donald would appreciate this information. I thought it might take his mind off videotapes. I was sadly mistaken.

He lit a cigarette. 'I have this theory.' Shit, here we go: the meaning of life according to a Kings Cross cop. 'I reckon the dumbest cunts of all are people who aren't stupid but who, for some reason, think they're geniuses. You know why? Because they always overestimate themselves and underestimate everyone else. Take you, for example: you're obviously not stupid but you expect me to believe that you can't remember who told you about Hanna. And you tell me that the victim of the murder I've been investigating for a month was a coke dealer, as if that's some sort of fucking revelation. You think you're smart, but you're not. You think I don't know my arse from a hole in the ground, but I do. One of these days, old son, those errors of judgement are going to sink you in a sea of shit.'

'Jesus Christ, I was only trying to be helpful . . .'

Donald was on a roll. 'Hanna was a piss-ant. His customers were recreational users, the sort who get some in for a dinner party. The sort who only buy it from someone they know, so it's not as if you could muscle in and take over his business. Besides, he didn't cross paths with the heavy operators, the ones who put guys away.' He dropped the butt and stood on it. 'The fact is, Mr Alabaster, Hanna didn't get killed because of drugs – we knew that from day one.

He got killed because of blackmail. We reckon he had stuff on tape that made his crotch shots look like aunty's holiday snaps. Find the tapes, we find the killer, it's that simple. That's why I've been going to all this trouble.' He stretched and rolled his shoulders. 'And that's why I'll bury you if I find out you've been jerking me around.'

He gave me a chance to say something. I had nothing to contribute so he tried another tack. 'If you know where any of those tapes are, you should say so now and we'll call it quits.'

I shrugged. 'Sorry, I can't help you.'

Donald folded his arms. He strummed the tip of his nose. His hooded eyes bored into mine like a streetfighter's thumbs. A minute went by, then he nodded. 'Okay, we'll leave it there. But you understand how it works from here on, don't you? If you've fucked me around – withheld evidence, obstructed justice, you know what I mean – you're going down, matey. And I'm not talking about a fucking country club. I'm talking about the real thing.'

He was talking about Cadbury Row.

Thursday morning. I rang Carla but she couldn't come out to play. Some moneymen from Switzerland were in town. Reece was taking them out on his boat and wanted her along. Why wouldn't he? It takes more than a harbour cruise and a seafood buffet to impress the gnomes of Zurich.

She'd heard from Alex, who'd found Gareth's farewell letter; it was waiting for us at reception. I said I'd pick it up.

'James, about the tape ...'

'Yeah?'

'Can I get it off you some time soon?'

'Sure, whenever you like.'

'It's nothing to do with you, okay? I just need that reassurance.'

'Carla, you can name a time now or give me five minutes notice any time of the day or night.'

'How about tomorrow?'

'Tomorrow's fine. Just on that subject . . .'

I was going to tell her about Donald but she cut in. 'Oh shit, they're here and I'm nowhere near ready. See you tomorrow.'

I caught a train to Martin Place and walked downtown. I told the receptionist on the fortieth floor who I was and why I was there. She picked up a phone and passed that information on, then invited me to take a seat. I asked if there was a problem. She said there wasn't and I had to take her word for it.

Lucy appeared a few minutes later. Alex wanted to talk to me; would I care to join her for lunch in her office? She just had a couple of urgent matters to attend to if I wouldn't mind waiting . . . I did mind but the message from Alex seemed to be no lunch, no letter. Lucy invited me to make a selection from a range of sandwiches and beverages. I went for the rare roast beef with horseradish and the mineral water with bubbles. I didn't have fond memories of lawyers' coffee.

Twenty minutes went by before Lucy escorted me through to Alex's office. Alex put the phone down as I walked in – every second counts. She had her hair up and was wearing a stylish dark, double-breasted trouser-suit. We sat on the sofa below Hillary Clinton and the Aboriginal art. As Lucy served lunch on the coffee table, Alex told me that when things got out of hand, as they often did around there, she always took time out to lie back on the sofa, put her feet up and let the view wash over her. It was a great pick-me-up. And, as I pointed out, a lot cheaper than cocaine. Lucy gave me a look that said, screw the view, give me coke any day.

Lucy left us to it. Predictably, Alex's sandwiches were full of shit like alfalfa and bean sprouts. Apart from sunbathing, she wouldn't have given her GP much to tut-tut about. She didn't speak with her mouth full either. When she'd finished her sandwich, she said, 'There's a couple of things about this which puzzle me. For instance, does Carla's husband know about it?'

'I think you should address that question to Carla.'

Alex raised her eyebrows. 'Well, she did say you were discreet – but I'm going to take that as a no. I can't say it comes as a surprise but it's a pity in the sense that someone of Reece Sully's means could clear this thing up in no time. Can I take it that Reece doesn't know about you either?'

'I really wouldn't know.'

She leaned forward to pour her herbal tea. The crossover of her jacket opened up, revealing a Wonderbra at work. 'But you could make an educated guess.'

'I suppose one follows on from the other but, frankly, I don't see what difference it makes.'

Alex smiled. Her off-duty smile was probably worth getting but this was the professional version and as empty as most of them are. 'I'm a lawyer; I like to have as many facts as possible at my fingertips.'

'Doesn't relevance enter into it?'

'I think it's a little early to be making judgements on what is or isn't relevant.'

It was stalemate. She wasn't asking straight questions and I wasn't giving straight answers. I said, 'Can I ask you a question?'

Her shrug said, yes but conditions apply.

'What's your recollection of the Bondi scene?'

She looked out the window. 'What stands out in my mind is the love–hate thing. Not just the boyfriends and girlfriends, everyone – it was like one big love–hate relationship. Hardly surprising, I suppose, given the circumstances. Do you know the background, the Peter–Carla–Adam love triangle and all that...?'

'Yeah.'

'Well, the friendships were the same. Peter and Gareth almost worshipped Adam but they also resented the way he manipulated them. Carla admired Shelley because she didn't agonise over what she should or shouldn't do, she just did exactly what she felt like, but it was always just a matter of time before they'd be at each other's throats again. And always over the same thing, of course.'

'Adam?'

She nodded. 'And didn't he enjoy it.'

'What about you?'

'My relationships weren't as intense as theirs. Gareth and I had some good times but it was never what you'd call a passionate love affair. When we started growing apart, we could both see what was happening, so there was no heartbreak involved. With Adam...'

I interrupted. 'I had the impression there was a bit more to it than just growing apart.'

Alex folded her arms. 'What did Carla say?'

'That Gareth got kind of weird.'

'I couldn't really argue with that.'

'Weird how?'

She shrugged. 'He just had some pretty strange ideas.'

'Like what?'

'Why are you so interested? This is ancient history.'

'You're a lawyer – I think you can work it out.'

'As a lawyer, I think you're getting a little ahead of yourself.'

'Okay, let me ask you a direct question: would you describe him as unstable?'

'I wouldn't go that far.'

'Would you say that, potentially, he was capable of violence?'

'Gareth?' With a derisive chuckle. 'Well, "potentially capable of" covers an awful lot of territory whether it's Gareth or the Queen Mother you're talking about. All I can tell you is that, when I was with him, he was the original gentle giant.'

It was like a mutual protection society: Carla vouched for Alex who vouched for Gareth. I just had to get Gareth's take on Carla and I'd have a matching set of glowing character references.

I said, 'You were saying something about Adam.'

Judging by her brief, self-satisfied smile, she felt that she'd won that round. 'I was just going to say that, with Adam, I was on the same roller-coaster ride as everyone else. When he was in a mellow mood, he was just one of those people you really liked being around; when he wasn't in a mellow mood, look out. He got a kick out of making fun of people – humiliating might be a better word for it – and being the straightest person in the group, I was an easy target. I got on well with Carla but, you know, she never stuck up for me with Adam, she never once told him to get off my back. I found that pretty hard to accept. I'd also have to admit I was a tad jealous of her. You know how it is at that age: appearance is everything and you couldn't help but be envious of someone who looked like that. I got over it, though.'

'But you never got over being bullied into playing a part in a porno movie?'

Alex's cheeks turned pink. 'I learned to live with it.'

I'd run out of beef sandwiches and Alex seemed to have run out of conversation. I stood up. 'You've got that letter for me?'

She went over to her desk. 'I thought about trying to get in touch with Gareth myself but it's probably better that you do it.' She handed me a white envelope with her firm's letterhead on it. 'It's a copy, so there's no need to return it.'

'Thanks – and thanks for lunch. We'll keep you posted.'

'There is one other thing.' I waited. She plonked herself on the corner of the desk. She was trying to be casual but her face was tight with anxiety. 'Do you know where the tape is?'

'More or less.'

'Could you get hold of it?'

'Uh, that'd be tricky.'

'I want that tape. Whatever Carla may say, our situations are poles apart. I've had to work like a slave to get here and that tape could wreck everything. I'm prepared to pay for it.'

I'd almost forgotten what it was like to be propositioned. 'Alex, I really don't think you need to worry about it. Carla's just as concerned as you are...'

'I don't think we look at it the same way at all. I won't feel safe till I see the damn thing burn whereas Carla, on the other hand, wants to keep it.'

'Why would she?'

'For its sentimental value. You've got to understand what her relationship with Adam was like. As far as Carla was concerned, he was it for all time. There were times you'd swear there was no way that relationship could possibly survive. They'd have a monumental bust-up, she'd move out, she wouldn't speak to him... Meanwhile, she'd be telling people that she still loved him and always would, no matter what.'

'She was what – nineteen, twenty? Shit, when I was that age, I thought Woody Allen was a genius. In the end, she dumped him.'

Alex's knowing smile seemed out of place on her scrubbed, open face, like a street-corner hooker in labrador-land. 'Is that what she told you? Well, I suppose we all tend to rewrite our romantic histories to put ourselves in the best light. So you tell me: if she doesn't want to keep the tape, why does it still exist? Why hasn't she got rid of it?'

Good point. 'Maybe it's not actually in her possession.'

'In other words, you've got it?'

'Well, not exactly...'

'For God's sake, one of you must have it.'

'Actually, neither of us does. It's on neutral ground, so to speak – under lock and key.'

With exaggerated calm, Alex asked, 'And who's got the key?'

It was time to lie. 'Both of us. But you need both keys to get access.'

'Oh?' She wasn't convinced and I couldn't blame her. 'That's a rather elaborate arrangement, isn't it?'

'Just playing safe.'

'You must be able to get the other key somehow?'

'Let me think about it.' Sure, I'd think about it. Right after I'd thought about female circumcision in the sub-Sahara.

'Okay.' Alex nodded, as if that was as good as she could hope for. 'Why don't you leave me your number?'

I wrote my phone number on her pad. As I left, she closed the door behind me.

Everyone wanted the tape but you can't always get what you want. C'est la vie, boys and girls. C'est la vie.

SEVENTEEN

It was a while since I'd been in town so I had a look around. I browsed in a couple of bookstores to see what might turn up in my local second-hand bookshop in due course. It was in the Cross, the sort of place where you'd find last year's Booker Prize winner between *Her Hot Honeypot* and *Rhonda's Moist Urge*. I guess there are worse places to be.

I checked out the magazine stand. You can't tell a magazine by its cover any more. It used to be that if there was a half-naked chick on the cover, you knew what sort of magazine it was. You knew what it was *for*. They might as well have sold them with a box of tissues. Now, they could be anything – fashion mags, women's mags, lads' mags, mags about sport, fitness, show biz, cars, motorbikes, tattoos ... They've all got cheesecake on the front.

Looking around for the crime section, I made brief eye contact with a big, wavy-haired guy in a dark suit. He looked vaguely familiar. I could tell he recognised me by the way he did a lightning eyes-front and stuck his nose in a coffee-table book on English country gardens. He was feigning enchantment with Dingle Dell and dreading the tap on the shoulder: 'I know you, don't I? Didn't you work on the Trigon Mining deal? No? It'll come to me. I'm James Alabaster, by the way. I expect you heard about my little spot of bother with the ASC . . .'

Then I noticed his shoes. They were brown. No, worse than that, they were yellowy-brown, the colour of baby shit. That's not an acceptable look in the world of high finance. In my day, you could wear any colour shoes as long as they were black. This guy had either changed careers or didn't date from that period. Whoever he was, he could relax. I didn't want a reunion any more than he did.

I exited the bookshop and moved on down George Street. I took a left at Market Street and hit David Jones' food hall like a fretful jockey. I bought an orange, a hydroponic tomato, a Spanish onion, a butterhead lettuce, some mince and a wedge of Tasmanian cheddar. I bypassed the artisan pasta, the fifty buck a litre Umbrian olive oil and the ten-year-old balsamic vinegar, reminders of the days when I signed credit card forms without bothering to check the total. I gave the wine section a wide berth. I thought about getting a few ready-made pasta sauces for the days when I didn't feel like cooking but how would I use the time I saved? I already had more time than I knew what to do with.

On the way out, I noticed the big guy in the dark suit over by the fish counter. I couldn't see his face but I could see his shoes. He'd been in the bookshop, now he was in DJ's. So what? He'd probably popped into the bookshop to scope this month's celebrity bush paparazzi shots in the girly mags, then strolled down to DJ's to get some fish for dinner. Like I used to.

I crossed Market Street to the Pitt Street mall without looking over my shoulder. I wasn't paranoid. On an impulse, I ducked into a below-ground music store; the only way in was down the stairs from the mall. I stood near the foot of the stairs, flicking through the discount bin. Thirty years of dross, thirty years of product that the market, insatiable and infinitely gullible though it was, is and always will be, simply wouldn't swallow: one-hit wonders, teeny-bop gimmick acts, whiny minstrels, production-line Motown, next big things who weren't, acid rock, glam rock, swamp rock, camp rock, slut rock, heavy metal, bubblegum, rock-a-billy, disco, techno, punk, funk, reggae, rap, world music, Britpop, AOR from the USA, old blues croakers and new romantics and yes, by God, rock 'n' roll's living dead, the Travelling Wilburys.

Five minutes passed, then ten. Brown Shoes didn't show. He wasn't following me. It was a coincidence and a tiddler at that. I went back up to the mall. Look left: nothing. Look right: Brown Shoes, with sunglasses but without a black and white DJ's shopping bag, sitting on a bench reading a paper. He didn't look up as I walked past.

I went right at King and left at Castlereagh, into Martin Place. I didn't look back. It was after two o'clock; the lunch-time crowd had drifted back to work. When I got near the top of the hill, I did a swift 180-degree turn. There was Brown Shoes, thirty metres behind me. He about-turned too and headed back down the hill, taking his time. He held out for half a minute before looking over his shoulder. When he turned into Pitt Street, I hurried on up to the station.

By the time the train reached Kings Cross, I'd placed Brown Shoes: he was the beefy specimen in the silver-framed photo on Alex's desk. Shaking him off hadn't achieved much because Alex had my phone number. It wouldn't take her long to put an address to it.

I walked down to the cafe trying to figure out what they were up to. Once again, there were two ways of looking at it, leading to two very different conclusions. One was more credible and a lot less terrifying than the other. Guess which one I favoured?

Maybe Alex was working on Plan B in case I didn't take up her offer. Putting a tail on me was unorthodox behaviour for a legal luminary in the making but then that was why she was sweating on the tape: it had the potential to derail her glittering career. Or maybe that was taking it way too lightly. I doubted it, though. Even if Alex was a killer – and what I'd seen of her tended to support Carla's view – I didn't think she'd be coming after me just then. Not when I'd been in her office twice in the past twenty hours; not unless Lucy and the receptionist were co-conspirators.

It wasn't that I was getting any braver, but the shock of the break-in had worn off. That was two weeks ago and it'd been all quiet on the western front since. I was coming around to thinking that it was probably just a random break-in after all, kids doing it for no other reason than that they could, then finding nothing worth stealing. I suppose I was getting used to being in the discomfort zone.

You can see what I was doing. We all do it. We all believe, as devoutly as we believe anything, that life's horrible tricks – plane crashes, house fires, incurable diseases, tidal waves, great white sharks, crazed or, for that matter, icily composed killers – are things which happen to other people. That is our creed. That's what gets us out of bed in the morning. That and statistics, but I was trying to keep statistics out of it: they pointed in a slightly different direction.

I got a coffee and opened the envelope. The letter was typed and datelined April 1995, Waihi Beach:

> Dear Ally,
> Of all the places in the world I thought I'd pitch up in, New Zealand was near the bottom of the list. Just above England in fact, and you know how I feel about the English. Well, this place is as close as you can get to England without actually being there – they still have 'Coronation Street' on TV every night! But here I am. I guess it just goes to show that our lives are shaped by forces beyond our control and understanding.
>
> Marie and I were looking for a base, a place where we can live the way we want, in a spiritual environment without hassles and distractions. I always thought I'd find that place in the east but Marie came down with a serious case of homesickness. Soon after we got here, we met a friend of hers who belongs to a group called the Children of Light. Yeah, I know, it sounds like a cult but it's not. Would I lie to you? It's just a bunch of cool people who happen to believe that spiritual growth is impossible if you're surrounded by

greed and soullessness. I think they're onto something! They've got this commune called the Valley of Light on a hundred beautiful acres just north of Auckland. It's completely self-contained – they grow all their own food etc. To cut a long story short, last week Marie and I joined up. By the time you read this, we'll be on the commune.

The bad news, Ally, is that when you enter the Valley of Light, you've got to cut all ties with the outside world for at least a year. The idea is to get members to really commit themselves to the commune and keep out negative thoughts and emotions from people on the outside who aren't prepared to live and let live.

Speaking of which, meet Marie's parents. (We're staying with them for a few days before we go onto the commune.) Wal and Jan don't approve – and that's putting it mildly – of the Children of Light or the commune or me. If they had their way, Marie would stay here, marry a local lad and settle down to be a good little Kiwi housewife and mother. You know how it goes – if it was good enough for your mother, blah, blah, blah.

I try not to be judgemental – you can vouch for that! – but Wal's got to be one of the most self-centred, materialistic you-know-whats on the planet. If he's not slagging off the Children of Light or bragging about how much money he's made (he owns several shops in Waihi) or describing the next extension to their house which is already too big for them, he's going on about his next career move – into politics! He's on the local council and plans to run for mayor. After that, who knows? Wal for prime minister. Then they'd have good reason to sing 'God Defend New Zealand'. Jan's easier to take, at least once she's had her first gin and tonic of the day – which is usually at about 11 a.m.

The no communication with the outside world thing is going to take a bit of getting used to but only in the sense of being cut off from some of my favourite people (take a bow). But it's only for a year but who knows, I might get to like it! Right now though, it just feels like everything's fallen into place.

I hope everything's fallen into place for you too, Ally. I hope you're getting what you want from your career but don't forget that, at the end of the day, a career can't give you what you need. To paraphrase the Stones. Anyway, even though you won't be hearing from me, you can rest assured I'll be thinking of you.

    Peace & love,
    Gareth

Gareth was obviously out there among the asteroids but at least he'd left a trail. I went back to the flat and rang international directory to get the number for the Waihi town council. It was quarter to four, quarter to six in New Zealand. The recorded message said the council offices were currently unattended but if I left my name, phone number and a short message outlining the nature of my inquiry, they'd get back to me. I didn't believe it.

At five past midnight that night, I came out of the video store, locked up, turned left and almost trod on Brown Shoes' toes.

He was leaning against a black BMW with his arms folded. He pushed off the car and stood in front of me, dangling his arms like a wrestler waiting for the bell. His mouth formed a crocodile grin. 'G'day, loser. Busy night in the video shop, was it?'

I heard footsteps behind me and looked around. We were being joined by a guy who could've been Brown Shoes' brother. His polo shirt was dark-green rather than black and worn outside his trousers, otherwise it would've been hard to tell them apart. They looked like front-rowers from an over-35s rugby team, the kind of guys who ruin social games by being too fit and way too serious.

'So you spotted me,' said Brown Shoes. 'I bet you thought you were James Bond. You didn't spot Danny though, did you? Okay, let's go.' I didn't move. 'Or do we have to make you?'

Danny dropped a heavy hand on my shoulder. Brown Shoes opened the BMW's rear passenger door and beckoned me with a mock-servile flourish.

I wouldn't pretend that I was unconcerned by this turn of events but I wasn't shitting myself just yet. It was Thursday night down the Kings Cross end of Potts Point: we weren't the only people on the street. I assumed this was Plan B. I also assumed that Alex would draw the line at broken bones, no matter how badly she wanted the tape. Maybe it was their preppy clothes – chinos, polos, boat shoes – but I picked them as amateurs, a couple of North Shore boof-heads who liked throwing their weight around, rather than genuine standover men.

There's such a thing as being too rational, especially under those circumstances. I shouldn't have assumed that Alex would draw the line at anything.

I said, 'Where are we going?'

'You've got a videotape we want,' said Brown Shoes. 'Just hand it over and we'll leave you to it – still in one piece.'

Danny put his hand on my shoulder again but I pulled away. 'I bet this was your idea. This strong-arm stuff doesn't seem like Alex's style.'

Brown Shoes' eyes darted to Danny, then back to me. 'Who's Alex?'

'Come on, you remember Alex – your sweetie-pie. You're obviously here on her behalf.'

If there was a signal, I missed it. Danny clamped one hand on my right arm, the other on the back of my neck and shoved me towards the car. Brown Shoes grabbed my other arm and they bundled me into the back seat. Danny got in beside me. Brown Shoes got behind the wheel as a couple of pedestrians hurried past, looking the other way.

Brown Shoes twisted around. The crocodile grin was back. 'Don't forget to buckle up. Okay, where to?'

I said, 'You know, if Alex wanted to keep her distance from this stunt – which would be understandable given that kidnapping and coercion are against the law – she shouldn't have a photo of you on her desk. Not that it isn't a nice photo.'

Brown Shoes shot another exclamation mark look at Danny via the rear-view mirror. He asked me again: where to? I told him where I lived.

He started the car and took off. I asked him, 'Has she told you what's on the tape?'

'Shut up.'

'Just in case she hasn't, let me put you in the picture. It's what you'd call home-made porn: it's got Alex and some fit young studs getting up to some frankly ...'

Danny terminated the review by elbowing me in the gob, not hard enough to loosen teeth but hard enough. I yelped and clutched my mouth. Brown Shoes watched me in the rear-view mirror. 'Get the message, loser? We're not playing games.'

I got the message. I stopped talking and started thinking. Brown Shoes parked outside my apartment building and we went in. I led them down the corridor to Roach Central. When I opened the door, Brown Shoes pushed past me. I followed him into the main room.

He looked around, hands on his hips. 'You really know how to live, don't you? Okay, let's have it.'

I said, 'I want to talk to Alex.'

'Forget it.'

'There's something she ought to know.'

Brown Shoes grabbed the front of my shirt and yanked me towards him.

'Wake up, shithead, it's way past that. Just give us the fucking tape.'

When he let go of me, I said, 'I bet Alex is sitting next to a phone, waiting to hear from you.' His expression confirmed it. 'There's something she needs to know about the tape – for her own good. It'll take a couple of minutes.'

Brown Shoes looked at Danny who shrugged, what the hell? 'Then we get the tape,' he said, 'or we kick your arse, big-time.'

I said, 'Let's wait and see if Alex still wants it.'

Brown Shoes plucked a mobile phone off his hip, punched in a number and started talking. 'It's me ... Yeah, we're at his place now ... He wants to talk to you ... No, no, he worked it out, I'll tell you about it later ... What? ... Yeah, he says there's something you ought to know ... Okay.' He thrust the phone at me. 'Two minutes.'

I said, 'Hello, Alex.'

'What do I need to know?'

'You didn't give me much time to think about it.'

'Basic negotiating rule: if you offer someone an unspecified amount of money and they don't immediately ask you how much, it means they're not interested.'

'I'll have to remember that.'

'Would you get on with it? I'm tired.'

'Okay. Have you come across a Detective-Sergeant Donald, Kings Cross police?'

'No.'

'He's heading the investigation into the murder of Ray Hanna.'

'How interesting.'

'What is interesting is that he knows about the tape.'

'You're lying.'

'Let me rephrase that: he knows there is a tape. He's got a fair idea what's on it but not, as far as I know, *who's* on it. He's just about as keen to get hold of it as you are because he thinks it's the key to the case. Why only yesterday he said to me, "Find the tape, we find the killer, it's that simple." That's a direct quote. Did I mention that I was the last person to see Hanna alive? I don't think I did. That's why I've been spending so much time with Donald.

Anyway, the point is, if I have to give you the tape, I'll tell Donald that you've got it. He'll be round to see you in a flash and if you can't produce it, I'd say you'd be facing criminal charges before you're much older – destroying vital evidence, conspiring to pervert the course of justice ... Shit, why am I telling you this? You're the fucking lawyer, right?'

Alex didn't respond. Brown Shoes' eyebrows bunched and collided, like caterpillars engaged in a territorial dispute over the bridge of his nose. I winked at him. 'You still there, Alex?'

She said, without much conviction, 'You're making it up.'

'I wish I was – I wouldn't have Donald badgering me. You see, the only things missing from Hanna's flat were a few videotapes. He had a little blackmail racket and Donald's convinced the real jackpot stuff was on one of the missing tapes. That's why he's so hot for it.'

'So our tape's actually not relevant to the investigation?'

'Maybe, maybe not. Even if it's not, Donald doesn't know that.'

'You won't go to the police.'

'Why not?'

'Because Carla's dead against it.'

'Carla's worried about what might happen if the cops get their grubby hands on the tape – copies of it turning up all over town, that sort of thing. If you destroy it, there's no risk of that happening, is there? Besides, if Carla's calling the shots, why hasn't she got the tape? Why aren't you talking to her?'

'So I'm not going to get it?' It sounded like surrender.

'I said I'd think about it, didn't I?'

'I didn't believe you.'

'And that was before one of your pet apes hit me.'

'You're out of your depth,' she said, 'You know that, don't you?'

'After tonight's performance, I'd say that makes two of us.'

'Maybe so, but I don't have to worry about Carla.'

She was just being a poor loser. I said, 'Nice talking to you, counsellor. Let's do lunch again, real soon.'

I gave the phone back to Brown Shoes and went into the kitchen to get a glass of wine. When I came back, my guests were leaving. I followed them down the corridor telling Brown Shoes, 'Well, thanks for the lift.'

Without looking at me, he said, 'Fuck off.'

I stood in the entrance as they walked to the BMW. As Brown Shoes was about to get in, I called out, 'Hey, by the way – does Alex still roll over?' Then I shut the door. Very quickly.

EIGHTEEN

Timing is everything. For the second day running, mine was lousy.

I rang Carla to tell her about Alex's ambush. She was on the move; her hello was accompanied by a rasp of static. I'd got as far as, 'It's James . . .' when we got a crossed line. A woman who sounded a lot like Carla babbled, 'I knew I'd forgotten something. Look, I'm terribly sorry but we decided on the spur of the moment to have a long weekend at the beach and I completely forgot to cancel the booking. Sorry about that. Can I re-book for same time next week? Great, thanks, bye.'

Certainly, madam, smoking or non-smoking? I wouldn't see Carla for three days, but the little charade provided a glimmer of consolation. It must've been for Reece's benefit and where there's deceit, there's hope.

I tried the Waihi town council again. Raewyn, the receptionist, sounded like the sort of breezy extrovert who'd share her husband's 'plumbing' problems with the next person in the supermarket queue. I explained that I wanted to get hold of a gent named Wal, a once and perhaps current councillor who owned several shops in town.

She said, 'That'd be Wal Gifford.'

'He fits the bill, does he?'

'Wal's the mayor.'

'He made it, eh? I heard he was planning to have a crack.'

Raewyn said, 'I'm having déjà vu – I had this conversation yesterday. You're not calling from Sydney, are you?'

'As a matter of fact, I am . . .'

'So was the woman who rang yesterday.' Alex again, saying one thing and doing another. 'What's going on over there? I know it's none of my business but this is a small town. You big-city types, you wouldn't know what it's like . . .'

'I grew up in a small town.'

'Then you would know what it's like,' she said. 'When not a lot happens, you've got to make a little go a long way.'

'What's the question?'

'Is Marie in some kind of trouble?'

'Marie, as in the mayor's daughter?'

'That's the one.'

'Not as far as I know.'

'It's just that when people start ringing from Sydney trying to contact Wal, you automatically assume that.'

'Why automatically?'

'Well, you know, you're in Sydney, Marie's in Sydney, you want to get in touch with her dad . . .'

'Marie's in Sydney?'

'Didn't you know that?'

'Last I heard she was on a commune near Auckland.'

'You're way behind. She got out of there about a

year and a half ago now, much to her parents' delight.'

'It's actually Marie I wanted to talk to. You wouldn't happen to have a phone number for her, would you?'

'Afraid not.'

'Okay, well, if you could give me the old man's number...'

'You haven't met Wal, have you?'

'No.'

'I didn't think so. Just between you and me, I can put you onto him but it probably won't do you much good. Unless there's something in it for him, Wal'd think twice about telling you the date, let alone how to get hold of his daughter.'

'So what do you suggest?'

She suggested I ring back in ten minutes. When I did, she gave me Marie's phone number. I thanked her. She said, 'Come on, give us a clue: what's it all about?'

That was the least I could do. 'It's actually about Gareth, her boyfriend...'

'Not any more he's not. Wal and Jan were pretty happy about that too.'

'Since when?'

'Since whenever she left the commune. Is he a friend of yours?'

'Never met the guy.'

'Good. For one awful moment, I thought he might be using you to track her down.'

I didn't like lying to this woman but I didn't want the folks back home fretting for Marie either. I told Raewyn I was helping to organise a surprise fortieth birthday party. My job was to trace some of the birthday boy's old mates who'd dropped out of sight. Gareth was one of them.

She said, 'Well, good luck', as if she thought I'd need it.

'Is there something I should know? Like, did he give Marie a hard time or something?'

She said, 'I wouldn't know', as if she did.

'I hear he's a bit different. Maybe we'd be better off without him.'

'Maybe you would.'

'From what you've heard of him . . .'

'From what I've heard of him, I doubt he'd be a big hit at your average Waihi knees-up, but maybe that's just us. For all I know, he might be a fun guy by Sydney standards.'

I sensed that Raewyn was starting to regret getting herself into this. Or maybe I'd asked too many questions for someone who was just organising a piss-up. I had one more: had she told the woman who'd rung the day before that Marie was in Sydney?

'No. She seemed in a hurry so I just gave her Wal's number. Wal goes easier on women – he's old-fashioned like that.'

I thanked Raewyn again. She said she'd been answering phones for twenty years and reckoned she'd got pretty good at telling what people were like from their voices. 'You sound okay, whoever you are.'

'I'm James. And thank you, Raewyn.'

'Are you okay, James?'

'Well, they'll never put up a statue of me but, yeah, I suppose I am. Put it this way, you could take me home to meet your mother.'

'I am a mother. I've got a seventeen-year-old daughter.'

'Well, she could take me home to meet her mother.'

'Don't even think about it, buster. I said you sounded okay; I didn't say you sounded suitable.'

'Too old, huh?'

'Among other things.'

'This daughter of yours, is she going to give you some headaches?'

'Headaches I can handle; it's the heartaches I worry about. I've seen a few parents go through them.'

'Wal and Jan?'

'Not mentioning any names.' There was a pause. 'James, promise me I won't regret giving you that number.'

'I can't do that, Raewyn – Marie mightn't take kindly to being asked about Gareth. But that's all I'm going to do.'

'That's not a bad answer, especially after that stuff about your friend's fortieth.'

'What about it?'

'I didn't believe a word of it.'

Alex hadn't believed me either. I used to be a pretty polished liar, even by merchant banking standards, but you know you've lost it when a stranger can pick the fiction down a telephone line. Who else had I tried to bullshit lately? Donald, for Christ's sake. The man was trained to recognise lies. He hacked through a jungle of them every day, searching for that endangered species, the truth.

Donald wouldn't have believed a fucking word I'd said and he probably wasn't bluffing when he threatened me with Cadbury Row. I could give him the videotape and the whole story and let the cards fall where they may. That'd get me off the hook. Or I could just destroy the tape. Who was to say otherwise if I insisted that there wasn't any tape? Hanna told me the story in the store one night and I made the rest up, using a non-existent tape to get next to Carla. Sure, I'd claimed to have it but, hey, I lie a lot. Ask Alex. Ask Raewyn, the human lie detector.

But I didn't do either. Carla and I had an unspoken agreement: she got the videotape and I got her. A piece of her, that is. Not that big a piece, either, and not for long. When you boiled it right down, that was the deal. She'd kept her side of the bargain, she'd played her part. Now she was signalling that it was time to wrap it up, time for me to deliver.

I wondered what she'd do with the tape. To Alex, the tape was like a deadly but dormant virus which she'd contracted through a shameful, albeit youthful, lapse of moral hygiene. If the virus became active, its symptoms would provoke such disgust that she'd be shunned like an untouchable. No wonder she couldn't wait to erase it, to wipe it off the face of the earth. Carla was far less spooked. If she'd ever felt guilt, she'd got over it. Whatever threat the tape posed to her, she hadn't been in any great rush to acquire it. Perhaps she knew that she wouldn't be able to resist re-living that moment of abandon and was afraid she'd find herself wishing she could change places with the girl on the tape.

Once she had the tape, I could see her rapidly losing interest in finding out what had happened to the others. And once she'd given up on that, how long before she gave up on me? What would I have to offer her?

But we'd made a deal and I'd stick to it. Because I was okay.

I couldn't bail out. I just had to keep winging it and hope for a soft landing. I dialled the number Raewyn had given me and got a Surry Hills bistro. I said, 'I'm trying to get in touch with Marie Gifford. A friend of hers gave me this number ...'

'Hang on, I'll get her.' Raewyn had hedged her bets: being okay wasn't enough to get the home number.

When Marie came to the phone, I began the tricky business of explaining myself without coming across as a waste of time or worse. She butted in, saying it was a really bad time, she was flat stick and going to get busier.

I said, 'I just need five minutes.'

'Okay, tomorrow's Saturday. I spend Saturday mornings at the cafe, reading the papers.' She named a place on Darlinghurst's espresso strip.

'How will I know you?'

'I could wear a leopardskin pillbox hat.'

'That would help.'

I hadn't seen anything more about the hit and run, so I rang Tony Stark at the *Herald* to find out why. I tried to grease the wheels by saying I owed him a beer, when would it suit him to collect?

He said, 'What is it this time?'

'What do you mean?'

'When someone phones up out of the blue offering to buy me a beer, it means they want something.'

'Well, when we're having that beer, I might, just in the course of conversation, raise the subject of Pete Grayson.'

'Pete Grayson, eh?' said Stark slowly. 'How about that? Guess what I'm doing a story on right now?'

'Does that mean there's been what they call a development?'

'That's what it means. You can get tomorrow's paper and save yourself a couple of bucks.'

'I'd still owe you a beer.'

'If you really want to buy me a beer, I'm aiming to lob at the Green Park in Darlinghurst about five. I'll be the short bloke with a tie.'

He left out scruffy. Tony Stark wasn't the only short bloke with a tie in the Green Park but he was definitely the scruffiest. His grey suit was a Saigon special – sleeves down to the knuckles, trousers which sagged at the crotch like hand-me-down longjohns – and his Hush Puppies were on their second time around the clock. The tie in question looked as if it'd been used in a suicide attempt.

Stark himself was tubby with an arrowhead nose, bright, foxy eyes and big hair. He looked like an out-of-work Elvis impersonator.

We shook hands and I bought a couple of beers. He said, 'I didn't think you'd front. As I said, that "let me buy you a beer" line is usually bullshit and ...'

He let it hang for a few seconds. I said, 'And what?'

'Your reputation preceded you.'

'Give me a break. Even when I was fleecing small investors, I always bought my round.'

He asked what Silverwater was like. I told a couple of stories and watched him lose interest. As Donald had said, it wasn't the real thing. Nor was I.

'So what's your interest in Grayson?'
'Friend of a friend.'
'Yeah? Being a friend of a friend of yours seems like a fairly fucking dangerous thing to be.'

I shrugged. He didn't know the half of it. He studied me like a bird inspecting a ploughed field. 'Mate, one of these days you'll have to tell me about it.'

'One of these days I will. I might have to change a couple of names, though.'

'Like that, is it?' Stark tipped back what was left of his beer and picked up the fresh one. 'They found the car that bowled Grayson. It was stolen from the long-term carpark at the airport and dumped back there, clean as a whistle. The average hit and run, right: the guy's pissed or speeding, he cleans up a pedestrian, panics, gets the fuck out of there. The average accident involving a stolen car is kids joyriding; if they can drive away, they either head for Dubbo or dump the car a block from home. Here someone's gone out to the airport, nicked a car which probably won't be missed till he's finished with it, shitcanned Grayson in Vaucluse, gone back to the airport and dumped the car without leaving a print, a smudge, a fibre, any fucking thing. Conclusion: the car was stolen for the specific purpose of nailing Grayson. Which makes it murder.' His bright eyes widened to let me know the best was yet to come. 'Maybe even a hit.'

'Jesus. Was he a likely target?'

Stark shrugged. 'That's what the cops are trying to work out – sometimes you don't realise the orange is rotten till you peel it. He might've been fucking someone he shouldn't have, his wife might've had her eye on the insurance – that sort of shit happens. Then they'll look at his business dealings. He could've stiffed some guys in a deal without realising they were the sort of operators who don't get even in court, you know what I mean?'

After that, he got talking about murder. It was obviously a subject close to his heart. I guess that's what journalism does to you. Political journalists live for elections and leadership challenges; war correspondents thrive on wars; foreign correspondents get off on revolutions and natural disasters. And police reporters dig murders. The big stories. The fact that your cholesterol's down and you're holding steady at four units of alcohol a day isn't even a little story. You want to be in the paper, get lost in the bush or bitten by a shark. Or stabbed eighteen times.

When he mentioned Ray Hanna, I said, 'Yeah, what's the story there?'

'Fuck, you're not going to tell me he was a friend of a friend?'

'No, he lived next door to me.'

Stark backed away. 'Mate, you're bad fucking juju. I'm going home to bed.'

'Don't most people die in bed?'

'Good point. I'm safer right here, plenty of witnesses. The story with Hanna is drugs – he was a small-time dealer. The cops think someone moved in on his patch or else he forgot the old rule: the customer is always right. Especially if he's a drug-fucked maniac with a carving knife.'

He was off the pace on that one. It made me wonder how good the rest of his information was. 'Shit, is that right?'

'Yeah, they're playing it close to the chest but I

got that from one of the crew the other day.'

'Would that be Detective-Sergeant Donald?'

He stared at me. 'Don't tell me: he's married to your sister?'

'My sister's a nun.'

Stark thought about taking that further but decided he didn't know me well enough.

Telling a police reporter the details of my fraught relationship with Donald didn't seem like a sensible thing to do, so I said, 'He knocked on my door the day they found Hanna.'

He nodded. 'Good old Duck.'

'Eh?'

'That's his nickname – Donald, Duck. Get it? Stupid fucking name, if you ask me – especially for one of the smartest cops in this town. He has to be, mind you, he wouldn't have lasted otherwise.'

'Why's that?'

'Duck's a lone wolf and that ain't the way to get on and get ahead in the New South Wales police service. There's also the odd whisper that he's not exactly squeaky-clean. They've never pinned anything on him but you know how it is: give a dog a bad name, it's usually enough to flush his career down the dunny.'

'By not exactly squeaky-clean, you mean corrupt?'

Stark sighed. 'Yeah, but shit, I've heard that whisper about dozens of coppers.'

'So you don't believe it?'

He shrugged and drank some beer. 'I don't believe it and I don't disbelieve it. In this job, if you're not careful, you can end up thinking the whole fucking world's bent.'

NINETEEN

The nights were getting slower at the video store. The place was going south, blitzed by the mega-stores like neighbourhood retail everywhere. I'd be scanning job ads by Easter.

I had plenty of time to ponder what I'd heard from Tony Stark. It looked like Donald had sold him a dummy on the Hanna murder. Donald wouldn't want the blackmail racket to come out in the media in case it sent the victims into denial. He was on safe ground playing up the drugs angle. They could blame El Niño on drugs and some people would buy it.

The news about Grayson was harder to decipher. If he was in fact the victim of a hit, then it probably wasn't connected to the others: as Stark said, he could've had a greedy wife or an unwise affair or unwittingly crossed people who didn't play by the rules, any rules. Unless, of course, the others were hits too. Four hits would add up to a major investment for whoever was signing the cheques, but then money wasn't a big issue for some of the people I'd rubbed shoulders with since I'd got into this thing.

On the other hand, what was done to Hanna didn't look like the work of a professional. That looked psycho or strung-out or deeply personal. Whoever took care of him was having far too good a time to bother trying to make it look like anything other than what it was.

Maybe Hanna was the odd one out. Or maybe they were four separate, self-contained, everyday tragedies with no significance beyond themselves and nothing new to tell us. Adam jumped because he was a guilty man or a broken man or to prove he could see something through. Shelley sleepwalked to the edge of oblivion and went one step too far. Grayson and Hanna got caught in the unpredictable machinery of the shadow world.

But there was always something I couldn't bring into my circle of logic. Like: if Hanna's murder really was a drug thing, then the blackmail racket was a smokescreen. Why would Donald make it up? Why would he pitch it to me?

He was an enigmatic bastard, Donald. It was easy to see why people wondered about him. Eddie had heard the rumours too. I hadn't taken much notice because Eddie was a criminal with a warped mind and a vicious tongue. But just as paranoiacs can have real enemies, in a vicious world a man with a vicious tongue can sometimes tell it like it is.

I rang Eddie on his mobile. He asked how come I wasn't dead yet – the last time he'd seen me was the morning after the break-in when I'd feared the worst. I said I might've over-reacted. Eddie had another explanation, the essence of which was that I was less than a man. There wasn't much happening at the club so he decided he'd pop down, just what I was afraid of.

He showed up with two burgers and a six-pack.

It wasn't a goodwill gesture or a peace offering. Eddie was no peacenik; turbulence was his normality.

I asked about Donald. Eddie slobbered over his burger. 'What about the cunt?'

'You said you'd heard he was bent. What exactly did you hear?'

Eddie guzzled burger and beer, heaving out burps and farts. When he was good and ready, he told me the story of the playboy, the dancer and the madman from across the water.

It began, as did a fair chunk of modern Sydney, with Julius Beca.

Beca was a classic New Australian success story, tramp steamer to gin palace. He emigrated from Lebanon in the late forties, twenty years old with broken English and chickenfeed in his hip pocket. After five scrimping years as a builder's labourer, he set up his own housebuilding business. The housebuilding business grew into a construction company which grew into a conglomerate spanning construction, engineering and transport. His self-transformation was epic: shitkicker to tycoon, pauper to philanthropist, wog on the make to nation-builder.

The upwardly mobile are rarely embraced by those they catch up with or overtake, especially when the upstart has an accent and an olive complexion. It was taken for granted that Julius Beca had bribed and bullied his way to the top of the construction industry, but then how many players in that game had clean hands? Unlike his competitors, though, Beca's fortunes seemed immune to the economic cycle and the Builders Labourers' Federation, hence the drug rumours. According to one version, Beca fell back on heroin trafficking whenever his legitimate operations stalled. According to another, he was Mr Big.

A story did the rounds: a state MP advised a few close colleagues that he intended to raise the Mr Big rumour in parliament and call on the police minister to confirm or deny it. Before he had a chance, a couple of cops pulled over his son for changing lanes without indicating and found a bag of heroin in the glovebox. The MP held his tongue. Some people swore by that story; others dismissed it as an urban myth.

Beca's youngest son, Joseph – Joey Pecker to his friends – liked the night-life. He and a crony were in a Kings Cross club. A dancer with the stage-name April, a Maori girl, not fully grown, brought Joey out in a heat rash. The manager advised him that April wasn't that kind of girl yet. He'd have to handle her with care.

Joey sent a bottle of champagne backstage. When April came out to thank him, he invited her to join them for supper at a tres chic restaurant. Joey said he knew the owner, he'd open the kitchen just for them. April was starry-eyed. But the boys decided to skip supper. They took April to an unoccupied office block in Parramatta and used her like a blow-up sex doll. April fled back to New Zealand the next day.

Twenty-four hours after April flew out, her cousin Miah flew in. Miah was a dread-locked monster with a facial tattoo, fresh from eight years of religious weight-training in a prison gym. When he turned up at the club, two bouncers tried to make him leave. Miah jumped up and down on them, then threw them down the stairs, knocked the bounce right out of them. He broke a bottle on the manager's forehead and the manager told him what he wanted to know. Miah told the manager that he was going to cut Joey Pecker and his pal in half. Then he skolled a bottle of bourbon, trashed the place and left. The manager warned Joey, who vacated his Kirribilli pad just before Miah let himself in with a chainsaw. He took the pad apart too.

A shooter came up from Melbourne. The madman from across the water, as they'd dubbed Miah, had been seen in Bondi. The shooter went out there looking for Miah and had the bad luck to find him. Miah used his chainsaw on the shooter, tossed the torso in a dump-bin and left the head in a butcher's shop window.

After that, it appeared as if the boys were on their own: no-one wanted to pick up the contract. But two days later they found Miah in the front seat of a stolen car with four rounds in his chest and two in the head to make damn sure. The madman from across the water would've been a career highlight for any hit-man but no-one claimed it.

The boys reappeared in the Cross. Joey got wasted and bragged that Miah had been taken care of by the best cop money could buy. A few people on both sides of the law immediately thought of Donald. He'd been linked to the Becas when he worked on the drug squad; he was investigated, cleared and reassigned.

Not long after Joey had shot his mouth off, drug squad detectives, acting on an anonymous tip, raided his pal's place in Balmain. They found three kilos of heroin in a wine carton in the cellar. Nothing more was heard of the best cop money could buy.

Eddie said, 'That's the story, morning glory.'

'So Donald set him up – as a warning to Joey to keep his mouth shut?'

'That's what they say. You know what else they say? The smack was supplied by Julius Beca himself. See, Donald was in his pocket, not Joey's – he blew that mad cunt away as a favour to the old man. When Donald found out that Joey was talking about him, he went to the old man and said we've got to make that boy shut the fuck up. They cooked it up between them. The old man had never gone much on that other fucker anyway, reckoned he was a bad influence on Joey. Can you fucking believe that? What a couple of real fucking operators.'

Eddie finished his beer and said, 'I got to have a shit.' He came around the counter heading for the toilet, which was off the storeroom. When I suggested that perhaps he should shit in his own nest, he said, 'What the fuck? Aren't I good enough to use your shithouse?'

I wasn't prepared to go quite that far.

Eddie would've just been getting under way when this big guy, about fifty, walked in. His well-cut navy-blue suit couldn't quite hide the thickening around the middle but he was still what my mother would've called a fine figure of a man. He had carefully deployed, very fine sandy hair which would've danced in the wind like ribbons on a kite, and a lumpy face with a nose from a Picasso painting. I wondered if he'd done some boxing and whether he got out before his brain went the way of his looks. It wasn't a face to commit to memory but it was the first new one we'd had in the store for a while.

I said, 'How are you?'

He nodded at me and looked around, taking his time. 'Quiet night.' He had a deep, rich voice. Perhaps he'd hung up his gloves for a career in radio, spinning golden oldies on the late-night shift. *Okay, night owls, coming up we've got Elvis. This one's for my old sparring partner, Ike the Spike O'Reilly. The Spike was an animal in the ring but when he heard the King singing 'Wooden Heart', he cried like a baby ...*

He completed his inspection. 'I seem to be your only customer.'

'You should've been here an hour ago.'

He closed the door and reversed the open/closed sign. No-one had told me we were closing early. I said, 'What do you think you're doing?'

'James Alabaster?'

Uh-oh. 'Who's asking?'

He came over to the counter. 'Never mind that.'

This was trouble. This guy was twice as scary as Brown Shoes and Danny put together. Without even trying.

'What do you want?'

'Come on, Alabaster, you know the answer to that. I want the tape. And don't ask "What tape?" because I'm not in the mood to play silly buggers.'

I'd bear that in mind. 'Why do you want it?'

There was a hint of a smile but the pale grey eyes remained flinty. 'A reasonable question, but you'll have to do without an answer.'

Stalling for time now. 'Is it for yourself or someone else?'

'Ditto on both counts.'

'Well, in that case, I don't see why I should ...'

'Pipe down.' He slammed his thick hands down

on the counter. They had knuckles like walnuts. 'A lot of the people I come across, violence is the only language they understand. I wouldn't have put you in that category.'

He loomed over me, letting me know it wouldn't worry him if he was wrong. The toilet flushed. He peered over my shoulder, frowning. The toilet door opened and closed. Eddie came out of the storeroom buckling up his studded black belt, saying, 'Fuck me, talk about a dead rat up the arse.'

The big man studied Eddie like someone trying to figure out how to assemble kit-set furniture – stare at it for long enough, it'll come to you. Eventually, he turned to me. 'Who's he?'

'A friend of mine.'

He raised unruly eyebrows. 'You really have come down in the world.' Without looking at Eddie, he said, 'Goodbye, friend.'

Eddie's eyes narrowed. 'You talking to me?'

I noticed the big man slip a button to undo his jacket. Still looking at me, he said, 'Mr Alabaster and I have private matters to discuss, so why don't you buzz off?'

There was a taut silence. It was up to Eddie now whether or not it turned ugly. My money was on ugly. I didn't think he'd go quietly, not in front of me.

Eddie thrust his jaw at the big man and snarled, 'Fuck you.'

The big man breathed heavily through his nose and gave a short, irritated shake of the head. Then he snapped out his right arm. Eddie never saw it coming. The backhander connected solidly and he went over backwards, taking a display stand with him.

The big man looked down at him. 'No, fuck you.' He turned his back on Eddie to ask me, 'Where is it?'

'It's not here.'

Out of the corner of my eye I saw Eddie get to his feet. He was wearing a lurid Hawaiian shirt outside his jeans. His right hand snaked under the shirt at the small of his back. There was a metallic ping and a flash of silver. The big man's head whipped around as Eddie lunged at him like a fencer. The big man groaned as if he was straining to lift a heavy weight. Eddie stepped back, holding the knife pointing at the floor. There was a film of blood on the blade.

The big man opened up his jacket. Blood was soaking into his white shirt, just above the hip.

The knife twitched in Eddie's hand. 'Hit the road, Jack, or I'll really fucking cut you.'

The big man said, 'I'd better get this seen to.' He could've been talking about his corns. He placed a handkerchief on the red patch and walked stiffly out of the store.

Eddie's cheek glowed and blood trickled from his nose. He said, 'Who the fuck was that?'

I was in a daze, shocked by the violence which had flared and disappeared like a firework. 'I don't know.'

He shrugged as if it wasn't that important. 'You reckon it was him who broke into your place?'

'Come to think of it, it probably was.'

'Well, that'll teach the cunt.'

He went to the toilet to wipe the blood off his face and perhaps off the knife. I could hear him talking to himself. He was complaining about the stench.

After Eddie left, I couldn't sit still; delayed reaction made me skittish and distracted. I tried to work out where the big man fitted in, but I couldn't concentrate. My mind kept sliding down blind alleys, like a wino looking for company.

I was in the storeroom doing something pointless to use up time when I heard the high heels. Please, I thought, please don't let it be one of those unattached good old girls, flushed, roguish and unstoppable after the pub, not sure what they feel like watching and wanting the A to Z on anything that catches their eye. They saw themselves as a brief, shining moment in a lonely guy's endless night. I saw them as half an hour's unpaid overtime.

I went out to the counter. Carla was standing there in a model pose – hip cocked, knee bent, foot rolled inwards. Her left hand rested on her thigh, holding a small handbag; her right arm was draped across her body, the hand on her left forearm. The contrived artlessness of her carefully tousled hair went with the cool mischief in her eyes. She was in a black party dress. There wasn't much of it and what there was fitted like a glove. A safe-cracker's glove.

I'd seen it all before – the outfit, the pose, the mystery, the promise. In my beautiful dreams.

If there was ever a time to show some style, that was it. But I was too deranged not to stumble into the whys and wherefores. I blurted, 'Carla, what are you doing here?'

'You don't sound very pleased to see me.' Not quite pouting.

'Hey, I'm delighted to see you. I just thought you were away for the weekend.'

'So did I. It wasn't till we got up there that Reece

informed me he's hosting an all-night poker school tonight. It was jacked up weeks ago but he conveniently forgot to mention it. I took it very calmly. I told him' – acting it out for me – ' "Darling, go right ahead but if you think I'm going to hang around and make sandwiches, you've got another think coming." And here I am.'

'You look great. Are you going out?'

She smiled. Her lipstick was dark, dark red, the colour of sin. 'We, James. We're going out.'

TWENTY

Carla knew this place in Chinatown which stayed open till three in the morning and did the best Peking Duck. First, though, she wanted to play pool. Playing pool at midnight struck me as kind of eccentric but apparently it was a cool thing to do. I really didn't care what we did. It was the *we* that mattered, not the what.

We walked up Victoria Street to the Soho bar. People were milling around on the pavement, mostly glassy-eyed girls waiting for someone to pay attention to them. There was a queue of sorts with a couple of hulks on the door weeding out under-agers and style victims. Carla wasn't disposed to stand in line; she walked straight to the head of the queue. The hulks' corrugated faces split into goofy grins and they waved us through.

The upstairs bar heaved. All these fun-loving people. Standing three-deep at the bar, impatient to refuel. Squirming to grinding dance music. Shouting and smoking their throats raw. Pulling back to wallflower a while and revise expectations. Scanning the room for a signal bounced back from another set of waving antennae.

Carla was trying to tell me something. I felt her warm breath in my ear, smelt the rose petal and gin tang of her perfume. She was nominating the drink I could get her while she found a pool table.

She weaved through the crowd, attracting hungry stares. It took me five minutes to push my way to the bar, another five to be acknowledged by one of the Valkyrie barmaids. I got a vodka and tonic and a beer and went in search of Carla. I found her in a two-table poolroom out the back, watching a game. As I handed Carla her drink, she said, 'We're on next.'

The game in progress pitted a thirtyish, business-suited mixed double against two young guys in jeans and T-shirts. It was a mismatch. The woman attacked the white ball as if she was trying to spear a fish and her partner never got out of damage control.

I said, 'We play the winners, do we?'

'Uh-huh.' Carla nodded towards the young guys who were standing together at the other end of the table. 'That'll be Marty and Tim. Marty's the one with the muscles.'

Tim was blond and forgettable. Marty was dark, a baby-faced heart-throb with a pumped-up torso gift-wrapped in a tight black T-shirt.

I said, 'He's probably gay.'

Carla said, 'I don't think so.' She was looking up the table, smiling. My eyes followed hers. She was looking at Marty. He was smiling too. They were smiling at each other.

I said, 'You make friends quickly.'

She shrugged, still eyeing Marty. 'You took ages.'

Marty sauntered to the table. He had a long diagonal pot to close out the game. Scarcely bothering to line it up, he rammed the black into the pocket. Then he glanced up at Carla and winked.

She said softly, 'Wow.'

I told myself to relax. She was just loosening up, admiring the scenery. Like me out in the bar, eyes roaming over all that boldly packaged flesh.

The players shook hands. Marty came over to us, cue at slope arms. 'Okay, Carla, let's see what you've got.'

She introduced me. Tim was setting up the balls; he glanced up, twitching his eyebrows indifferently. Marty smirked and asked, 'How's it going?'

He tossed a coin. Carla called correctly and decided to break without bothering to consult her partner. She went to the top of the table and bent over the cue. Marty stood behind her, his eyes crawling up the backs of her legs. Carla miscued. The white ball dribbled down the table, barely disturbing the triangle of coloured balls. She said, 'Shit, I hate that. What'd I do wrong, Marty?'

He put a hand on her shoulder. 'Don't worry, I'll give you some coaching.'

Tim came down to take his shot. Carla stayed where she was, voting with her feet. I concentrated on the game, which wasn't that easy with Carla's playful laugh as background noise. I was tingling all over. I felt a drop of sweat slide down my ribcage. What the fuck was she up to?

Tim broke up the triangle. A few balls rolled close to pockets but nothing dropped. I hadn't played for a couple of years and was never that good but pool is, after all, a pub game, a lowest common denominator game. I knocked down a couple of gimmes and finished with a safety shot which left the white up against the cushion, behind one of ours.

I went back to my spot. Carla was still standing with Marty. She called, 'Way to go, partner.' I forced a thin smile.

Marty said, 'Okay, let's get serious here.'

He tried an ambitious rebound shot which didn't quite come off. It was Carla's turn again. I sat down on the bench along the wall. I had a feeling this was going to take some time.

First Marty talked her through the options and their respective degrees of difficulty. Then Carla decided she needed a cigarette. She came over to get one out of her handbag, which was on the bench next to me. I got a dim smile. 'Okay, James?'

I said, 'I'm fine', as if I couldn't imagine why she needed to ask.

She went back to the table. Marty wondered if she could spare him a cigarette. She made another trip to the handbag, this time without getting sidetracked. She offered him a light. Operating her lighter suddenly seemed to require two pairs of hands. They discussed her shot some more, then she hunched over the cue. Marty stood behind her, very close. From another angle, it would've looked as though he was taking her from the rear. As he leaned forward to adjust her bridge, he murmured in her ear, prompting a low laugh.

Tim craned his neck to see how I was taking it. I was taking it badly but trying not to let it show. I felt like a share trader sitting in front of a screen, watching a stock I'd bet the farm on go into freefall. It was turning to shit right in front of me and there was nothing I could do about it.

Carla played her shot. The white ball cannoned off a colour and clipped the black which disappeared down a pocket as if magnetised. Game over. Carla boo-hooed. Marty yelled, 'Fucking what?' I said, 'Got to hand it to you, coach.'

Marty put his arm around Carla. She looked up at him, making a poor-little-me face. I went to find a toilet.

I found the toilet. Not a toilet, the toilet. The anteroom was jammed even though guys were pissing in tandem. Each change-over was marked by the squelch of shoes on tiles sticky with urine.

I managed to calm down. That performance out there didn't mean anything. Okay, it was a little perverse of Carla but it wasn't for real. I was her date. She wasn't going to offload me for a pea-brained hunk a few years out of high school, whatever he might think.

I went back to the poolroom. Another group had taken over the table. There was no sign of Carla or the others. On the way back to the bar, I saw Tim walk out onto the balcony. I followed him out, intercepting him as he moved in on a girl.

I said, 'Where's Carla?'

'How should I know?' He was barely restraining himself from laughing in my face.

'Well, where'd you last see her?'

'In the bar – with Marty.' As I headed that way, he added, 'I wouldn't bother, mate. You can kiss that one goodbye.'

The bar was Sardine City. I squeezed through cracks in the wall of bodies, trying not to stand on toes or rub up against women in a way they might misinterpret. I was near-frantic, wanting this nightmare to end but afraid that I wasn't dreaming. I was beginning to think the unthinkable when I spotted them over in the dance corner. They were dancing, if you could call it that, standing face-to-face, blasted by percussive music, just shifting their weight from one foot to the other. I couldn't see Carla's face but Marty's was stretched into a lopsided grin. He thought he was home and hosed.

I was trembling with rage, burning with humiliation. I shoved towards them, way past politeness now. A woman swore at me and someone thumped me on the back. I took no notice. I came up behind Carla as Marty ran his hands down her bare arms.

As they joined hands, I tapped her on the shoulder. She turned around, flinching at the ugliness in my eyes. She mouthed, 'Where've you been? I thought you must've gone.'

What could I say? There was no point in asking what was going on or what it meant. The fact that I'd been discarded for this piece of meat spoke for itself. There was no relationship, there never had been. It was a pipedream, the forlorn fantasy of a two-time loser. I turned away, ignoring a tug at my sleeve.

I went down the stairs fast. They were still queuing up outside. I saw a girl light a cigarette and I wanted one. And a bottle of hard liquor. That wasn't going to be a problem: the Cross exists to feed the cravings that seize damaged people after midnight.

I was crossing the road when I heard Carla call, 'James, wait.' She was on the opposite footpath, waiting for a car to go by. When it was clear, she skittered across the road, high heels click-clacking. I waited for her, torn again, hovering between wild hope and the urge to fuck her off as brutally as I knew how.

She came up to me. Her face was frozen, immobilised by uncertainty. 'James, don't look at me like that.'

'Can I have a cigarette?'

She blinked. It would've been the last thing she expected me to say. 'What?'

'I'd like a cigarette – if you can spare one, that is.'

'But you don't smoke.'

'Fuck, forget it. I'll get my own.'

I walked away. She caught up with me. 'Jesus, what's the matter with you?'

I slowed to a stop, then turned to face her. 'Got you stumped, has it? Try as you might, you just can't figure it out?' I could feel the sarcasm twisting my mouth into mean shapes. 'I wouldn't have thought it was quite that much of a mystery myself but I guess it depends on your point of view.'

She didn't answer and she wouldn't look me in the eye.

I let it all out. 'You know what I don't understand? You want to go out and pick up a toy-boy, that's fine, go right ahead. But why the fuck drag me along?' She was looking at the ground now. 'To make a fool of me – was that the idea? To hurt me?' Her bowed head rocked gently. 'Because that's what you did. And tell me, Carla: what did I do to deserve it? I'd really like to know.' I waited for an answer but there wasn't one. 'But hey, don't worry about it – I wouldn't want it to spoil your night. You're off the leash, make the most of it. A young stud like Marty, I bet he can fuck all night.'

She finally looked up. Her eyes had a film of moisture but her voice was steady. 'I don't want him.'

'You could've fooled me.'

She fumbled in her handbag, extracting cigarettes and lighter. She offered them to me. 'Go on.'

I took them. I lit a cigarette and gave it to her, lit another one and inhaled cautiously. It made my head spin.

She said, 'Do you want to go to Chinatown?'

'No.'

'What are you going to do?'

'Get pissed.'

'Where?'

'At home, where else?'

'Can I come?'

I took another drag. It felt good. 'You wouldn't like my place.'

'Please?'

Her eyes were dry now and solemn as a child's. A shadow of vulnerability softened the pure lines of her face and touched me like a fond memory. I couldn't hate her and I couldn't deny her, so I had to forgive her.

TWENTY-ONE

I should've just put the whole episode out of my mind and salvaged what I could from the evening. But I couldn't. I wasn't tough enough to live with it.

We were taking a shortcut through Kings Cross station to Darlinghurst Road. I said, 'So what was going on back there?'

'I assume you mean Marty?' She said it reluctantly, as if no good could come from revisiting it. 'Remember the Elle Macpherson scenario?' She shrugged. 'That's what was going on.'

'He wasn't a once-in-a-lifetime opportunity,' I said stiffly, 'and you weren't a long way from home.'

'Come on, James, don't be so literal.'

'Oh, I see, so it doesn't actually have to be a supermodel in New York? It could be . . .' – I remembered Donald's definition of a scrubber – '. . . a trainee hairdresser with a tattoo on her bum?'

'Wouldn't you agree,' she said lightly, 'that most guys' idea of the perfect woman for a one-night stand would be young, horny, gorgeous, brainless, not interested in conversation, definitely not interested in a relationship, not really interested in anything except getting you into bed as quickly as possible?'

'Yeah, but that's a fantasy.'

'A fantasy which works both ways.'

I had to ask, didn't I? We were passing a liquor store. I asked her what she wanted; she told me to suit myself. I got a bottle of vodka and a four-pack of tonic.

Walking through the Cross towards Potts Point, I started on Marty again. I couldn't leave it alone. I had a morbid need to know how close she'd been to succumbing to temptation. 'So the fact that Marty's an insufferable turd was part of the attraction?'

She raised her eyebrows. 'Still on that subject, are we? No, it wasn't part of the attraction, it was irrelevant. I had no desire to get to know him, so his personality didn't enter into it.'

'What did you desire to do?'

'Ah-ha, the sixty-four thousand dollar question.' Ten minutes earlier, she'd been looking at the ground, shuffling her feet; now she was mocking me. 'And the answer is, that much and no more.' She stepped in front me. The mocking smile faded. 'I certainly didn't want to take him home, although I don't blame you for thinking that. I was in the mood and ...' – she made a down-in-the-mouth clown's face – '... I got a bit carried away.' She reached for my hand. 'I didn't think you'd gone, James, but you looked so angry, I just said the first thing that came into my head. I knew you wouldn't give up that easily.'

It didn't taste great but I could swallow it. And keep it down.

We picked up Carla's Audi from a side street. As she reversed into a parking spot across the road from my apartment building, she said, 'Shit, I didn't bring my mobile. Reece's bound to've phoned in and left a message.'

'He wouldn't expect to hear from you now, surely?'

'He's having an all-nighter, remember. I'd better get home.'

I'd been half-expecting her to find an excuse to bail out. I turned away and opened the car door, dejection settling on my shoulders like a heavy overcoat. Carla put a hand on my arm. 'Hang on, you're coming too. I'm not losing you twice in one night.'

My smile was as guarded as smiles get. It'd been a bruising night. I was still standing but I wasn't sure how much more punishment I could take.

Carla U-turned and headed back up Macleay Street. At the Greenknowe Avenue lights, I told her to pull over.

'Why?'

'I won't be a minute.'

She swung into the kerb. I got out of the car, ran up the steps to the post office and went into the alcove housing the post office boxes. I still had the key taped to my foot. I retrieved the videotape and went back to the car.

I showed it to her. 'This belongs to you.'

'That's it?' She laughed nervously. 'Oh my God, it's all happening tonight.'

Rolling east on New South Head Road, sharing her last cigarette. Carla pushed a button on the dashboard. 'You'll like this,' she said. It was late-night music: moody piano, swelling strings. A crooner breathed, 'You were an innocent child before I laid my hands on you.'

Carla sang along: 'You can drink a little more and hurt a little less and you get that butterfly feeling underneath your dress.' She laughed again. This time, there was nothing nervous about it. 'Ain't that the truth?'

Talking about the video-orgy, she'd said booze loosened her up, there'd been times she'd drunk too much and done things she'd regretted in the morning. Maybe she'd had a couple before coming out tonight; maybe it was as mundane as that. I dwelt on the implications of her having a couple more for thirty action-packed seconds.

I said, 'Who's this?'

'Lloyd Cole. The album's called "Don't get weird on me, babe". You can relate to that, can't you?' She grazed her knuckles along my jawline. 'I'm glad you got mad.'

I asked why but she just smiled and shook her head. We drove on, listening to Lloyd's unclean thoughts about his little butterfly.

We turned off at Vaucluse Road, heading down to the water. We came to a high white wall stretching the best part of a block. Carla pointed a remote, the gates swung back and she turned in. Dead ahead was the biggest private residence I'd ever seen. It was a mix of architectural styles – Italian Renaissance meets Spanish Colonial with a few French Rococo touches thrown in for good measure. What's known in the trade as the more-money-than-sense look.

I said, 'Holy shit.'

She nodded. 'That's pretty much the standard reaction.'

'How many architects did you go though?'

'I lost count. If we ever build another one, Reece'll have to design it himself.'

Carla followed the drive over to a low white building which housed Reece's car collection. She parked next to the Ferrari and told me to leave the vodka, there was enough booze inside to fill the swimming pool. We walked towards the house through a Japanese garden. In the ponds below the arched footbridges, foot-long goldfish drifted like airships.

I said, 'I don't see any security guards.'

'They've got the weekend off.'

I looked sceptical.

'You don't believe me, do you?'

'Should I?'

'Of course. I took your advice.'

'What'd Reece say?'

'He thought it was a good idea. He said off the top of his head, he could think of at least a dozen people who'd like to kill him.'

We reached the portico entrance. Getting in required a swipe card, a security code and a key. The door opened into a two-storey octagonal entrance hall the size of the average duplex apartment. Carla punched in another code to deactivate the alarm.

The message light on the phone on the antique console was blinking. It was Reece, his voice roughened by a night of grog-sodden men's stuff. 'Jesus, Carla, where are you? Your mobile's switched off and it's . . . what the fuck time is it anyway? Ten to one. What sort of time is that for a respectable married woman to be out and about? I'm not looking good here, baby – the boys are giving me a hard time.' The guffaws in the background made Carla grimace. 'Ring me as soon as you get in, eh? If I have to worry about you, it'll fuck up my concentration and you know what'll happen then – I'll lose money and I fucking hate that.'

Carla said something under her breath, then told me, 'I better ring him.' She pointed to one of the five doors in the wood-panelled walls. 'There's a bar down there, just help yourself. I'll have a cognac.'

Down there was a grown-ups' playroom. It had a full-size snooker table, a milkbar jukebox, a curved wooden bar with dull brass, padded barstools and a footrest, and a semicircular black leather lounge suite facing a panelled wall. The bar was an Aladdin's Cave. There were three mini-fridges – one with beer, one with champagne, one with mixers – and shelves stacked with the sort of booze you see in the exclusive shops, locked away in glass cabinets.

I was pouring fifty-year-old cognac into brandy balloons when Carla arrived with the videotape and a fresh packet of cigarettes. She pressed a button on the wall; the panels opened up to reveal a giant TV screen. She inserted the tape in the built-in VCR and sat down. I took the drinks over.

She lit cigarettes for both of us. 'How long since you watched it?'

'Quite a while.'

'Sick of it, huh?'

'You asked me that before. It wasn't a matter of being sick of it, it was a matter of keeping it in a safe place.' I thought of all the troubling things I hadn't told her about – the break-in, Alex and Brown Shoes, Donald, the big man. They were mounting up. I wondered if there'd ever be a right time to mention them. 'Besides, I didn't think you'd want me to keep watching it.'

She shrugged. 'It was a long time ago. I'm not that person any more.'

That's what they all say but you can't fold up the past like out-of-fashion clothes and send it off to charity. What we are today is what we did yesterday. I knew that better than most.

She said, 'I want to have one last look.'

'Would you prefer to do that in private?'

'No, I'd prefer to do that with you.' She tucked her legs underneath her and leaned against me, resting her head on my chest. 'I can't hear your heartbeat.'

'You will.'

The low, suggestive laugh, which had tormented me earlier, now triggered a rush of desire. She started the tape and Alex and Gareth went at it. I brushed a strand of hair off her face. She caught my hand and kissed the palm. I longed to kiss her but her eyes were fixed on the screen.

The video left me cold now. It was like watching some ponderous documentary full of flickering black and white home movie footage – Hitler playing with his dog at Berchtesgaden or Edward and Mrs Simpson playing deck quoits off the Isle of Capri.

After twenty seconds of her solo performance, Carla grabbed the remote. 'That's enough of that,' she said. When the action resumed, Shelley was going down on Adam. 'Adam once told me that Shelley was better than me at blow-jobs,' she said matter-of-factly. 'I said that didn't surprise me, it was the difference between doing something because you want to and doing it because you feel obliged to. You know what he said? "There are chicks all over town who'd kill to suck my dick – how come I ended up with you?"'

'A fool for love, that boy.'

'No, that was me.'

Shelley was relentless, the hardest working woman in show business, slip-sliding with Carla, sixty-nining with Gareth, planting the cucumber. Carla shook her head in wonder. 'Look at her go.'

We got to the threesome – Carla, Adam and Pete. Carla winced. I said, 'We don't have to watch this.'

She shook her head quickly as if I didn't understand that it was something she had to do. We watched. Pretty little Carla lay on her back. Adam was nosing around between her legs while Pete licked her breasts like a dog cleaning its dinner bowl. Then they flipped her onto her hands and knees. Adam went in from behind while Pete positioned himself in front of her, his hips thrown forward.

I took the remote from Carla and stopped the tape. She sat up. I said, 'That's my least favourite bit.'

'Doesn't look good, does it?'

'It looks like you're being used.'

She nestled against me again. A minute went by. I was about to ask what she was thinking when she tilted her head back to look at me. 'I think you are bored by it. I couldn't help but notice' – dropping her eyes – 'that it didn't do much for you.'

'I'm on my best behaviour.'

'At least I can hear your heartbeat now.'

'So can I.'

She got up onto her knees and put her hands on my shoulders, forcing me backwards. Our faces were only a few centimetres apart. 'So what about the first time – did it turn you on then?'

'What do you think?'

Her eyes glowed. 'Did you ... ?'

'Yep.'

'Over which bit?'

'The bit you fast-forwarded.'

She made a dreamy noise. 'So, in a way, we got ourselves off together?'

'I guess you could say that.'

Carla went 'hmmm' again. Her eyes were half-closed now. 'I think it's time we took the next step. Don't you?'

Before I could answer, she kissed me, softly but with great deliberation. Her tongue swirled across my teeth and fluttered in my mouth. Then she slid off the couch and stood up. 'I'm going to have a bath.'

She walked over to the bar carrying her drink. Her dress was bunched at the tops of her thighs. She stopped at the bar, threw back what was left of the cognac and put down the glass. She placed her hands on her buttocks to smooth down the dress. 'When you're ready, James' – looking over her shoulder – 'I'll have another one of those.'

She wasn't a mystery any more. She wanted me. It wasn't a fantasy, it was going to happen and not by serendipity in some foreign hotel room. She'd had plenty of time to think about it.

Stars tell interviewers that they always knew they'd make it, right from the time they were kids. They're espousing the golden rule of show business: if you work hard and believe in yourself enough, the sky's the limit. Maybe so, but most kids think they're special and, by the way, who *are* all those losers on the Boulevard of Broken Dreams? But I knew what they meant. I'd caused our trajectories to intersect,

I'd persisted, I'd endured. I'd made myself destiny's agent.

I gave Carla five minutes or so then set forth to collect my reward, cognac bottle and glasses in hand. After a couple of wrong turns, I found my way to the foot of the main staircase. On the upstairs landing, I was wondering where to now when I saw the black high heels down the corridor.

The corridor led to a baronial bedroom via an adjoining sitting room with bookshelves, a sofa, several armchairs, a television and a fireplace. The curtains were closed and the bedside lamps turned down low. Carla's party dress was draped over an ottoman at the end of the bed.

The Sullys had his and hers bathrooms but light showed under the door to the left of the bed and a pair of black panties hung from the door-handle. I pushed the door open with my shoulder and entered a world of gold plate and marble. On one side was an enclosed shower, on the other a marble vanity with a ceiling-high mirror and a cross-legged stool with a leopardskin seat. Inlaid marble floor ended in steps up to a raised bath. The only sound was the hum of the whirlpool.

Carla sat in the bath up to her neck in bubbles, her back to a large window. She said, 'You found it okay.'

'I followed the trail.'

Another tantalising laugh. 'Clever boy.'

I sat on the top step and poured her a drink. As she reached for it, the brown slopes of her breasts broke the surface. She said, 'Come on in, the water's fine.'

I unbuttoned my shirt, willing away self-consciousness. This was it. I had to do it right, I had to be worthy. I dropped my shirt on the floor, kicked off my shoes, fumbled with my belt. Carla watched me over the rim of her glass. I hoped she couldn't see me shake. I yanked down my boxers and stepped into the bath. It was the right heat, warm but not enervating. I lowered myself onto the underwater seat, stretching out. Our legs bumped. She slid a feathery foot up my leg making my skin prickle.

Carla came to my side of the bath. She was sleek and firm. She straddled me and we kissed, much harder this time, mouths open wide. Her fingers were in my hair, twirling and kneading. When my hand slipped between her legs, she hissed in my ear. A little later, she reached down. We hurtled into ecstasy, her hair flying. When I touched her face, her mouth sought my fingers.

Afterwards, we dried off and Carla led me to bed. We lay with our foreheads touching. She whispered, 'James, what happened at the Soho . . .'

'Hmmm.'

'It wasn't what I said it was.'

'What was it, then?'

'I was making sure.'

'Of what?'

'Of what I wanted. Of how you felt.'

I propped myself up on an elbow. 'You already knew that.'

'You don't give much away, you know – not as much as you think.'

'So when were you sure?'

'When you forgave me. I was sure of everything then.'

My hand skimmed over her flat stomach. When I stroked her, she shuddered, scissoring her legs. Her skin was flushed and damp. She writhed against me, chewing hotly on my chest and neck and making purring noises which came from deep inside her.

Her fierce desire thrilled me. I wanted to drive it higher and higher, until it rolled over me like a wave and swept me away.

TWENTY-TWO

I woke up with a burnt-out mouth and a deadening headache when Carla switched on the bedside lamp. She climbed onto the bed with a tray containing fruit juice, toast and honey. The message on her knee-length white T-shirt said, 'Forget the shrimp, honey – I'm coming home with the crabs.' She didn't look anything like I felt.

She dabbed a kiss on my forehead. 'Juice?'

'Thanks.' I took the glass from her and swilled the grapefruit juice in one mouth-cleansing gulp. 'What's the time?'

'Just after five.'

My hearing wasn't too good either. 'Just after nine, did you say?'

'No, I said just after five – F-I-V-E. Comes between four and six.'

That didn't make sense. 'I know I sort of lost track of time last night but we can't have had much more than a couple of hours sleep?'

She was spreading honey on the toast. 'If that.'

'So when did you first realise you were an insomniac?'

'I'm not.' She passed me a piece of toast, then

licked her fingers. 'I'd love to sleep in but it wouldn't be a good idea – there's no telling what Reece'll do in these situations.'

These situations?

Carla crunched through her piece of toast as if she was anxious to get breakfast out of the way. 'What'll probably happen,' she said, 'is the poker game will wind up about eight. Reece and his cronies will go off for a big breakfast, then get a few hours kip before golf. That's the most likely scenario. But Reece mightn't feel like bacon and eggs, he might feel like an early lunch at his favourite Italian restaurant, which happens to be in Paddington. Or, another possibility, if the cards didn't fall his way, he might've spat the dummy an hour ago and kicked everyone out, in which case he could be on his way here as we speak.'

'How did you get back last night?'

'In the Ferrari.'

'So how's he going to get back?'

'We keep a car up there.'

'Why didn't I think of that? What sort?'

'A Volvo.' She smiled, but briefly and without much conviction. 'Reece doesn't mind if it gets sand in it.'

I didn't want this night to end in a scramble, being hustled out the door with my shoes in my hand. I wanted a lingering till-we-meet-again. 'Why don't you ring him, find out what's happening?'

'I can think of three good reasons.' Letting me know she was being patient. 'One, he's probably got the answer-machine on so I'd be none the wiser. Two, I might wake him up. Three, if I ring him at a quarter past five to find out what he's up to, he's going to wonder what I'm up to.'

'Is he that suspicious?'

'It's not so much a matter of being suspicious... Put it this way, if something doesn't make sense to Reece, he wants an explanation. And if you give him a reason to be suspicious, doesn't matter how trivial the thing is, he'll make damn sure he gets to the bottom of it. Basically, he just can't bear the thought of anyone putting one over him. Any more questions?'

I shook my head.

'In that case, if you'll kindly shift your arse, I've got to change the sheets. You're on dishes.'

It wasn't the most romantic morning after but I couldn't fault her reasoning. I just wished it'd been a little more off-the-cuff. The exercise had a practised feel to it, like a fire drill. By twenty to six, we were on our way; by ten to, we were outside my apartment building. Carla left the motor running. I asked her what she was going to do now.

'Head back up to the beach – nothing like a body-surf to clear away the cobwebs.'

'What cobwebs? I don't see any cobwebs.'

This time she put some effort into the smile. 'I don't think you're seeing too well, James – you're still half-asleep. You should go back to bed.'

'Yeah, I might do that. I've got a few hours before I have to meet Gareth's ex.'

'Who's that?'

'Marie's her name – she's the one he joined that commune with. She lives over here now.'

'You didn't tell me about her.'

It was as good a time as any. 'There's a few things I haven't told you.'

Her eyes narrowed. 'Such as?'

I started running through them. Carla's frown

deepened and she switched the engine off. When I finished, she said sharply, 'Why didn't you tell me all this at the time?'

I sighed. 'The break-in could've been something or it could've been just another break-in – I didn't want you to worry. I was going to tell you about Donald when the Swiss bankers arrived. I tried again the next day but you had Reece with you in the car. Then last night, well ...'

She squeezed my arm. 'There's a time and a place for everything and last night wasn't it. Fair enough. Jesus, it never fucking ends, does it? Where do you think that guy last night fits in?'

I shrugged. 'I don't know. Maybe it was Alex again, this time using a pro. On the subject of the video ...'

'It's okay,' she said. 'I took care of it.'

'For keeps?'

She nodded. Her expression was unfathomable. I couldn't tell if she had nothing to hide or was concealing a lie. I couldn't tell if she was looking forward to next time or thinking that she didn't need me any more. She must've thought I was going to get emotional, because she went 'Sssshhh' and put a finger to my lips. Then she kissed me. Not passionately but a burst of passion, like a delicious aftertaste, would've only left me wanting more.

She said, 'See you next week.' I got out of the car and she drove off. Early-morning sun was splashing day-glo orange across the rooftops. It was going to be a beautiful day, a real beach day.

No-one at the Darlinghurst cafe was wearing a leopardskin pillbox hat. There was a woman in the right age bracket with a floppy-brimmed purple velvet number, a la the fey chick with the haystack hair in Fleetwood Mac. She also had a Celtic bicep tattoo, silver bangles up her forearm and the slightly tragic aura of someone who felt the suffering of all creatures great and small. That was my girl.

As I homed in on her, a waiter arrived with her order and she put her newspaper aside. Wait a minute, how many hippies read the *Financial Review*? Even fewer than have sausages, bacon and eggs for breakfast. I skirted her table, eyes sweeping the cafe for another candidate. A female voice came from the vicinity of my right elbow: 'You looking for me by any chance?'

The speaker was a sweet-faced little thing with a cluster of very fair, almost white, ringlets. She wore granny spectacles, a short floral dress and clumping, lace-up boots. She looked twenty-five, tops.

I said, 'Marie?'

'That's me.'

I pulled up a stool and sat down. She looked over my shoulder at the woman in the purple hat. 'You thought that was me?' As if I couldn't tell shit from brown bread.

'Well, yeah . . .'

'As if. What gave you that idea?'

'You said you'd be wearing a hat.'

'A leopardskin pillbox hat – when was the last time you saw one of those? That was a joke – it's the name of a Bob Dylan song.'

'He was a bit before my time. I also thought you'd be older.'

'Why?'

'Because of Gareth, I guess. He'd be, what . . . ?'

'Thirty-nine this year. I'll be twenty-four.'

'Jesus, how old were you when you met him?'

'Nineteen.'

'That's pretty young to be back-packing around Asia on your own.'

'How old do you have to be?' Before I could think of a number, she said, 'How do you know that?'

'I saw a letter Gareth wrote to an ex-girlfriend...'

'An older woman, right?'

Wait till you hit thirty, cookie. 'Yeah. It was to let her know he was going to live on the commune. He mentioned your parents, which is how I got onto you.'

'You talked to Mum and Dad?'

'No, a woman called Raewyn who answers the phone at the Waihi council office.'

Marie looked puzzled. 'She wouldn't know how to get hold of me.'

'She told me to ring back, so I guess she asked around.'

'That was helpful of her.'

I hadn't done Raewyn any favours but I couldn't protect my sources and expect Marie to open up. 'I must've convinced her it was important.'

'Oh yeah?' Rolling her eyes. 'What's so important about Gareth?'

'I'm getting to that. Is he still on the commune, by the way?'

'Last I heard.'

'When you were with him, did he ever talk about his days in Bondi?'

'Now and again.'

'Did he mention any names?'

She closed her eyes to show that she was trying.

'There was one guy he talked about a lot – you'd've thought he was in love with him or something, the way he went on about him. It used to piss me off, to tell you the truth.'

'Was that Adam?'

'Yeah, that's right, Adam. Jesus, it was Adam this, Adam that . . .'

'What sort of stuff?'

'Basically hero-worship – what a fucking genius he was, that kind of thing. You can see why I got a little tired of it?'

I nodded. 'Well, four of Gareth's friends from those days, including Adam, are dead. Three of them have died in the last couple of months.'

'Fuck. What'd they die of?'

'Adam fell off a high-rise balcony. One of the others overdosed, one was run over, one was stabbed. I thought Gareth would want to know.'

'What makes you think he doesn't?'

'Isn't the commune more or less sealed off from the outside world?'

She snorted. 'That's what they tell new members – it's half the attraction for some of them. Gareth's a main man in the Children of Light these days, he suits himself. I mean, shit, he was over here not that long ago, which is why I assume he probably already knows.'

'He was here – in Sydney?'

'That's what I said.'

'When?'

'I don't know, five or six weeks ago.'

'Did you see him?'

'Get off the grass – I had enough of the prick to last a lifetime. No, I keep in touch with a couple of girls in the valley. One of them found a boarding pass for a Sydney–Auckland flight in Gareth's jeans when she was doing the laundry. She thought he might've come over to hassle me.'

'So why did he come?'

'To see the girlfriend, I suppose.'

'You mean Alex Towle?'

'I don't know her name – he never told me. It wasn't a subject we could have a rational discussion about. All I know is, she's quite a lot older than me and she pre-dates me. Does that sound like this Alex whatever-she's-called?'

'Well, yeah.'

'Have you met her?'

'Yeah.'

'What's she like?'

'She acts her age – takes herself pretty seriously, in other words. But listen, are you absolutely sure about this? According to her, they were just pen pals. She reckoned she hasn't seen him for ten years.'

'Well, then, she's obviously as big a fucking liar as he is.'

Marie was getting warmed up. She ordered another coffee and went to work on Gareth.

They met on a beach in Bali and made a quick connection, one flake to another. Their spiritual quest took them to Nepal, where Marie caught a bug. After a week in Katmandu spouting from both ends, she'd convinced herself she was going to die if she didn't get home. Gareth talked her into a Sydney stopover on the way.

They stayed in a backpacker dump in Victoria Street and Gareth showed her around. Then he went off to catch up with an old friend and didn't come back. For four days, Marie lay on a bed reading tattered women's magazines, her imagination churning out one-reel shockers with unhappy endings. Gareth's story, when he finally turned up, was that he and his mate had got ripped on hash and tequila and zombied out for sixty hours solid. Marie was so relieved he hadn't been erased by random big-city evil that she took his word for it.

They crossed the Tasman. The homecoming was a blur of changing faces, refilled glasses and late nights, so it was a few weeks before it registered with Marie that Gareth had gone off the boil sexually. She mentioned it to a friend who reckoned a stalled sex drive usually meant the guy had another woman on his mind. The penny dropped: the old friend Gareth had spent four days and nights with was female. When Marie confronted him, he confessed that he'd met up with an ex-girlfriend and the auld lang syne had got right out of hand. He promised to break off contact.

The Valley of Light throbbed with sexual activity dressed up as free love and encouraged by the cult's male-dominated hierarchy. When Marie discovered that Gareth was practising what the hierarchy preached, she joined in on the basis that what was good enough for him was good enough for her. Gareth didn't see it that way: he went berserk.

He faced expulsion on two counts: disturbing the karma and breaching the entry conditions by making surreptitious calls on the commune's sole phone. By this stage, though, Gareth's zeal had propelled him into the inner circle, which closed around him. The guy he'd mauled was smeared as a sower of discord and the phone calls were justified as arising from a death in the family.

Marie could see what was happening. She persuaded a woman who worked in the administration office to slip her a copy of the relevant phone bill. They showed that Gareth had called Sydney, not the land of his fathers.

She'd had a gutful of Gareth and the Children of Light. When she started packing, he turned nasty, telling her she was immature and ignorant, a silly little bitch compared to the woman in Sydney. Now there was a real woman, an intelligent, sensitive adult, a soul-mate. Marie walked out of the Valley of Light and caught the bus to Auckland. She hadn't seen or spoken to Gareth since.

I asked, 'When was that?'

'October ninety-six.'

'And Gareth's still there. What do your friends say about him now?'

She shrugged. 'That he's the same only more so – pretty out there, in other words.'

'In what way?'

'Well, he wasn't exactly normal to start with, but now it sounds as if his ego's out of control. The thing is, you don't have to be screwed up to join a cult but it helps. Most people in cults, they don't want to be individuals. They want to be programmed, they want to play follow the leader – that's why most of them join in the first place. So when someone like Gareth looks around that closed-off little world, he sees all these inadequate people who look up to him as if he's some kind of superior being. And why shouldn't they? He's not like them. That scene can go to your head – you start to believe God's got something special in mind for you. And once someone gets into that mindset . . .' – she shook her head – '. . . well, let's just say, it's only a matter of time before they start taking some far-out attitudes on all sorts of things.'

'Like what?'

'Sex, for instance.'

'Has he got hang-ups about sex?'

'I told you how he went apeshit and beat that guy up.'

'You don't mean to say he's the only guy you know who has double standards when it comes to sex?'

'Course not, but it went way beyond that. As far as he was concerned, when other people had any sort of sex which wasn't, like, in the missionary position, with their partner for life, with the lights out, it was sinful and disgusting, you know, they were behaving like animals. But because he was on a higher plane, so he thought, he wasn't bound by the rules. He could do whatever he wanted.'

This was getting interesting. 'Would you say he's got a violent streak?'

She dropped her chin onto the heel of her hand and studied me. 'You want to know a hell of a lot about him for someone who's just passing on bad news.'

I said, 'The four dead friends – it's possible they were all murdered.'

Her chin slipped off her hand. 'I thought you said . . . ?'

'We've got one definite murder, right? Another one looks like a carefully planned hit and run, which would make two. The others might've been murders, made to look like accidents.'

She nodded slowly. 'Now I get it – you think he killed them, don't you?'

I shrugged. 'Someone did. Do you think he's capable of it?'

'Why would he do that?'

'No idea,' I said, which wasn't quite true. 'But if he's nuts, he might have reasons which wouldn't make sense to anyone else.'

'I didn't say he was nuts.'

'You implied he was in the ballpark. And you haven't answered the question.'

She played distractedly with her hair. 'What do you want me to say? Sure, I spent two years of my life with this guy; sure, there were even times I thought I might be in love with him. But you know what? I always had this feeling that, one day, he'd go out and kill a bunch of people. Is that what you want to hear?'

'I'm not trying to put words in your mouth. If you don't think he's capable of it, just say so.'

She stared into her empty coffee cup. I waited. Without raising her eyes, she said, 'I really wouldn't know what he's capable of – and I doubt he would either.'

TWENTY-THREE

Back at the flat, I had another look at Gareth's letter. It was written a few weeks after Alex, so Marie said, had pumped him dry, but there was no mention of that. In fact, you wouldn't know from reading it that they'd seen each other recently or that he'd even been in Sydney. Plus, the tone was all wrong: it wasn't a love letter, it was a communique.

Marie must've been mistaken. With a little help from me, admittedly, she'd jumped to a conclusion: Alex was an old Sydney flame, the soul-mate was an old Sydney flame; Alex was older than her, the soul-mate was older than her. Therefore, Alex was the soul-mate. But Gareth had lived in Sydney long enough to have more than one old flame, and who *wasn't* older than Marie?

I was tossing up between a bite of lunch and a nap when another possibility occurred to me: the letter was a fake. How did it come up? Alex was talking about Gareth, saying she hadn't seen him for years but he dropped her a line occasionally. She wouldn't have expected me to ask for a copy of his last letter.

If she didn't want me to see the real letter, why not just say she hadn't kept it instead of going to the trouble of typing up a fake? No, that wouldn't be clever enough for Alex. She'd see it as an opportunity to plant misinformation, to show her and Gareth as old friends heading in opposite directions, about to lose touch.

The relationship was the key. That was why she had to hide it, that was why she'd bother faking the letter. Once you saw Alex and Gareth as a pair, a partnership, it all fell into place. I couldn't see Alex doing the killing but, if I put my mind to it, I could see her doing the thinking. I could see her working out the when, where and how to make it look like an accident and Gareth doing the dirty work.

Motive? Years ago, Carla had promised her that the sex videotape had been destroyed. Alex found out otherwise. Someone saw it, someone heard about it, somehow word got back to her. She was paranoid – if that tape ever got into circulation, she'd be dog-shit. Copies would do the rounds of every big law firm and every major company in town. Imagine walking into a meeting with a group of men who'd just been huddled around a TV set, roaring like beasts at the sight of Ms Too Good To Be True with that big boy between her legs. Imagine the vileness she'd have to put up with. Imagine what they'd say behind her back. She'd never be taken seriously again.

She went looking for the tape and found . . . what? Perhaps that there was more than one copy out there: Adam had one, Shelley had one, Pete had one. Even that sleazehound Ray Hanna had one.

But why kill them? Why not just get the tapes? Maybe Alex's bitterness boiled over as she imagined the tape blighting her life like leprosy and she conceived a fearful reckoning. She told me that she'd never got over being bullied into taking part but she'd learned to live with it. Did that get a little easier each time a bully died? Was Carla spared because she was browbeaten into it too?

More questions. What was in it for Gareth? Alex was his soul-mate and, anyway, he was off his head. Dirty sex – as practised by other people – got him frothing at the mouth. Alex could've nurtured that psychosis, channelled it towards the videotape and all who screwed on it. Except them, of course; they were on a higher plane. That would explain her character reference: how had she described Gareth? That's right, the original gentle giant. Well, if Gareth was the original gentle giant, you wouldn't want to meet a cheap imitation. A gentle giant who was capable of rabid rage, who'd retreated from society, who thought he was superhuman – textbook schizophrenia. The loony-bins were full of people who didn't have that many strings to their bows.

Why did Alex send Brown Shoes and maybe the big man? I wasn't one of the bullies, so it was just a matter of securing the tape. For that matter, how did Brown Shoes square with the Alex–Gareth axis? Turn it around: why should Alex wake up alone when Gareth was taking his pick of the female intake? Besides, she probably hadn't told him.

I had a tomato sandwich and kept looking for holes in the theory. I couldn't find any; it made sense. I was thinking of running it past Carla when I remembered that a woman had rung the Waihi council office from Sydney. I'd assumed it was Alex trying to track down Gareth, but that didn't fit. Either it wasn't Alex or that wasn't why she'd called. Christ, maybe she was trying to track down Marie because Marie knew about her and Gareth.

Late that afternoon I rang Marie at the bistro. I said, 'I forgot to ask you: can Gareth type?'

'What?'

'I'm beginning to wonder if he really wrote that letter.'

'Yeah, he can type. He can do shorthand too – he did a journalism course when he left school. Dad told him he just had to learn how to do blow-jobs and he'd make a perfect secretary. Gareth wasn't amused.'

If Gareth couldn't type, that would've proved the letter was a fake. The fact that he could didn't prove it wasn't.

'Listen, Marie, I don't want to make you nervous but just be careful, eh? I've been heavied a couple of times and someone broke into my flat.'

That pissed her off. 'You should've thought of that before you dragged me into it.'

'Hey, you were involved before I came along. If you hear from Gareth, can you let me know straight away?' I gave her my number. 'And if he shows up on your doorstep, don't let him in, whatever you do.'

'That's really useful advice,' she said. 'Any more where that came from?' She hung up before I could tell her to look both ways before crossing the road.

Marie had a point, of course. Warning her to watch her step was the very least I could do. I thought about taking my theory to Donald, but it wouldn't be that simple: he'd take a lot of convincing. In the end, I'd have to choose between making a credible case against Alex and keeping Carla out of it. That was no choice at all.

A courier pressed my buzzer at 8.30 on Monday morning: delivery for Mr Alabaster. Mr Alabaster wasn't expecting anything, so he asked who it was from.

'A Mrs Carla Sully,' said the voice.

You mean *the* Mrs Carla Sully. I buzzed him in, wondering what it was. As usual, my expectations careered across the spectrum, like the needle on a drag racer's speedometer flipping from zero to the red zone in a few incandescent seconds. A diamond ear stud? A Dear James letter? The courier knocked as I remembered I'd left the bottle of vodka in her car.

I opened the door to a couple of sunken-eyed jumbos in dark-blue trousers and short-sleeved white shirts with City Security logos on the breast pockets. They were empty-handed.

I said, 'So where's the delivery?'

The jumbos silently debated who'd do the talking. Eventually, the crewcut one, whose nametag said Daryn Jenks, did it. 'We haven't actually got anything for you. Mr Sully wants to see you.'

'Who?'

'Mr Reece Sully.'

I shrugged. 'Don't know him.'

Daryn sighed and scratched the bristles on the back of his neck. 'Well, he'd like to talk to you . . .'

'What about?'

'He didn't say.'

'What if I don't want to talk to him?'

'Our instructions were not to take no for an answer.'

I'd heard of passive resistance; this was passive attack. They stood there like a couple of trees, reluctant to manhandle me but not open to negotiation.

I said, 'Whose idea was the shit about a delivery from Mrs Sully?'

Daryn glanced at his mute mate. 'Put it this way, it wasn't ours.' Then, earnestly: 'We don't want any trouble, Mr Alabaster.'

'That makes three of us. What about Mr Sully, though – can you say the same for him?'

'He just wants to talk to you, that's all.'

I could've refused to go but there didn't seem much point. I put on some shoes, locked up and went with them, as curious as I was anxious. How much did Reece know? How badly was he taking it? Would Carla be there and, if so, which corner would she be in when the bell rang?

On the drive to Vaucluse, I tried to work out how we'd been sprung. It was all too easy: Carla had given Reece a reason to be suspicious, so he'd put a tail on her. The all-night poker game might've even been a trap – give her some rope, see if she hangs herself. Jesus, lambs to the slaughter.

They parked on the street in front of the white wall. Daryn spoke into an intercom and the gates opened. He walked me to the front door, where we were met by a young guy clothed in a two-thousand-dollar suit and private school self-assurance. I saw recognition stir in his eyes and realised I'd seen him before.

I followed him through to the rear of the house. The informal dining area off the kitchen opened onto a wide, semi-enclosed loggia with lounging chairs, an eight-seater table and a built-in barbecue. A forked Italianate staircase descended from the loggia to a kidney-shaped swimming pool. To the right of the pool was a glass-fronted cabana, presumably changing rooms.

Beyond the pool, lush lawn weaved through flowerbeds down to the water's edge, where a launch built for comfort and debauchery on the high seas sat at a jetty. Beyond the jetty was a scene from a travel agent's window: a symmetrical little bay, the sea deep-blue and sparkling under a cloudless sky, yachts swaying at anchor, lavish houses dotting a green hillside. Easy to be an optimist if you woke up to that view every morning. Easy to believe that all was for the best in the best of all possible worlds.

Mr Armani led me down the staircase to the cabana. The front room contained a giant TV set ringed by sofas and a bar, a replica of the one inside. The inner wall was half glass and half not, divided by a corridor. On the other side of the glass, three rows of gleaming exercise machines faced a mirrored wall. Reece Sully, in a white towelling robe, stood behind the bar with a mobile phone to his ear. His dark gaze landed on me like a vulture.

Reece ended the call. He told the flunkey, 'Okay, Gerard, I'll see you later', grinding the words out as if his voice was computer-generated. Gerard left us. Reece opened a manila folder and leafed through the contents. 'I've been reading about you. You don't look dumb enough to get caught insider trading. How come you let those maggots get you?'

'Someone I worked with dobbed me in.'

It wasn't a very bright answer. Reece let his mouth fall open. 'No fucking kidding?'

He put on sunglasses and came out from behind the bar carrying his phone and the manila folder. 'We'll sit outside.' He walked past me trailing eau de toilette, his bare feet slapping on the slate floor.

I followed him. 'Will Carla be joining us?'

Without turning his head, he said, 'Carla's out of town.'

We sat at a granite-topped table beside the pool. He asked, 'Were you any good at making money?'

'I was okay. I wasn't an ace but I got the job done.' I nodded at the folder. 'What does it say in there?'

He shook his head. 'It's just factual stuff – date of birth, address, criminal record, credit rating ... doesn't really tell me much.' He paused. 'Like, it doesn't tell me what made you think you could have a relationship with my wife without me finding out about it.'

So much for small talk. I said as blandly as I could, 'I never thought about it – it's not that sort of relationship.'

He opened the folder and consulted his notes. 'You meet for coffee; you have lunch at the Bayswater Brasserie; you have a scene on the footpath late on Friday night which looked and sounded like a lovers' tiff ...'

'Does Carla know you spy on her?'

He bared his teeth like an attack dog but his voice remained a metallic monotone. 'I don't spy on her, I don't fucking have to. Gerard, who was here a minute ago, he goes to the same cafe as you, he was at the Soho the other night. He's just one. I've got lots of eyes and ears out there, keeping me posted on what's happening around town.'

I relaxed a little. If he didn't have a pro on the job, he probably didn't know what came after the tiff.

Reece planted his elbows on the table. 'I'm going to ask you once: what the fuck's going on?'

'Why don't you ask your wife?'

'I'm asking you.'

'Nothing's going on. We're just friends, that's all.'

'Just friends, eh? That's what they all say.'

'In this case, it happens to be the truth.'

'And how long have you been just friends?'

'A month or so.'

He closed the manila folder. He'd seen and heard enough to reach a conclusion. 'Well, I don't happen to think you're a suitable friend for Carla.' I started to protest but he talked over me. 'I got you here to tell you that, as of now, the friendship's over. Find yourself another friend. That shouldn't be too hard, it's a big city. And stay away from Carla — or I'll keep you away. Do you read me?'

'Can I make a suggestion? I think you and Carla should communicate more.'

'Here's a suggestion for you,' he said quietly. 'Don't make the same mistake twice, don't overplay your hand. Take your profit and walk away while you still can. One other thing: this is between you and me, okay? It doesn't get back to Carla.'

I said, 'Look, I realise you're used to people shitting their pants whenever you growl at them but I don't work for you. I'm not even in the industry any more. You've got no leverage with me.'

Reece showed his teeth again. 'You plan to spend the rest of your life in a video store?'

'I'm not planning on it, no.'

'Well, if you ever want to work in the markets again, you'd better fucking believe I've got some leverage.'

I stood up. 'I take it a reference is out of the question?'

He leaned back in his chair. 'You know, when

you've got as much money as I have, you can do just about any fucking thing. I could buy you more trouble than you could possibly handle – at zero risk to myself, you know what I mean?' He put one foot up on an empty chair and rested his arm on his knee, aiming a thick forefinger at my forehead. 'Stay away from her – or I'll fuck you for all time.'

TWENTY-FOUR

I didn't even get a ride home. Daryn escorted me off the premises. As the gates closed, he told me a taxi would be along shortly. A little reminder from Reece that I was playing by his rules now.

I took his threat seriously. Reece was famously vindictive in his business dealings, so he could be expected to come down hard on anyone who messed around with his wife. But I figured that sending in the legbreakers was Plan B. That performance back there had been as much for Carla's benefit as mine. The carry-on about it not getting back to her was a double bluff. Reece wouldn't mind if I ran to Carla, telling tales; in fact, he was counting on it. She'd get the message: I know what's going on; dump the loser now and we'll pretend it never happened.

I cabbed it as far as Edgecliff, where I picked up some supplies and got the train to the Cross. I'd been back in the flat two minutes when the phone rang. It was Carla. She was on her way back from the beach. I asked how her weekend had gone.

'No drama, if that's what you mean. Reece was sleeping like a baby when I got there – if you can imagine a baby whose snoring scares the birds. Guess who just rang me?'

For no particular reason, I said, 'Alex?'

'How did you know?'

'I didn't. You said guess, so I guessed. What'd she want?'

'To apologise for what happened the other night – you know, with her fiance.'

'That guy's her fiance?'

'That's what she called him.'

'How come she apologised to you? I'm the one who got the elbow in the chops.'

'You, my dear, are getting an apology in person. We're invited to her place tonight, for a drink and a pow-wow. She thinks she's got a pretty good idea what's going on.'

'She's not the only one.' I passed on what Marie had told me and outlined my theory.

'You are having me on, aren't you?'

I said, 'I think it makes a lot of . . .'

Carla chuckled. 'It might make sense to you but if you knew Alex . . . She's probably the most law-abiding, stitched-up person I've ever come across. That's her problem.'

'Come on, Carla. So she was a goody-goody when you knew her in Bondi – that was fifteen years ago, for Christ's sake, and you've hardly set eyes on her since. People change.'

'From goody-goody to serial killer? That's some change, I mean, that's straight out of "The X-Files". Of course she's changed – we all do – but not that much. When we were with her the other day, I wasn't sitting there thinking, I don't know this person, this isn't the Alex I remember.'

This was starting to shit me. While she was frolicking in the surf at Palm Beach, I was doing the legwork and the brainwork and what did I get for my trouble? This X-Files crap, just because she knew Alex from way back. 'Tell me, if she's such a fucking model citizen, why did she send her fiance and his mate to push me around?'

'She admits she lost it for a while there, when she found out about the video.'

'What about the big guy who came into the shop?'

'I asked her about him: she said she had nothing to do with it.'

'Oh, well, that's good enough for me.'

'I believed her. So would you if you'd heard her. Anyway, your theory doesn't make sense. She could survive the video. It mightn't do her career any good but it wouldn't, like, terminate it. She couldn't survive being a murderer.'

'She couldn't survive getting caught but she doesn't expect to. I bet that's why she backed off in such a hurry when I threatened to go to Donald: that's the only way she's likely to come to the cops' attention.'

'Sorry, James, no sale. A rush of blood over the tape is one thing; murder is something else altogether. I just don't believe Alex is capable of it.'

'Carla, people say that sort of thing every time a murderer gets arrested.' I put on a batty old duck voice: '"Oooh, he was such a nice young man, always helped me across the road."'

'You'll have to do better than that,' she said coolly.

There didn't seem much point in trying. 'So you're going tonight?'

'Yes. On my own, by the sound of it.'

I had too much faith in my theory to let her go by herself. On the other hand, stepping out with her the same day as I'd been warned off by Reece was just asking for trouble. 'I didn't say I wouldn't go with you. But if we're venturing out in public together, there's something you should know. I've just been hauled out to your place by a couple of security goons. Reece wanted a word.'

After a long silence, Carla said, in a level voice, 'What did he say?'

'His parting words pretty well summed it up: "Stay away from my wife or I'll fuck you for all time."'

'Very subtle. Someone's seen us, right – one of his little spies?'

'Yeah, including outside the Soho. I'm pretty sure that's where the surveillance stopped, though.'

'If it's any consolation, you're not the first guy I've hung out with who's had that treatment.'

'When you say hung out with . . . ?'

'Don't play with words, James – it won't get us anywhere. I'll pick you up at seven, all right?'

'What about Reece?'

She said crisply, 'Fuck Reece.'

Yeah, why not? You only live once.

I put down the phone and stared at the wall until I had an idea. Or a moment of madness, time would tell. I rang Eddie to ask if he was available for back-up duty that night.

He said, 'What's it worth?'

'What's your rate?'

'Half a grand.'

'Fuck off.'

'Okay, for you, three-fifty.'

'For that sort of dough, I'd expect the full service.'

'What the fuck does that mean?'

'The other day, you mentioned that you sometimes carry a gun.'

'You want me to bring it?' As if he couldn't believe what he was hearing.

'I think we should have something up our sleeves, just in case.'

'I'll have something up my sleeve, don't you fucking worry about that.'

At five to seven, Eddie – it had to be him – put his finger on my buzzer and left it there. I locked up and went outside. We crossed the road to wait for Carla. I asked him if he'd brought the gun. He had on another wild beach bum shirt over a white singlet. He opened the shirt to show me the pistol stuck in the waistband of his jeans.

'What sort is it?'

'What fucking difference does it make? It's just for show, right?'

'Let's hope so. We're going to meet a woman who may or may not be responsible for several murders. I tend to think so. My friend, who's picking us up, thinks she wouldn't hurt a fly.' Eddie's lip was curling. 'I know what you're thinking: what does he need me for? Well, if I'm right, her boyfriend won't be far away. He's the one who actually does the business.'

'Big cunt, is he?'

'Big enough. He's also a head case.'

'Yeah?' He patted the pistol. 'They're all the fucking same to this guy.'

'Eddie, promise me you won't kill anyone unless it's absolutely necessary.'

He grinned savagely. 'You should've thought of that earlier, mate.'

Carla's Audi peeled off from the single file of traffic and swung into the kerb. When she came to a stop, I opened the passenger door and started to explain what Eddie was doing there. I sensed him manoeuvring behind me, trying to get a good look at Carla. Her eyes switched back and forth without finding anything that pleased her.

She turned the engine off and joined us on the footpath, svelte in white capri pants and a black and white striped top. The outfit and her grave expression reminded me of those adorable, enigmatic French actresses I flipped over as a student, walking back to the hostel after a film society evening with another aching crush.

Eddie had never been that close to a woman like her. He stared at her like a down-and-outer looking in a restaurant window. She responded with a tight little smile. 'Eddie, would you excuse us for a moment?'

She drew me away from the car, hissing, 'Is he the one who stabbed that man the other night?'

I nodded. 'Look at it this way: if it wasn't for Eddie, that bloke, whoever he was, would've got the video. He's our insurance, in case I'm right about Alex.'

'And if you're wrong?'

'If I'm wrong, I'll be embarrassed.'

'*You'll* be embarrassed?' She watched Eddie circle her car as if she expected him to make off with the hubcaps. 'God, I almost hope you're right.'

The drive to Mosman was tough going. Eddie lolled in the back yapping away, trying to get something happening with Carla. It was excruciating, like having to listen to some daffy basket-weaver's solution to poverty. After a few minutes of stoic politeness, Carla put some music on.

At least it distracted me. I'd had a dragged-out, nervy afternoon boxed up in Roach Central, imagining what was in store for us. If Carla was right, we'd get an apology, a glass of wine – unoaked chardonnay, no doubt – and the benefit of Alex's finely tuned mind. I wondered if they'd discussed the video and, if not, whether a chastened Alex would settle for Carla's assurance that she'd taken care of it.

But if I was right, we were probably heading into a trap. This was the endgame and we were the only pieces left on the board.

I was very glad I'd hired Eddie to ride shotgun. I glanced over my shoulder at him; he waggled his eyebrows and grinned lewdly, like a character in a Benny Hill sketch. He was too busy salivating over Carla to become prey to anxiety. I couldn't help but admire his casual fearlessness, even though it derived from a lunatic and primitive code of hoodlum machismo.

Eddie had come for the money and he'd have to earn it. He wouldn't be relying on me for much of a contribution if things got desperate, but he'd expect me to keep a lid on my fear; he'd expect me to stand my ground, at least until headlong flight was the percentage option. If I couldn't manage that, his contempt would be scorching. That would make me lower than the most degraded junkie whore.

Alex lived in a short avenue of speed bumps,

densely leaved plane trees and million-dollar redbrick federation bungalows. On a hot day, with the wind gusting from the south, she would've got a musky whiff of Taronga Zoo. Her house was as tidy as any in the street. There was a birdbath on the tablecloth of lawn out front and a new model Honda Accord in the carport.

It was an unlikely setting for a deadly ambush. Now that I came to think of it, turning her own home into a deathtrap seemed unnecessarily risky, especially as Alex couldn't assume that we'd told no-one where we were going. But I took limited comfort from these thoughts. I'd been seeing both sides of the argument for so long, I couldn't make up my mind about anything any more.

Carla parked right outside. I said to her, 'Okay, this is the plan. You stay here while we check it out. If we're not back in ten minutes or if you see or hear anything that makes you nervous, get the hell out of here and ring the cops.'

She said, 'So you're just going to barge in there and what, search the place?'

'Pretty much.'

'What if Alex objects?'

From the back seat came, 'Tough shit.'

I said, 'She's only got herself to blame. And if I'm wrong, well, we'll be all square. It'll be apologies all round.'

Carla looked away, shaking her head in silent protest. Eddie and I got out of the car. I opened the gate and we went up the tiled path to the porch. I pressed the intercom button and we stood there for a couple of minutes, me worrying about making a fool of myself. A mind as supple as mine can always find a way to postpone confrontations with harsh reality, if only for a few seconds.

I pressed the button again. Another minute went by. The fear was coming in waves now. Tiny vibrations shook me from head to foot and I could feel a slick of sweat on my face and palms.

Eddie fidgeted, muttering, 'Come on, fuck you.' I peered through the pane of frosted glass but couldn't make out any movement in the well-lit corridor.

I said, 'Maybe this thing doesn't work,' and we hammered on the door. Still no-one came.

I looked at Eddie, shrugging. He jerked his chin at the closed-circuit TV camera above the intercom. 'She mightn't like the look of us.'

'Hard to believe.'

'Fuck this,' he said. 'She's not here. Tell you what, why don't you wait for her and me and Carla'll go and have a drink somewhere?'

'Hmmm, I'm sure she'd like that.' Trying to be cool with my nervous system humming.

I tried the door-handle. The door opened and we looked down a long corridor, Tibetan rugs on polished floorboards. I called, 'Anyone home?' That didn't flush Alex out either.

We went in. All the doors off the corridor were open, but the rooms were unoccupied. Nothing was out of place in the formal dining room or the sitting room or the guest bedroom or the toilet or the study. Classical music floated up from the rear of the house. At the end of the corridor, there were steps down to an open-plan kitchen/living area with French doors. The stereo was playing; the TV was on with the sound off; water sloshed in the dishwasher. There was a broached bottle of white wine – French and expensive – in an ice bucket on the coffee table. In the kitchen, there were plates of finger food covered with clingwrap on the stainless steel bench and a bottle of red breathing on the table.

The trap had been set and the victims had walked in, right on cue.

The French doors were open. We went out to a paved courtyard containing a jarrah table and wood-framed canvas chairs, dozens of pot-plants, a covered barbecue and a miniature swimming pool. Alex wasn't there and she wasn't putting the rubbish out in the lane over the back fence.

With every still, ominous second that passed, panic bubbled a little closer to the surface and the urge to be gone from that place became harder to resist. If Eddie hadn't been there, I would've cracked. I would've cut and run.

We backtracked. I turned down the stereo and heard a faint radio voice coming from behind the door in the corner of the living room. I knocked without getting an answer. The door opened into a short corridor with doors in either wall and at the end. The door on the right was open: his-and-hers tennis gear was heaped in the middle of the laundry floor. The radio was in the room at the end of the corridor. A broadcaster with a honeyed voice was wishing paedophiles everywhere a slow, painful death. I knocked and called Alex's name.

Eddie and I looked at each other. He pulled out the gun and brushed past me, his face set like a fighter entering the ring. He wrenched the door open and went in pistol-first. I heard, 'Fucking Jesus', in a voice I hardly recognised.

I said, 'What? What is it?'

Eddie just stood there, shoulders slumped, the gun dangling from his right hand. I looked over his shoulder. Blood had turned the white bathroom two-tone. It was sprayed on the walls and smeared on the fluffy towels and spread over the floor, trickling into the overflow drain beside the bath. It came from the well-built man who lay naked and face-down on the white tiles. Lynch mob sentiments were still oozing from the transistor on the ledge above the basin.

I was deeply afraid but not scared out of my wits like when I found Hanna. It was partly because Eddie was there, partly because it wasn't such a shock. All day I'd had a feeling I'd want to run from whatever was waiting for us down that kempt avenue where happy families and high-fliers were living out the Australian dream.

Eddie whispered, 'You know him?'

I squeezed past him to get a better look. It was Brown Shoes. His throat had been hacked all the way back to the spinal cord.

I turned away, hearing myself groan. Eddie stood aside to let me past. I went out to the courtyard to gulp fresh air and rub the goosepimples off my forearms.

Eddie watched me from the doorway. 'Was that the boyfriend?'

'One of them,' I said. 'Not the one I expected.'

He shrugged. 'What the fuck? Let's go.'

I went back inside. 'There's one more room.'

We hadn't seen the main bedroom; it had to be the other room off the short corridor. The reason I didn't want to go in there was the reason we had to.

This time I went first. Alex was propped up on a pile of plump, bloodied pillows, as if on display. She looked like a vandalised Barbie doll. Her head was thrown back and her mouth was stuffed with lingerie. She'd been slaughtered, ripped open from the groin to the chin.

I don't know how long I stood there with a hand clamped over my mouth, getting cold. Long enough for Eddie to start shaking me, pleading, 'Come on, man, we've got to split, man, we've got to get the fuck out of here.'

He dragged me from the bedroom and herded me down the corridor. I stumbled out onto the footpath. The Audi was still there but Carla wasn't. She was gone.

TWENTY-FIVE

Alex had warned me I was out of my depth. That made two of us, I said. We were both right. She'd added that at least she didn't have to worry about Carla. Now Alex was dead, Carla was gone and I didn't know what to think any more.

So I thought the worst. Alex wasn't Gareth's long-distance lover, Carla was. Alex hadn't programmed him to exterminate all knowledge of her dirty little secret, Carla had. Alex hadn't invited us over for a drink; her place was the final killing ground, where all the loose ends would be tied up. I qualified as a loose end but they hadn't counted on me bringing Eddie. When Gareth saw him instead of Carla on the closed-circuit TV, he'd aborted the mission. He'd slipped out the back way and doubled around to collect her.

Eddie thumped me on the shoulder, bringing me back from a dark place. 'Get a fucking grip, man, we've got to shift.' He kept his voice down, not wanting to attract the neighbours' attention. 'Where's Carla?'

'She's gone.'

'Gone?' He looked up and down the street. 'Where the fuck to?'

'I don't know.'

'That's fucking great,' he spat. 'That's all we need.'

I tried the car door. The Audi was unlocked, the keys were in the ignition. If Carla had masterminded the killings, would she've left her car at the scene? That was as much of a giveaway as leaving your wallet behind. And much harder to do without realising it.

'Fuck it,' said Eddie. 'Just get in. We're out of here.'

I slumped in the passenger seat. There was a second possibility, as chilling as the first: I was the patsy. The object of the exercise had been to place me at the scene of the crime; Carla would explain away the car by claiming she'd lent it to me for the night. It followed from there that I'd been groomed to be the fall-guy from day one. She'd just been stringing me along, softening me up for the big day, like a Christmas turkey.

Stretching out my legs, I kicked something on the floor: Carla's handbag complete with wallet, credit cards, address book, lipstick, mobile phone. So what was she going to do – claim I stole the car and her handbag? That seemed over-elaborate and, given our association, unlikely to be swallowed without a murmur. And if the idea was to place me at the crime scene, where were the cops? Wouldn't she have made an anonymous call as soon as Eddie and I went inside?

This train of thought rolled on to a third stop: Carla hadn't gone with the killer; the killer had taken her.

Eddie gunned the Audi through back streets. I sat there like a crash test dummy, paralysed by despair.

When we came out onto Military Road, he said, 'Got to hand it to you, mate, you can pick 'em.'

I waited for it.

'The chick back there with her guts hanging out . . .'

'Yeah, I know, I thought she was the murderer.'

I felt Eddie's eyes on me. Whatever he saw persuaded him to change the subject. 'You reckon the psycho's got Carla?'

It was time to fall back on instinct. People weren't laboratory rats – inject them with this or that hypothesis and see how they run. There was a lot about Carla I didn't know. There'd been moments when, whether out of carelessness or calculation, she'd given me glimpses of a private agenda. But, in the end, it wasn't within me to transform her into a monster. I couldn't sustain the suspicion that, beneath the unimpeachable surface, she was riddled with evil.

I nodded.

'You better get that fucking big brain of yours working, bud, else she's dead meat.'

'You know what'd be a big help?'

He shut up. We were whistling off the Cahill Expressway down into Woolloomooloo when it came to me. I rang directory on Carla's mobile to get the number of the bistro where Marie worked. I dialled it, muttering, 'Be there, baby, please be there.' She was.

I said, 'Marie, it's James Alabaster . . .'

'What is it with you? You always ring at a really bad time . . .'

'Marie, listen to me. There were two more murders tonight, no ifs or buts or maybes this time.

Whoever did it kidnapped a friend of mine. He's going to cut her up too if we don't find them real soon.'

'Christ almighty. You think it's Gareth?'

'That's what I want to know. Can you ring your friend at the Valley of Light, find out if he's there? If not, see if they have any idea where he is – he might've told someone or left a contact number. Can you do that?'

'Of course I will. I just hope someone answers the phone. They're two hours ahead over there and they go to bed early in the valley.'

'Let it ring till someone answers.' I gave her my number. 'One more thing: get your friend to check the phone bill for calls to Sydney. I need a number.'

Eddie steered the Audi into a parking spot outside my place. He said, 'What if that doesn't work?'

'We don't have a choice – we have to go to the cops.'

'Fuck that.'

'Get real, Eddie. We'll be talking to them before the night's out, whatever happens.'

'No fucking way, man – that wasn't part of the deal.'

The bottle of vodka and four-pack of tonic I'd bought on Friday night were still on the back seat. We were on the second round, drinking to fill in time, when Marie called back. Two days earlier, without a word to anyone, Gareth had done a midnight flit from the Valley of Light. The last phone bill showed a flurry of late-night calls to a Sydney number. It wasn't familiar.

I started to thank Marie but she cut me off. 'Good luck, keep me posted.'

I dialled the number. The phone was picked up on the third ring. A voice I recognised said, 'Irene Lomas speaking.'

I cut the connection, unhinged again. Irene Lomas the secret lover? Irene a methodical taker of lives? She couldn't be. She was too old, too civilised, too sad ... Then I remembered how Gareth had described his soul-mate: adult, intelligent, sensitive. Irene was all of those. And she'd suffered a monstrous loss, her sister lured to self-destruction by her son's corruptive sensuality. Could that have driven her to call down the furies?

Eddie was on tenterhooks. 'Come on, mate, who is it?'

'A woman I talked to a couple of weeks ago. I wouldn't have thought of her in a thousand years.'

'You know where she lives?'

I nodded.

'You got any better ideas?'

I shook my head.

Eddie put down his glass. 'Let's go. If Carla's not there, she's fucked anyway.' There was a trace of pity in his magpie eyes. 'So are you.'

We drove over to Edgecliff. Outside Irene's apartment building, a fat man in a tight suit was juggling a briefcase and a jailer's keyring as he checked his mailbox. He eyed us suspiciously when he caught on that we were planning to ride into the building on his coat-tails. 'Which apartment are you visiting?' he asked.

I said, 'Irene Lomas.'

'Oh, yes.' He nodded at the intercom. 'Fifty-seven.'

'We want to surprise her.'

He tucked in his chin, causing his jowls to ripple. 'Well, I hope you're not expecting me to let you in. That sort of thing defeats the whole purpose of a security system ...'

Eddie snapped. He seized the fat man by his lapels and jerked him onto his toes. 'Open the door, motherfucker.'

The fat man dropped his briefcase. It bounced once and popped open, spilling its contents – a tupperware lunchbox, half a dozen needle-sharp pencils bound together by a rubber band, a transistor in a button-down leather pouch, a calculator, documents in plastic folders, that morning's newspaper, a *Reader's Digest*. He had some grit, though. He swelled up and barked, 'Take your bloody hands off me.'

He was one of those stiff-necked busybodies with an overdeveloped sense of duty and self-importance, the sort of citizen who'd wind down his window at the traffic lights to tick off a posse of cro-magnon bikers for changing lanes without signalling. In a time of war, he'd probably have been a hero. Then again, you could say the same about Eddie.

I had a vision of Carla being put to death while we bickered five floors below. We had to get into that fucking building. I stepped in, telling Eddie to take it easy. He let go of the fat man's lapels and backed off.

'The bloke you should be worried about's already inside,' I said, earnest as they come. 'He's just murdered two people in Mosman. If we stand here arguing for much longer, he'll make it three.'

The fat man looked affronted, as if I'd insulted his intelligence. 'I don't believe you.'

'It's true, I promise you.'

'Then why haven't you called the police?'

'By the time they took us seriously, it'd be too late.'

It all sounded pretty bloody unlikely to him. He bent over, wheezing, to gather the contents of his briefcase. He was out of time; maybe we all were. I glanced at Eddie. 'You want to try again?'

Eddie took a long stride and slammed his right knee into the fat man's ear. He went over backwards, thrashing his stumpy legs like a capsized cockroach. Eddie got hold of his right hand and wrenched back a couple of fingers, snarling, 'Give us the keys, you fat fuck.' The fat man squealed and his key collection clanged on the concrete.

The fourth one I tried opened the door. As Eddie went to get the lift, I gave the fat man back his keys. 'Sorry about that,' I said, 'but there's a life at stake.'

He was cradling his damaged fingers, his face pale. In a shaky voice, he announced that he was going to call the police.

I said, 'It's about time someone did.'

In the lift, Eddie checked his pistol. I wasn't worried about him shooting someone any more. He could shoot on sight for all I cared. I wasn't even all that worried on my own account. I was being bombarded with sickening visions of butchery that we'd be one minute too late to prevent.

Outside Irene's apartment, Eddie flattened himself against the wall, holding the pistol down his leg. I was muttering 'Come on, come on, come on,' and about to press the doorbell for the third time when I heard heavy footsteps approaching. Bigfoot examined me through the peephole. None the wiser, he asked, 'Who's that?'

'James Alabaster. Mrs Lomas knows who I am.'

'What do you want?'

'I need to talk to her. It's very important.'

'Wait a sec.'

After a two-minute hiatus, the door was opened. Irene's palace guard was taller, wider and older than me, with sloping shoulders and a huge head coated in hair of many colours. Thick blond hair with a tinge of yellow framed his broad face but the fuzz on the upper lip was pure white; his beard was ginger around the chin and light-brown from the ears to the jawline. Everything about him jarred. Despite his bulk, his boulder-like head seemed too big for his body, like a bison's, and his outfit – black polo shirt, tan chinos and boat shoes – clashed with the natural man shagginess. His eyes belonged in a machine rather than something made of flesh and blood: they were hard and silvery, like ball-bearings.

I said, 'You must be Gareth?'

He still hadn't blinked. He gave no indication that he'd heard me. In a soft voice with a faint sing-song Welsh accent, he said, 'Come in.'

Eddie stepped away from the wall. The gun wobbled slightly at the end of his stiffly extended right arm.

Gareth finally blinked. 'What's that for?' he asked, as if he'd never seen a gun before.

'It's not for show,' I said. 'Let's go and see Irene.'

He shrugged and turned his back on us. We followed him down the hall to the living room, where Irene sat on the oriental sofa, drinking tea. This was a different Irene to the faded casualty of my last visit.

She was out of mourning and into a jaunty new hairdo, bold make-up and sheer black nylons. Carla wasn't there.

A cool change swept across her face when she saw Eddie and his gun. She sat up straight, uncrossing her legs. 'What on earth's going on?'

Gareth said, 'I think it's what they call a home invasion.'

Eddie told him to sit down and shut up. Gareth put his hands on his hips and sneered, daring Eddie to make him. Irene said calmly, 'Do as he says, Gar.' He went to the other side of the room and plonked himself down in an armchair.

In a harsh, ragged voice, I asked Irene, 'Where's Carla?'

'Carla?' She tried to look and sound baffled, but the theatrics were laboured. 'Why are you asking me? I wouldn't have the foggiest.'

'You won't mind if I look around, then?'

Irene sighed, 'Oh, all right.' She tossed me a key and pointed to the door in the far corner. 'She's in my bedroom – in the wardrobe.'

'She better be okay.'

'Of course she's okay. Why wouldn't she be?'

'I can think of a couple of reasons.'

Eddie had taken up a position against the wall. He held the gun in the crook of his folded left arm, aimed at Gareth. Gareth squirmed on the chair; his otherworldly serenity had all but evaporated. Irene told him, 'It's all right, Gar, it's all right.'

The double bed in Irene's bedroom was unmade and the scent of sex hung in the air. Sex and death went hand in hand tonight, as they'd done from the start. Still going strong after all this time, like a beauty and the beast couple whose relationship, they said, would never last.

The wardrobe was old and massively solid. Carla could've screamed blue murder without causing the neighbours to turn up their televisions. I put the key in the lock, steeling myself for more horror. I was praying that Irene had told the truth and wondering what I'd be capable of if she'd lied.

I opened the wardrobe door. Carla was balled up in the corner, like an airline passenger braced for an emergency landing. She looked lost, fearful, all out of hope. But she was unmarked. She was intact.

It took a few seconds to sink in. She brightened slowly, like a child coaxed out of a tantrum with an extravagant bribe. 'James? Oh, thank God.'

As she emerged from the wardrobe, I put a tentative hand on her arm, longing masquerading as concern. 'You okay?'

She fell into me. When we broke apart, she asked, 'Gareth . . . ?'

'He's still here,' I said. 'So's Eddie. It's all under control.'

'How did you know?'

I told her about Marie's call to the Valley of Light. She told me what had happened outside Alex's place. Bored with sitting in the car, she'd got out to stretch her legs. She was grabbed from behind, scooped up like a shop window mannequin and tossed into the boot of a car. Forty minutes of claustrophobic terror – Gareth either got lost or took a roundabout route – ended in an underground carpark. She recognised Gareth, of course, but he was deaf to her pleas and dumb to her questions. He marched her up six flights of stairs. She almost fainted with relief when

Irene opened the door. Then Irene told her they'd been saving her till last and the relief drained away. Then the doorbell rang.

She asked if Irene's remark meant what she thought it meant. I said, 'You're the only one left.'

She shook her head, dazed. 'They must be completely insane, both of them.'

'Let's find out.'

The tension in the living room was close to breaking point. Gareth looked ready to charge; Eddie looked ready to shoot. Irene's eyes were closed and her face was clenched with concentration, as if she was trying to bring telepathic powers to bear.

I asked Eddie if he was okay. He nodded, still locked in a staring contest with Gareth. 'Look at that mad fuck.'

Gareth said, 'Yeah!'

I told Eddie, 'Carla's fine, everything's cool. Let's keep it that way, okay?'

I left them to their face-off. Irene sat up rubbing her eyes, as if she'd just woken up. She said, 'So you're off then, are you?'

I said, 'Why did he bring Carla here, Irene?'

'So we could talk about old times. Happy times.' She smiled fondly at Carla. 'You and Adam made such a darling couple.'

'What did you mean when you said you were saving me till last?' asked Carla.

'I didn't say anything of the sort, dear. You must've misheard me.'

I said, 'It started with your sister, didn't it?'

Irene looked mystified; her acting was getting better. 'I'm sorry, I don't know what you're talking about.'

'You know bloody well what I'm talking about: the six people, including your son, who've died from unnatural causes.'

The green cat's eyes clouded over. 'If you don't mind, Adam and Lesley are painful subjects for me. I'd rather not talk about them.'

'You want some advice?' I said. 'Don't try that line on the cops – they won't give a shit.'

My head felt like it was four in the morning. I'd been over this ground too many times. I'd had enough. Irene wasn't going to explain anything, she was already working on her exit strategy. Ring the cops, I told myself. Let them sort it out.

I looked over at Eddie and Gareth, who were still engaged in their private psychological battle. There, right in front of me, was the explanation for a couple of things which had been nagging at me. I turned back to Irene. 'One thing I don't understand is why you didn't stick to making it look like an accident. If you'd done that, you might've got away with it. But bloodbaths like tonight, the cops'll be all over it – that psycho-killer stuff scares the shit out of the taxpayers.'

'This has gone beyond a joke,' said Irene sniffily. 'Would you please leave?'

'Am I doing you a disservice, Irene? Maybe you did cook up something clever but your nutty boyfriend didn't do as he was told. What happened, Gareth? Did you go apeshit when you found your old flame had discovered the joy of sex?'

Gareth made a low growling sound. He was out of the chair before Eddie lined him up. 'Sit the fuck down or I'll blow your fucking head off.'

Gareth smouldered for a couple of seconds, then

dropped back into the chair. Now I had Irene's attention. I said to her, 'He hasn't told you, has he? The Manson family act wasn't what you had in mind at all. What was he supposed to do – stick a bikini on her and drown her in the swimming pool? Well, I'm here to tell you, Irene, your boy got right off the leash – the place looked like a fucking abattoir. Did I mention that he chopped up Alex's fiance as well? I was wondering how he managed to avoid getting blood all over himself, but of course he didn't – that's why he's wearing the fiance's clothes. Carla, did he have a bag with him when he brought you up here?'

'Yeah, one of those airline ones.'

I asked, 'Where's the bag, Gareth?'

The contemptuous smile was back on his face. 'In the laundry, where else?'

Carla went and got it. The first item I pulled out was an extra-large T-shirt the colour of Alex's bathroom – red on white. I shook it out and held it up. 'Get the picture, Irene?'

Irene looked appalled. 'Oh my lord, Gar, what've you done?'

'You know, lovely,' said Gareth in an injured tone. 'I did what had to be done. I purged her.'

'I don't know anything of the sort,' she said, her voice rising. 'This is your doing, Gar, it has nothing to do with me.'

Gareth lurched to his feet. 'Don't say that, lovely,' he pleaded, 'don't disown me. We made a vow ...'

Eddie stepped up to Gareth, pushing the gun into his face. Gareth snatched at it, fast enough to pluck a fly out of the air, too fast for Eddie. In a blink, the pistol was out of his hand, skating across the floor.

Carla and I went for it, but Irene beat us to it. She straightened up swinging the pistol in an arc which covered us both.

Gareth swung Eddie off his feet, dashing him against the wall. Eddie wilted. Gareth teed him up with his left hand and planted a pile-driving right in the centre of his face. Eddie went down and out. Gareth tried kicking him in the head but the second-hand boat shoes weren't up to it.

He turned to Irene with a whipped-puppy expression. 'You didn't mean it, did you, lovely?'

She beamed back a loving look. 'Of course not, sweetheart.'

Happy now, Gareth rummaged in the airline bag. He brought out a long knife with a blood-streaked blade. His gaze settled on me. 'You first,' he said. 'We're saving the whore till last.'

Behind me, Carla screamed, 'Stop him, Irene, don't let him do it.'

We backed away. Gareth sauntered towards us, turning the blade so it caught the light. His ball-bearing eyes glittered.

Irene moved away from the sofa holding the gun like a used tissue. As Gareth went past, she jabbed it into his side and pulled the trigger. He staggered, his face slack with confusion. She shot him again. Gareth went into a slow spin. He clutched at the silk screen but it couldn't support his weight and he keeled over.

He still wasn't done. He heaved himself up onto his knees. Irene dropped the gun and walked over to him. She brushed hair off his face, murmuring, 'My sweet boy.'

Gareth ran out of life. He went limp and flopped

forward, banging his forehead on the floor as if kow-towing to an imaginary idol.

Irene went into the bedroom and shut the door behind her. I had just enough time to find her copy of the sex video before the cops arrived.

TWENTY-SIX

Reece and a snowy-haired lawyer of the old school took Carla home. The paramedics took Gareth to the morgue and Eddie to hospital to have his crushed nose rebuilt. The cops took me to the Kings Cross police station. I don't know where they took Irene.

In an interview room smelling of exhaustion and unwashed socks, I told my tale to a couple of detective constables. They sat there wooden-faced, in their short-sleeved nylon shirts. They were about twenty-five, not necessarily stupid, just doing it by the book, the only way they knew how.

I told the truth, but not quite the whole truth. I left out the stuff that could've landed me in trouble: the fact that I'd inherited Ray Hanna's videotape; the various attempts to take it from me; the fact that I'd been in Hanna's apartment that morning; the fact that I'd dropped Irene's copy of the tape down the incinerator chute.

I told them I'd met Carla at the cafe. She was spooked by Hanna's murder and confided in me. Back in 1983, she and some friends had made an embarrassing home movie. Hanna was the third person from that group of seven who'd met a premature end. I had time on my hands, so I volunteered to look into it. What I found out about Adam Lomas and Shelley Lendich was inconclusive, but Pete Grayson's death defied the law of averages. I talked to Alex and Marie and got interested in Gareth. Then Alex had an idea. We went over to her place to hear it and ... Well, guys, you know the rest.

They left me alone for half an hour. Another duo arrived. They wanted to know about the gun. I said I thought Eddie had found it at Alex's. Given what else we found there, he'd decided to hang onto it.

There was a long silence. Then one of them said, 'Let's try again, shall we?'

At that point, Detective-Sergeant Donald made an uncharacteristically low-key entrance. He leaned against the wall while I re-told my story, then left without saying a word. It was well past midnight. I was told, Go home but be back here at two tomorrow afternoon. I asked what for, I'd told them everything I could. The cops looked at each other as if I'd said something funny.

Sleep was a long time coming that night but it came to stay. Waking up was like taking a slow lift to the seventy-fifth floor.

I was back at the Kings Cross station at the appointed hour, like a good citizen. They wheeled me into the same room and forgot about me. An hour later, Donald strolled in with a mug of tea and an ashtray.

He sat across the table from me and lit a cigarette. 'Sorry to keep you waiting.'

I went back to looking at the wall. 'Yeah, right.'

'You want a cup of tea or something?'

'Like what, a pina colada?'

Donald studied me, smoke streaming from his nostrils. 'You're pretty cocky for a bloke who got a couple of people killed last night.'

I stared back. 'Oh, so that was my fault, was it?'

'Too right it was. I gave you three chances to tell me what was going on. If you'd told me the truth, the lawyer lady and her friend would still be alive. But you had other priorities, didn't you?'

'Such as?'

'You were cunt-struck. You were far too busy sniffing around another bloke's wife to give a shit that people were in danger.'

I shrugged. 'I guess that's one way of looking at it.'

Donald said something unflattering under his breath.

'You seem to have overlooked the fact that Mrs Sully was also in danger,' I said. 'And just for the record, I warned Alex, I told her what I thought was going on. But she didn't take me seriously – any more than you would've.'

'Oh, I would've taken you seriously,' he said, 'because I knew there was a tape.'

'Yeah, and you kept that to yourself, didn't you?'

'What's that supposed to mean?'

His instant caginess reinforced my hunch. I said, 'Last night, four of your guys heard my version of events. None of them seemed to notice that I didn't mention Hanna coming into the video store the night he was killed or any of that buggering around with you over the tapes. Why was that?'

He reached for another cigarette even though he'd just stubbed one out. 'You tell me.'

'Okay. They didn't pick me up on that stuff because they didn't know about it – because you didn't tell them. You know, I could never understand why the man heading the investigation, the famous Duck Donald, kept dropping in to see me, or why you slogged your way through that carton of tapes and checked every cover in the store. You've got plenty of people to do that sort of shit work, but you chose to do it yourself. Was that because you're a lone wolf?' He opened his mouth to say something but I beat him to the punch. 'Or had it occurred to you that a videotape featuring some of Hanna's high society clients playing hard-core games could be worth a lot of money?'

I got a jolting stare to remind me who I was dealing with. He said, 'An old cop once warned me not to get into the habit of questioning everyone's motives, because not everyone's a crook.' A haze of cynicism descended on his heavy-lidded eyes. 'No fucking wonder he never got past constable, eh?'

He stood up, pocketing his cigarettes. 'Just as a matter of interest, what happened to the tape?'

I said, 'I heard it was destroyed.'

'Probably just as well.' He paused in the doorway. 'You know, I can't say I really blame you for being cunt-struck. I got an eyeful of Mrs Sully when I was going through Hanna's crotch shots. She's all woman, isn't she?'

On the way out, I was accosted by a bouncy little fellow whose quivering energy was fending off middle age. He stuck out his hand. 'Mr Alabaster, my name's Gil Savage. I'm your lawyer.'

If clothes maketh the man, then Gil Savage was a gentleman. He was Savile Row from the toes of his gleaming black brogues to the cutaway collar of his white silk shirt. But the tailor-made threads weren't the whole story. There was the sharky overbite, for instance, and the larrikin glint in his eyes. I was pretty sure he wasn't a gentleman.

I said, 'I didn't know I had a lawyer.'

'You do now. Reece Sully has retained me to look after your interests.'

That seemed unlikely. 'Why would he do that?'

'He didn't say. He just made it plain that he wants this dog's breakfast wrapped up ASAP. Where can we get a decent cup of coffee around here?'

I suggested the cafe.

'How far away is it?'

'Five minutes walk.'

'That's four-and-a-half too many. We'll get a cab.'

He waved one down in Darlinghurst Road. In the back seat, I asked him if he was looking after Carla's interests as well.

'No, horses for courses. You've got me; Mrs Sully's got Old Silver-Tongue himself, Teddy Jonas QC.'

'So what's your speciality?'

'I fix things, Mr Alabaster, that's what I do. I sort out messes, I get people out of jams. You ever heard that song, "Send lawyers, guns and money, the shit has hit the fan"? That's the kind of lawyer I am.'

I nodded. 'Where were you when I needed you?'

'Believe me, Mr Alabaster, you needed me today.'

Over coffee, Savage told me how it would pan out. The killings would be classified as the work of lone nutter, Gareth Pugh. Irene would walk. There'd be no charges, no trial, no need for Carla or me to appear in the witness box. All in all, exactly the outcome his client desired.

I said, 'You mean they're going to let that murderous old bitch get away scot-free just to keep Carla Sully's name out of the papers?'

'That murderous old bitch saved your life,' he said mildly. 'In doing so, she eliminated the only person who could implicate her – which of course was the object of the exercise.'

'Jesus Christ, surely they'll find something to show she was calling the shots?'

'Well, they haven't so far,' he said. 'And you can bet your bottom dollar that anything they do find will be circumstantial at best. What's more, you're talking about a woman who's lost a sister and a son and had to shoot her lover to save your ungrateful bacon. Unless her lawyer was a complete dud, the jury would see her as a victim.'

'Hang on a fucking second, what sort of a dud would that make the prosecutor?' I demanded, starting to get worked up. 'I mean, that's her fucking motive right there. Adam, her son, has an affair with her sister. The sister's marriage breaks up, she loses the kids, she ends up committing suicide. Adam goes to pieces and tops himself as well. Irene sees a sex tape that Adam and his friends made back in the eighties and somehow convinces herself that it's the friends' fault that her little boy turned into the sort of degenerate who'd fuck his aunty.'

Savage nodded. 'You may well be right, but here's the problem: how do you prove Pugh was only following orders when he's not around to confirm it? No-one else can. Apart from that, she's almost certainly round the bend. You might as well face it, Mr Alabaster – she's going to get away with it. The woman's simply not convictable. If it's any consolation, she must be a prime candidate for suicide herself. It obviously runs in the family.'

'I doubt it,' I grumbled. 'I would've thought the way she took Gareth out of the equation indicated a pretty healthy survival instinct.'

'Ah, yes, but guilt is a slow-acting poison. Give it time.'

I grunted and changed the subject. 'What's happening with Eddie?'

'Your shady friend, Mr Sarkis? I understand they're planning to charge him with various firearms offences.'

'Can you fix it?'

'At Reece Sully's expense? I don't think so.'

'Eddie won't lie down, you know. If it gets to court, what's to stop the whole lot coming out? Surely someone's going to ask why Mrs Reece Sully was ferrying around a Kings Cross hustler with a criminal record and a hot firearm.'

After some swift and sober reflection, Savage changed his mind. 'You've got a point there. I'll see what I can do.' He handed me a card with just his name and a mobile phone number on it. 'You shouldn't need me again, but give me a call if you do. It's paid for.'

'So that's it?'

'Yep, all over. Fixed.'

'Is Donald on side?'

'He is now. He was hard work but we got there in the end. That's why you had such a wait.' Savage popped out of his seat like a jack-in-the-box. 'Well, got to keep moving.' As we shook hands, he said, 'I almost forgot, I've got a message for you, from Reece. He asked me to tell you that nothing's changed.'

'Is that some kind of code?'

Savage's face creased. He had a good set of laughter lines for a lawyer. 'Reece doesn't really go in for subtleties or hidden meanings. In my experience, you're safe to assume that what he says is what he means.'

So nothing had changed as far as Big Reece was concerned. From where I sat, everything had. I had nowhere to go and nothing to do, so I stayed at the cafe. I had another coffee, I had a slice of lemon tart, I read a couple of magazines. Then Donald showed up wearing an arsehole grin. Something had made his day.

'I thought I might find you here.'

I said sourly, 'Is this official police business?'

'Yes and no.' He sat down. 'What's the matter, Alabaster? You got the shits with me because I saw your fancy woman's hole?'

I ignored him.

'Maybe I lied.'

I said, 'That'd make you an even bigger cunt.'

He chuckled. 'True, but it'd make you feel better, wouldn't it?'

I didn't pursue it. Donald would've just led me on and left me up in the air. It was another uncertainty I'd have to live with. 'Would you mind getting to the point?' I said. 'I thought it was all over. My lawyer said he'd sorted it out with you.'

'Oh, well, your Mr Savage got a bit ahead of himself. It's not over. How the hell can it be over when we've still got an unsolved murder on our hands?'

'Whose?'

'The one I've been working on all along – Ray Hanna's.'

'What are you talking about?'

'Pugh didn't do it,' said Donald. 'We've checked the immigration records. He was here for the overdose and the hit and run; he wasn't here when the son went off the balcony and Hanna got the chop.'

'Maybe he had more than one passport.'

'Believe it or not, we thought of that. Take it from me, he couldn't have done it – he was in New Zealand.'

'What about Irene?'

He shook his head. 'She claims she's never heard of Hanna. Obviously we didn't take her word for it, but guess what? She wasn't here either; she was on holiday in New Zealand – with Pugh. She's got the stamp in her passport and the credit card statement to prove it.'

'It doesn't make sense – they *must*'ve fucking done it.'

Donald leaned forward, slowing it down to make sure I got the message. 'Listen, old son, when it comes to making a little evidence go a long way, I'm your man, but there are some things even I wouldn't try. Fitting up people who weren't in the fucking country at the time is one of them. It's not over – for either of us. You could say we're back to square one.'

'What does that mean? Am I officially a suspect?'

The arsehole grin was back. 'I'm not too sure,' he said. 'I've kind of lost track of what I did and didn't put in the case file.'

TWENTY-SEVEN

I wanted to talk to Carla, but it was too soon. She would've been in aftershock, having moments when she just had to let it all out.

I knew because I'd had a couple myself in the privacy of Roach Central. I'd be sitting there thinking about the things I'd seen, thinking, Did it really happen? It was like trying to recall a dark, dark nightmare on one of those bright, shining mornings which make optimists of us all. Suddenly I'd start trembling. I'd watch my hand shake, wondering what was going on. I'd get this feeling as if something inside me was swelling to bursting point and realise I was crying. It was strange to be weeping steadily without knowing why, without feeling pain. I cried a few times during the insider trading saga, self-pitying sniffles late at night when I was so drunk I couldn't undo my shoelaces. This was something else. These were the selfish tears of a survivor. These were the relieved tears of a man who'd almost caved in to fear.

But it didn't end there for Carla. She also had to deal with a husband who'd now want to pore over every footnote in her sexual history.

I had some pasta and went to work. As usual, I had plenty of time to think. I started at the beginning, the night Hanna slapped the videotape down on the counter and hurried on to his fate. We knew everything now except who killed Hanna and who sent the big man. I no longer took it for granted that the big man had broken into my flat, because now there was a second suspect: Duck Donald, the best cop money could buy. But if it was the big man, he'd had two serious cracks at getting hold of the tape. Whoever he was working for wanted that tape badly.

Alex claimed it wasn't her. I believed her now. And I didn't think Irene had hired him to stand in for Gareth. She didn't want the videotape; she just wanted to annihilate everyone on it.

I came up with a plan. Find the big man. Persuade him – by means yet to be determined – to reveal his client's identity. Feed that information to Donald, thereby chalking up a few brownie points. Look for another job. Don't let Carla slip away. That seemed to cover it.

The next morning I rang Tony Stark. Before picking his brains again, I returned previous favours. I told him that the bloodletting in Mosman and Edgecliff had its origins in a group sex scene in Bondi back in the eighties. I didn't name the sole survivor. I explained how an incestuous affair was the trigger for four murders. He loved it. How much of it he could actually use was another matter. As long as Irene was free to walk the streets, she'd have the law of defamation on her side.

I gave Stark a detailed description of the big man, asking, 'Does that sound like anyone you know?'

'It sounds a hell of a lot like Frank Lamont.'

'Who's he?'

'Frank's what we hacks call a colourful Sydney identity. That's how we describe people in or on the fringes of the criminal underworld who might sue the arse off us if we said so in print. Frank started out as a fighter, first boxing then pro wrestling. He called himself The Wild Irishman and apparently looked a treat in a green leotard. Then he graduated to the real thing: bouncer, trade union standover man, bodyguard for a couple of even more colourful Sydney identities, private investigator, repo man ... You name it, if it involves violence or the threat of violence, it's a lay-down misere that Frank's turned his hand to it at some stage.'

I said, 'You mean he's a heavy?'

'If you wanted the *Reader's Digest* version, why the fuck didn't you say so? I was giving you a bit of colour.'

'How heavy is heavy?'

'He's not a hit-man, if that's what you're getting at.'

'Even at a pinch?'

'Well, shit, you're talking about a bloke who's knocked people around for a living, so I don't suppose it'd be such a huge stretch. I hear he's cleaned up his act lately, though.'

'What's he doing these days?'

'Last I heard, he'd set himself up as a security consultant.'

'Which means?'

'Fucked if I know. I suppose he shows people how to make their homes burglar-proof and tells bosses how to spy on their staff.'

'Have you ever run a photo of him?'

'We must've at some stage. I suppose you want me to dig it out and fax it to you?'

The fax was waiting for me at the cafe. The big man was Frank Lamont all right. For once, the easy part had been easy. I had a feeling the hard part was going to be really fucking hard.

As I drank coffee and studied the blurred likeness of Frank Lamont on what was, for him, a good hair day, something Carla had mentioned in passing came back to me: when Penny Wheat's marriage began to unravel, she'd hired a private investigator to dig up dirt on her husband.

I was right, it was too soon to ring Carla. She greeted me like a polite atheist doorstepped by evangelists. After hello, how are you, she told me Reece had taken a couple of days off work. I said I thought that was a good idea.

It obviously wasn't going to be a long conversation, so I skipped the Hanna update – she'd get that from her lawyer sooner or later. 'Carla, one quick question: you know you told me Penny Wheat hired a private investigator when her husband kicked her out?'

'Hmmm.'

'I don't suppose you'd remember his name?'

'No, I don't. I very much doubt I ever knew it. Why do you want to know?'

'It's a long story . . .'

She wasn't in the market for one. 'Do you want me to ask Penny?'

'No. In fact, I'd prefer you didn't. I know this must sound odd, but I'll explain it some time. Any idea how she got onto the guy? I mean, did she look in the yellow pages or what?'

'No, what she did was ask me to ask Reece if he knew anyone. He put her onto a lawyer, well, you know him – Gil Savage.'

'Savage? That figures – I bet he'd know all sorts of desperadoes.'

'Didn't you hit it off with him?' Her tone was slightly wounded.

'On the contrary, I wish I'd met him a couple of years ago. Was that your idea?'

'It was the least I could do.'

'I really appreciate it. It's reassuring to have someone like him on your side.'

'Well, we all need some reassurance at the moment. James, I'm sorry but I've really got to go . . .'

'That's okay.'

'It's a delicate situation. It could take a while to sort itself out.'

'Hey, I understand . . .'

'I doubt it. I'm not even sure I do.'

Savage's mobile was switched over to an answering machine, so I left a message. He rang back after lunch, expecting that I'd want to talk about Hanna.

I said, 'Donald brought me up to speed. He enjoyed leaving me in some doubt as to where I stand.'

'You want me to talk to him?'

'No, leave it for the time being. Right now, he's just having fun playing mind-games.'

'Watch him, he's a snake.' Savage's tone was deeply respectful.

'The reason I called: a few years ago, you put a friend of Carla Sully's in touch with a private investigator . . .'

'That's right, the unforgettable Mrs Wheat. She wanted some mud to throw at her husband and Frank duly supplied a bucketful.'

'Frank?'

'Frank Lamont, the private investigator.'

'Would you recommend him? I've got a friend in a similar situation.'

'Well, I haven't crossed paths with Frank for a while . . . In fact, I'm not even sure if he's still doing that type of work. If he is, I'd recommend him in the sense that he gets results, but there is a proviso: Frank's got quite a smooth bedside manner, so to speak, but the fact is, he's a hard man. To put it bluntly, he doesn't fuck around. If your friend's led a sheltered life, exposing her to Frank may not be such a good idea.'

The next afternoon, Thursday, I met Carla in a Paddington art gallery. The meeting was my idea; the gallery was Carla's. She wanted it to look as if we just happened to bump into each other. That seemed a little far-fetched to me, but then I wasn't married to Big Brother.

Most of the stuff on display was abstract and I have a problem with abstract: I don't really get it. I wasn't getting a piece which looked like a rejected design for a banana republic's flag when Carla bumped into me.

'James Alabaster, as I live and breathe,' she exclaimed. 'Gosh, it's a small world.' She threw an arm around my neck and kissed me on the mouth, then collapsed against me shaking with laughter. Seeing her like that – beautiful, radiant, not giving a damn – I felt truly blessed.

She was wearing a dark pinstripe double-breasted trouser suit with a white shirt and a navy-blue polka dot tie. She could afford to dice with mannishness. The dice were loaded in her favour.

I said, 'I like the outfit.'

'Do you? Reece loathes it, that's why I wore it.' She laughed some more. 'He simply wouldn't believe that I could get up to mischief dressed like this.'

'Let's hope there aren't too many dykes around here – I'd be trampled in the rush.'

She folded her arms, a gesture which went with the costume. 'Are you being rude?'

'Absolutely not. It was meant as a compliment.'

'I don't believe you. Do you think I look like a dyke?'

'No, I think you look like every dyke's damp dream.'

She shrugged, unsure what to make of that. 'I happen to think it's quite a sexy look.'

'So do I.'

'So what does that make you?'

'Normal. Didn't you know that most men would like to be lesbians?'

'No, I didn't. I must've missed the announcement.'

'You know, it's that porno fantasy thing – good-looking chicks giving each other endless orgasms.'

'I'm not sure it's like that in real life.'

'No, in real life it's more likely to be thunder-thighed bull dykes with five o'clock shadows giving each other endless orgasms.'

She made a face. 'Thank you for that. I actually meant the orgasms – most women I know would settle for one and a good night's sleep.'

'Who are the exceptions?'

She gave it five seconds thought. 'Only one comes to mind – Shelley.'

'What about Penny Wheat?'

That drew a sharp look. 'Why this sudden interest in Penny?'

I said, 'I found out who the big man is – he's a jack-of-all-trades called Frank Lamont. The very same Frank Lamont that Gil Savage put Penny onto when she was looking for a muck-raker.'

'So what?'

'So maybe she hired him to get the tape.'

'Penny doesn't even know about the tape.'

'Are you sure of that?'

'Well, I certainly haven't told her.'

'What makes you think Hanna didn't?'

Carla clapped a hand to her forehead. 'Jesus, I'm slow. I just never thought of it. Of course he would've. All those long, liquid lunches, swapping gossip and talking dirty, dissecting other people's lives ... He must've told her, there's just no way he could've kept that to himself.'

'And I bet somewhere along the line you told her that I worked in a video store?'

Her eyes slid away. 'I might've. She was curious about you and she's pretty good at extracting information ...'

'I couldn't care less,' I said, 'but I'd say that's when she clicked. That's when she worked out what Hanna had done with the tape.'

She shook her head. 'But why would Penny go to all that trouble? I mean, okay, I can believe she got a kick out it, but not that big a kick.'

'How about money?'

Carla's face got tight. She was beginning to

wonder if something repulsive would crawl out from under the rock I'd dislodged.

I said, 'Put one copy of that sort of tape into circulation and in six months time, half the country's seen it. How much would Reece pay to stop that happening?'

Carla stiffened as if I'd made an obscene suggestion. When she finally spoke, the words came out slow and disjointed, as if she was under hypnosis. 'That fucking bitch.'

I touched her arm. 'Hang on, Carla, it's just a theory. Before you go to war, we need to make sure . . .'

She snapped out of it. 'Penny wasn't going to do it that way,' she said calmly. 'She wasn't going to threaten Reece that unless he paid up, she'd put a copy of the tape out there. She was just going to go ahead and do it and wait for Reece and his money to fall into her lap once he'd dropped me like a hot potato. You see, there's something I haven't told you. For a while now, I've been pretty sure – like ninety-nine per cent sure – that Reece is having an affair. Now I know who with.'

TWENTY-EIGHT

Carla got me a hire car and a mobile phone and I started staking out Penny Wheat's place. I was happy to do it. I couldn't see anything but upside in catching Reece with his pants down.

Penny lived a block from the water in Double Bay, in a white weatherboard cottage with blue window-frames and a white picket fence. It bordered on twee; I'd expected something bordering on vulgar. Carla explained that Penny needed run-around room for her canine fluffball, Versace.

I did two shifts a day: lunch-time and early evening. Like Gordon Gekko, Reece believed that lunch is for wimps. Lately though, he'd been difficult to get hold of in the middle of the day. He'd switch his mobile to the message service and disappear from the office without telling his secretary where he was going.

He'd also got into the habit, once or twice a week, of stopping off for nine holes at Royal Sydney on the way home, just tagging along with whoever happened to be on the first tee. This from a guy who normally liked everything organised to within an inch of its life and had zero tolerance for the company of strangers.

Shortly after noon on the fourth day, I was dozing off listening to John Hiatt when a taxi stopped in front of the white picket fence. Reece Sully got out. He hooked his jacket over his shoulder, walked up the path to Penny's front door and let himself in.

I rang Carla to tell her, 'The turkey has landed.'

A quarter of an hour later, the Audi pulled up behind me. I got out of the car. With the wind in her hair, Carla looked glamorous and carefree in Raybans and a roomy white trouser suit. But her smile blinked on and off like a neon sign and she couldn't wait to get a cigarette going.

I asked how she was feeling.

'So far, so good.'

'How do you think they'll take it?'

We started walking towards the love-nest. 'Reece'll beat his chest,' she said. 'He believes attack is the best form of defence. Penny? Hard to say. She'll probably suggest we all go out for lunch.'

We crossed the road and went through the gate and up the flagstone path to the front door. The curtains were drawn. Carla pushed her sunglasses up her forehead and said, 'Coming, ready or not.' Then she pressed the doorbell and waited with her arms folded.

The third ring brought quick footsteps. From the other side of the door, Penny said, 'Who is it?'

'Carla.'

'Carla?'

'As in Carla Sully. Remember me?'

'Listen, darling, no offence but this really isn't a good time.'

'Oh? Why not?'

Penny's voice dropped to a stage-whisper. 'I'm entertaining an admirer.'

Carla shot me a cold smile. 'Well,' she said, 'tell your admirer his wife's here.'

A few seconds later, the door opened. Penny peered at us through a tangle of blonde hair, looking as dissolute as a woman could without a glass in her hand and a cigarette in the corner of her mouth. She had lipstick smears on her chin and upper lip and her breasts were throwing their weight around beneath the careless folds of the white peignoir.

Carla looked at her, not moving a muscle. Eventually she said, 'Darling, you look absolutely fucked.'

We gathered in the sitting room, a Mills and Boon setting of soft curves, pastel shades, gilt frames and swag curtains. Reece, shirt-sleeved and barefoot, started in on me. Carla cut him off, her voice a whip. He blinked and reddened as if his face had been slapped.

Penny lounged on the sofa in skimpy shorts and a white singlet, cuddling her toy dog. Like Reece, she believed the best form of defence was attack. Like me, she could see some good coming out of this. Straining for sophistication, she said, 'Well, this is all very dramatic but what exactly are we trying to achieve here? I mean, is this a post-mortem, or a group therapy session, or what?'

I said, 'Think of it as a post-mortem, on Ray Hanna. Who killed him, Penny – Frank Lamont?'

Penny gave up on sophistication. She buried her face in the dog. 'I don't know what you're talking about,' she said in a muffled voice.

I said, 'You hired Lamont to get hold of something

that had belonged to Hanna. He wasn't fussy how he went about it. That makes him a suspect and makes you a potential accessory.'

She baby-talked the fluffball, ignoring me. I went to the sideboard and picked up the phone. 'Suit yourself. I'm just going to give Detective-Sergeant Donald a ring. I didn't tell him about Frank and I think it's high time I started acting like a responsible citizen.'

Penny hugged her dog. She didn't look worldly any more. She looked gawky and vulnerable, like an overgrown fourteen-year-old whose precocious physique had got her in over her head. She made helpless eyes at Reece, imploring him to take charge.

He flapped his hands at me. 'Okay, just hold it a minute, would you? Before anyone calls the police, I'd like to know exactly what the fuck we're getting into.'

I said, 'Penny knows but she's not telling.'

Everyone looked at Penny. She was curled up in the corner of the sofa, resting her head on the arm. Her eyes were troubled and unfocused. Reece gave her a minute. 'Come on, Pen,' he prompted. 'Let's hear it.'

She lifted her head slowly. 'All right. You won't like it though.'

Penny had known about the videotape for months. At first, Hanna just mentioned seeing it years ago, not letting on that he actually had a copy. Then one night, he invited her back to his apartment for 'a little treat'. She assumed that meant a molehill of cocaine followed by another futile bid to get into her pants. She got those plus a private showing. Penny laughed off the video and Hanna's advances and went home to bed. She didn't give it another thought until she fell into an affair with Reece Sully.

She was quite partial to married men. A girl got the best of both worlds: a few weeks of champagne and roses and frantic sex in the afternoon, then when they started mumbling about ditching the wife and kids and moving in, you got yourself a new mobile phone number and went to Noosa for a couple of weeks. But with Reece, the roles were reversed. Penny was the one daydreaming about a new life together, while Reece was quite happy with the status quo. And why not? He had the best of both worlds.

Penny was past the stage of wanting to be a rich man's mistress, expected to sit around in full make-up and dirty weekend lingerie, permanently on heat, waiting for his call. She either had to give Reece up or find a way to break the deadlock, to make him reassess the situation. That was when she started giving serious thought to the videotape. Her take on it was that if Carla's sexual antics became the talk of the town, Reece would cut her loose in a heartbeat.

Penny hadn't told Hanna about the affair, although once or twice she'd joked that if Carla wasn't a girlfriend, she'd move in on Reece like a great white shark. She asked Hanna to make her a copy of the tape, just for her own twisted amusement. Typical Ray: he asked, What's it worth?

At first, he wanted plain old sex, so she let him have plain old sex. Like that old joke: a guy asks a woman, do you want a fuck? She says, no. He says, well, would you mind lying down while I have one? Then he wanted kinky sex, the kind of stuff which obliged her to take a more active role, the kind of stuff she could take or leave even with a guy who got her motor running. She said, If I do that, I get the tape, right? Hanna told her the tape wasn't there, he'd lent it to a client. He promised, next time. Except next time, he'd forgotten to get it back. But listen, darling, now that you're here ...

Hanna was stringing her along, trying to maximise his return, but she'd had enough. If he wouldn't keep to his side of the bargain, she'd take matters into her own hands. She found Frank Lamont's number in her old filofax and got him on the case.

She invited Ray over for dinner to give Lamont a clear run. Later she worked out what must've happened. The night before, Ray had sat up late watching videos and smoking that killer dope he used. On his way out that morning, feeling like shit and running late for a shoot over in Hunters Hill, he remembered that the Hitchcock video was due back. He ejected a tape from the VCR, whacked it into the Hitchcock cover and dropped it in his satchel. What he forgot was that the very last thing he'd watched before crawling off to bed was a sex sandwich with sweet little Carla as the filling ...

Hanna left Penny's place about 11.30, after she'd made it clear there was nothing to follow dessert. She sat by the phone waiting for Lamont's call. He rang shortly after midnight with news that was worse than bad. He'd checked every tape in the apartment: none of them fitted the bill. There was a sex tape, but not with a bunch of kids. This one featured her and Ray and his collection of mail-order toys. Hanna had secretly videoed one of their sessions. He had her on film, doing hard-core.

Penny blew a fuse. She jumped in her car and drove over to Potts Point. Hanna was still up. By the time she got out of the lift, she'd cooled down a bit. She wasn't going to get hysterical, but she wasn't leaving without both of those tapes.

Ray was pleased to see her; he assumed she'd changed her mind about afters. Penny set him straight: she was there for one reason and one reason only – the videotape. Hanna cracked up. She was kidding, right? How could an old campaigner like her, a woman who, let's face it, had been around the block a time or two, be so fucking naive? He knew why she wanted the tape – to fuck things up between Reece and Carla. Well, forget it, honey. He had other plans for Mr and Mrs Sully. He had other plans for the tape.

Hanna let her in on his scam. Next time Reece had a big deal in the works – something which was making headlines, a takeover bid, say, or a greenmail play – he'd make his move. He'd go to Reece and tell him, throw some large money at me, big guy, or I'll carpet-bomb this town with videotapes of your gorgeous wife a-fucking and a-sucking.

That tape was his meal ticket, his rainy day money and his superannuation all wrapped into one. Did she really think he'd let her screw that up? And while he was on that subject, he didn't want her rocking the boat in the meantime: she could stay the fuck away from Reece until further notice. There was another video nasty floating around which made Carla and co. look like the Brady Bunch. If she didn't do as she was told, that'd go in a jiffy bag addressed to Reece . . .

It took a fair bit to shock Penny. She'd never been under any illusions about Ray: fun to be around, especially when he was flush with marching powder, but basically a sleaze. But nothing, not even the sex, had prepared her for this. He'd made a promise he never intended to keep. He'd tricked her into acting the slut. He'd filmed her acting the slut to gain a hold over her. And now he was laughing at her for swallowing it.

What was he saying now? He'd had a long day, he was off to bed. She was welcome to join him, otherwise she could see herself out. Don't take it personally, baby – it's just business. It doesn't mean I don't love you any more.

Still in a daze, she listened to Hanna go through his bathroom routine. She heard the toilet flush. She stood up and walked around to clear her head and found herself in the kitchen. There was a knife block on the bench. Ray used to boast that he kept his knives razor-sharp. It was true – she'd seen him slice raw meat as if he was drawing shapes in the air.

He called down the corridor, I know you're still here, pretty Penny, let's kiss and make up.

She took a knife from the block. Just to get the feel of it, just to fire her imagination as she played with the idea. She saw herself going down the corridor. She visualised the bedroom. She remembered what she'd had to do in there – *for nothing*! – and hate swept through her like a flash flood.

She slipped out of her dress and walked down the corridor in her underwear and high heels. The bedroom door was open. She looked in, holding the knife out of sight. Hanna lay on the bed, legs splayed, fondling himself.

She lowered her eyelids and ran her tongue around her lips. Hanna grinned, wrinkling his face like a fat man with a pole-dancer on his lap. The situation made her want to howl with laughter: her coming on all wanton, Ray lying there with half a hard-on, thinking he was about to get the fuck of the century. She cooed, Close your eyes and see what the fairies bring you. Hanna closed his eyes. He didn't open them again until she slammed 20 centimetres of high carbon German steel into his chest. The knife went in so easily, her arm didn't even get tired.

The video of her was in the pile by the VCR. She went looking for the other one, methodically at first, but after a while frustration got to her. She was wiping sweat out of her eyes after turning the study upside down when reality sank in. Unless she got professional help, she was fucked. The rest of her life would be a wasteland. She had just enough presence of mind to use her mobile to call Frank Lamont.

When Lamont arrived, she told him everything. She promised that if he got her out of this mess and helped her find the videotape, he'd be on the drip for evermore. He took one look in the bedroom and said, You bet I will. Lamont's fingerprints were all over Hanna's collection of videos, so he took them with him when they left.

We knew the rest.

I picked up the phone. Reece said, 'What do you think you're doing?'

'Ringing the police,' I said. 'Maybe you weren't listening, but your girlfriend just confessed to murder.'

'Put the phone down,' he said. 'We'll handle this.'

'What?'

'If the cops get involved, we'll all be in the shit – you, me and Carla.'

I shrugged. 'I'll take my chances.'

'What's the big fucking deal?' he demanded, as if Penny had forgotten to renew her dog licence. 'The prick asked for it. He was a fucking parasite.'

I said, 'Well, I'm sure the jury will take that into account.'

Reece turned to Carla. 'Can you talk some sense into him? You know as well as I do what'll happen if this ends up in court: we'll be fucking crucified.'

Carla gave a half-apologetic shrug. 'He's got a point, James.'

'So what do we do – just pretend it didn't happen?'

'It's not a matter of that,' Reece droned, 'it's a matter of getting it in perspective. Or are we supposed to believe that you actually care what happened to that turd?'

Carla hushed him with a narrow-eyed glare. 'We'll take responsibility for Penny,' she told me. 'We'll make sure she goes away and stays away.'

'Who's we?'

She looked at Reece. He nodded. The deal was done, just like that.

Carla looked back at me. 'Reece and I.'

I wanted to laugh at them, standing there like tin gods, but my throat was too tight and my mouth was too dry. Reece was nodding smugly, as if he'd just figured it all out. 'He wants to know what's in it for him,' he said.

Carla said, 'What do you want, James?'

That was more than I could bear. I said, 'I just want to get the fuck out of here.'

A month later: I was sitting outside at the cafe in one of my fifteen suits, reading the business pages. A woman laughed and said, 'Go, girl.' I looked up to see Carla beating a ponytailed jerk-off in a Porsche to the only parking spot within walking distance.

She got out of the Audi and came over to the cafe, doing an Emma Peel in second-skin black leather. I hadn't seen or spoken to her since that afternoon at Penny's. Nothing had changed. She looked the same and I felt the same.

She said, 'Hi, James, how've you been?'

'Okay,' I lied. 'How about you?'

She shrugged and pulled up a stool. 'So-so. It hasn't been a lot of fun.'

'What, being responsible for Penny?'

'That too.'

'What did you do with her?'

'Packed her off to London.'

'Not exactly Siberia.'

She nodded, closing her eyes. 'I know. Let's not get into that. You're looking very smart. I don't think I've ever seen you in a suit.'

'Last time I wore one, I copped a seventy-five grand fine and a year's periodic detention. I went off them after that.'

'You look good. You should wear one more often. So what's the big occasion?'

'It's not that big. I've got a job interview.'

'Hey, good for you.' She was more excited at the prospect of me getting a proper job than I was. 'What is it?'

'Analyst with a little funds management outfit. If I get it and if I do a good job and if I don't steal the stationery, I might make fund manager in a decade or so.'

'What's the name of the company? We might be able to put in a good . . .' She saw my eyebrows take off and her voice trailed away.

'Thanks, but I'd settle for Reece not putting in a bad word.'

'You needn't worry about that – right now, he's got other things on his mind. He's convinced there's going to be a crash, so he's selling most of his shares and scaling down the business.'

I made a mental note to casually drop that into the interview. 'What's he going to do when he's all cashed up?'

'Take time out.' Carla lowered her eyes. 'We're going to France for a while. I want to get a feel for what it's like to, you know, actually live there rather than just do the tourist thing.'

'A year in Provence?'

She smiled weakly. 'Something like that.'

I'd been resigned to a life without Carla for weeks. I thought I was prepared for it. But I still felt sick, I still buckled under the weight of desolation. It was an effort to keep my voice under control. 'So all was forgiven?'

She nodded. 'We decided to wipe the slate clean.' She was trying to be matter-of-fact but her expression kept changing. It was like watching a long close-up in fast-forward.

'What happened to the ground-rules? I would've thought an affair with a close friend of yours was a bit different from a one-night stand on the road.'

'It wasn't all one-way traffic, don't forget.'

Numbness was setting in. She'd made her decision and I couldn't change it. Now she wanted me to go along with it, but that was asking too much. I just shrugged.

'Reece can be the world's biggest arsehole,' she said, 'but there is another side to the coin. He's not one of life's spectators, he's always out there doing things. Say he'd been in your position, you know, like, lost the lot: he would've just picked himself up and started again, found another way to make money.'

I said coldly, 'I'd say, "Who's counting?" but I guess that'd be a silly question.'

Carla sighed. Her hands shook as she lit a cigarette. 'You think it's just the money, don't you? It is and it isn't. I loved a boy once and look where that got me. That's when I stopped believing in happily ever after.'

'Yeah, it must've been a bummer but, shit, Reece would've just picked himself up and started again.'

She took it more seriously than it was meant. 'I don't think Reece has ever believed in happily ever after.'

I had one last try. 'That's the whole fucking point. You haven't given yourself a chance. You're not even looking in the right place.'

She said gently, 'That makes two of us, James.'

And that was that. She leaned forward, reaching for my hand. I had to look away.

She let go of my hand and stood up. 'I better get going.'

I looked up at her. 'You were just sending Reece a message, weren't you – two can play that game? That's all it ever was.'

She examined me carefully. Perhaps she was looking for something worth committing to memory. 'Even if that was true,' she said slowly, 'I still had to choose.' She paused. 'And there are plenty of fish in the sea. Goodbye, James.'

I watched her walk to the car, get in and start the engine. She didn't look back until the car was moving. It was only for a moment and nothing showed on her face except perhaps curiosity.

Don't feel sorry for me. I'm a big boy. I knew what I was doing, I went in with my eyes wide open. There were no promises, no guarantees, no safety net. It doesn't work that way.

And no happy ending? Well, that depends on how you look at it. I got what I wanted more than anything else in the world. Only for a little while, maybe, but how many people can even say that?

And I never told her I loved her.

BLACK TIDE
Peter Temple

Darkly evocative, genuinely thrilling, wryly funny, this is a fabulous book.
'READ OF THE WEEK', *INSIDE MELBOURNE*

Jack Irish – lawyer, gambler, part-time cabinetmaker, finder of missing people – is recovering from a foray into the criminal underworld when he agrees to look for the son of an old workmate of his father's.

It's an offer he soon has cause to regret, as the trail of Gary Connors leads him into the world of Steven Levesque, millionaire and political kingmaker. The more Jack learns about Levesque's powerful corporation, the more convinced he becomes that at its heart lies a secret.

What he's destined to find out is just how deadly that secret is ...

This novel ... puts Temple at the forefront of contemporary Australian crime fiction.
STUART COUPE, *SYDNEY MORNING HERALD*

Bantam Paperback
ISBN: 0 73380 159 5

CAT CATCHER
Caroline Shaw

A stunning debut novel ... Shaw's writing is sharp and witty, the plot well crafted and cat catcher Lenny Aaron is irresistible.
ADELAIDE ADVERTISER

Meet Lenny Aaron, a Zen-cool young ex-cop with a few left-field addictions, a cuttingly droll style and a seedy little office of her own in downtown Footscray. Sworn off true crime after a harrowing experience on duty, Lenny earns a living tracking missing cats down Melbourne's alleys and byways. She is making OK money, smoking like a chimney and sort of coping with life when she gets a call about the missing cat of Melbourne's wealthiest and most powerful dysfunctional family. Suddenly she's back in the murder business – and confronting her own haunting past.

A gripping first novel by an exciting, new young Melbourne-based crime writer.

Bantam Paperback
ISBN: 0 73380 170 6

THE BLACK PRINCE
A Cliff Hardy Novel
Peter Corris

The Black Prince *is a wonderfully written, well-paced and plotted novel ... This is vintage Corris and Hardy. Long may they run.*
STUART COUPE, *SYDNEY MORNING HERALD*

They call him the Black Prince. Southwestern Uni's top athlete, Clinton seemed to have it all: he was destined for sporting stardom and luck in love – then it all went terribly wrong.

Now Clinton won't rest until he's avenged his girlfriend's death. He's after the dealer who sold Angie bad steroids and nothing's going to get in his way. Can Cliff Hardy find him before he ends up on a murder charge – or dead? The trail leads the Sydney PI to an Aboriginal community in Far North Queensland and back to the shadowy world of illegal boxing.

Bantam Paperback
ISBN: 1 86325 132 4